ECHOES OF EARTHSHINE

A Melded Earths Standalone

MEL HARDING-SHAW

CORUSCATE PRESS

ISBN 978-1-99-117785-8 (Paperback)

ISBN 978-1-99-117784-1 (ePub)

Edited and proofread by Madeleine Collinge

Cover design by Getcovers

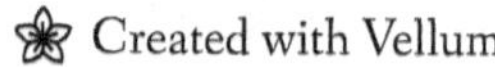 Created with Vellum

CHAPTER 1
RA

"You can't just shove it in there. It's a seduction. You need the right prep," Ra said, keeping his gaze on the busted security camera he was fixing.

The damage caused to the City of Souls during the recent invasion had given him the perfect opportunity to upgrade their defensive surveillance using the tech he and Zee had developed. This camera was the last one he needed to retrofit. The final box he needed to tick before he could leave everything behind.

"For fuck's sake, Ra. It's a computer, not a person. It's six o'clock in the morning and I was already out all night fixing the Greenhaven overbridge. I need to be out of sight before your ex arrives so I don't cause a diplomatic incident. I don't have time to master your human coding," Zee shot back.

Ra winced in sympathy. Zee did look tired. Their wings of copper shot through with a blue-green like the oxidised form of the metal were draped lax on the floor behind them. Zee was the city's magical engineer, so they'd been working round the clock to repair structures across the city after the battle.

"He's not my damn ex. It was one kiss," Ra grumbled. One kiss and a decade of flirtatious messages and intense connection before it all went wrong, but who was counting? "You need to learn this before Mica gets here because there's no one else I trust to maintain the soul database if he lets me accompany Kaia back to the Earth Court with him."

Zee was a fairly competent coder for a centuries-old elemental who'd never come across a computer before their worlds melded together. Ra hadn't needed to teach them much, given the two of them had built the system from scratch, fusing human tech with elemental magic. Zee's power was already woven through every conductor and they had an innate understanding of the system. He knew Zee was just tired and frustrated at how much longer it had taken them to complete the Soul Court's usual reports than it would Ra and that was showing through in the violent clacking of the keyboard behind him.

"I thought Lord Mica already said no to you going. Repeatedly. There's no way he's going to risk having the second-in-command to the lord of a rival court in his territory. Especially one he so publicly rejected," Zee pointed out.

Ra forced his hands to relax before he tightened the final screw almost hard enough to snap and turned to face his friend. He really hadn't needed the reminder of Mica's words at the global summit—*Bastion. Get your human under control.* But if there was anyone who knew how the Earth Lord thought, it was Zee, who'd grown up in his court.

"I have to try one more time. Kaia woke screaming again

last night and just about blasted through the wall with her power before she realised where she was," Ra said.

The deep concern they shared for the girl was clear in Zee's expression. "She should've left for training months ago."

"She was in no state to move to another continent on her own. She still isn't. And you know Ana wasn't ready to let her go when she'd only just got her back," Ra said.

Zee wasn't wrong about the urgency, but there was nothing they could do about it now. All the most powerful young elemental mages needed to receive training in one of the sentient strongholds of the other four courts to gain control over their magic. Otherwise, they burned out in horrific accidents in their early teens. Despite being only twelve and half-human to boot, little Kaia was fast approaching that point. Her kidnapping and assault at the hands of the Air Court months earlier had massively accelerated her magical development and the trauma had left her a shadow of her former gregarious self.

The Earth Lord Mica had agreed to train her as political leverage, the bastard, but to his credit he'd also committed to providing her with access to a counsellor. He just hadn't budged on letting anyone from the Soul Court accompany her. Ra was going to change Mica's mind this morning, no matter what it took, because the niece of his heart had only just started healing and there was no way he was going to let her feel alone again.

"That may be so, but how on the earths are you going to convince Lord Mica? Can you even be civil to him?" Zee asked.

His response was cut off by a knock at the door and Rose, one of the elemental scouts, let herself into the room. It was just as well because he had nothing to say in response to Zee's question. He had no clue how he was going to convince Mica of anything. Given a choice, he'd dropkick the Earth Lord back to the sentient magical cave system of his stronghold and never see him again. Mica's actions had almost cost Bast and his mate Hel their lives. Bast was like a brother to him. It wasn't something Ra could forgive.

"Lord Mica's incoming in five. Tir's on the roof to set up the portal," Rose told him.

Ra gave her an up-nod in acknowledgement. "Thanks. I'll head up now."

"Are you sure that's a good idea? Are you going to behave?" she teased, arching an eyebrow.

Ra smirked and pretended a confidence he didn't feel. The bad blood between him and the Earth Lord was no secret to anyone in Soul Tower, or the world for that matter. Mica had made sure of that with his little outburst.

"You know me, sugar. I'm more fun when I don't," he flirted back.

He'd shared a hot night with Rose at The Crypt nightclub further down the Tower several years back, but they both knew the score. He wasn't into repeats. And these days he spent more time in the DJ booth than on the dancefloor, anyway. It had been too many months since he'd really let loose. He wasn't going to count exactly how many because then he'd have to admit it was the same number since he'd first met Mica in person after years of flirty communications that started as official court business and quickly became something more. The slow seduction he'd been reeling the Earth Lord in with had been the light in his days right up until Mica showed his true colours. The elemental had known exactly what Bast meant to Ra when he made his choice to betray them. He deserved everything Ra had thrown at him since.

Rose grinned and waved a lazy salute to them in farewell.

"I won't see you before you leave if you succeed," Zee said, standing up from the computer they'd been working at.

Ra pulled them into a hug, careful to avoid brushing up against their sensitive wings. "I'll be back before you know it, but we can have one last whiskey before I go," he said, heading to his drinks cabinet to pour them both a measure of the whiskey he saved for special occasions.

He'd lovingly distilled and casked the liquor in barrels he'd carved and assembled himself twenty-one years earlier. Back when he'd still been mentally adjusting to being a human who suddenly had all the time in the world because the magical mark Bast placed on him to save his life had left him with an elemental's immortal lifespan.

"Three years is a long time, Ra. And I'm not so sure he'll let you go again if he lets you back in."

Ra took a long sip from his glass and closed his eyes to savour the taste. "You managed to get away," he said.

Zee rolled their eyes. "I was no one to him. With you, it's personal."

"He hates me. Just like I hate him. He's not going to want me around a minute longer than is absolutely necessary," Ra said.

"Hate and love are just two currents holding the same wing aloft. Go well, my friend," Zee said, raising their glass in a toast before finishing the drink.

Ra shook his head and gave Zee one last squeeze before heading for the elevators. "You can bunk in my spare room here until he's gone so you don't have to cross the city. Love you!" he called over his shoulder.

The sun was rising over the sparkling waters of the harbour as he stepped out onto the roof terrace of Soul Tower. His friend Tir stood in the circle of black obsidian tiles where they'd taken to setting up portals when needed. The ubiquitous winds of the city chilled Ra's skin as he walked closer and he wished he'd grabbed a jacket. Tir was never bothered by the cold. There was no sign of discomfort visible in the tentacles draping from their scalp and undulating gently down to the ground. Tir's multiple jaws split into a wide smile as Ra approached, revealing rows of predatory razor-sharp fangs. The teeth had taken a bit of getting used to, especially when the ceptae children smiled so sweetly in the exact same way.

"Hello, Sunshine," Tir said.

Ra smiled at the nickname. Sometimes he felt distinctly underpowered compared to all the amazing species now occupying the city—the lethal monster-hunting ceptae with their rare portalling ability, the elementals with their wings and magic, the blood-drinking vampyr who had healed so many of the fallen in the battle. At times like this he was reminded he still had influence as a human—even if sometimes that influence was the tendency to come up with ridiculous nicknames and drop f-bombs. Someone needed to make sure they all remembered to have fun.

"Hey there, T-Bird. Ready to get this party started?" Ra asked, faking a nonchalance he definitely wasn't feeling at the imminent arrival of the elemental he despised only a touch more than he desired.

"Of course," Tir said, angling their head in agreement.

Stretching out a slender hand, the ceptae gathered the

liquid shadow of their power to them and started forming the rift in the air that would open into the Earth Court on the distant Asian continent.

"I need to speak to him in private once he's through, please," Ra said, keeping his voice soft so as not to distract Tir.

"I doubt he will notice me leaving once he sees you," Tir said, flashing him another toothy grin.

Ra rolled his eyes at the gentle teasing and turned to face the coalescing swirling shadows. He didn't have long to wait.

The sun's rays catching on the sparkling metallic copper of Mica's wings as he emerged from the portal threw Ra back to the first time they'd met in person on this same rooftop. There had always been a tension between them over the decades their messages had shifted from official business to something more personal, but it hadn't been until they finally stood face to face that he'd felt the full effect.

Just like he had that day, he drew in a sharp breath as he took in Mica's sculpted muscles, perfectly framed by his formal suit. The wind chose that moment to shift direction and Mica's familiar scent of forest and the deep stillness of the caves he called home filled his lungs—clean, fresh, and far too tempting.

The Earth Lord was wearing a tux and bowtie despite the early hour, because of course he was. Bast used to tease Ra about how hot he found the image of Mica as his personal fallen angel—like Lucifer poised at a piano with a whiskey in one of his too-tempting hands and that annoyingly delicious three-day scruff gracing his jaw. Thank the earths he'd never revealed that weakness to Mica, either in the days they'd spent together in the city or in the endless string of messages they'd shared before Mica's actions destroyed everything growing between them.

As Tir's portal disappeared, he noticed a tension leave Mica's body, which was strange given he'd just arrived at a court he had only a tenuous truce with. It was as if Mica had been straining to carry a great weight and it had suddenly lifted. The relief he witnessed was short-lived. They were both snapped back to reality as his gaze finally met the Earth Lord's and Mica processed his presence on the roof. The blue-green of Mica's eyes widened with surprise and the thin line of the copper of his power ringing his pupils flashed as they dilated.

Stalking forward until he was right up in Ra's space, Mica's voice was barely more than a growl when he spoke. "Where is the Soul Lord? Would Bastion insult me by sending you to greet me?"

Ra tilted his head to keep their eyes locked. He used to love that Mica was taller and more imposing. The perfect size to wrap around him. Now it just pissed him off.

"Nau mai, haere mai, Lord Mica. As a member of our ruling partnership, I am honoured to welcome you back to the City of Souls," he replied, taking perverse pleasure in rubbing Mica's nose in his failure at basic diplomatic protocol. For whatever reason, the Earth Lord who was renowned for his calm, staid presence and formality always seemed to lose it all in Ra's presence.

As close as they were, Ra could now see the signs of fatigue and strain in Mica's face—the smooth bronze of his skin was marred by deep shadows beneath his eyes that were almost as dark as the ebony of his hair. Ra frowned as he took it in. He'd known the Earth Court had been reeling since the damage to their sentient stronghold caused by Hel's abduction, but they'd thought Mica would've been able to heal his home by now. The stronghold was what was supposed to keep Kaia's power stable as she trained there. If it was still damaged, would she be safe?

"Are you well, Lord Mica?" Ra asked.

"That is none of your concern."

"It sure as fuck is if the reason you look like one of Bast's reanimated corpses is going to put Kaia in danger!" Ra snapped.

So much for diplomacy. Maybe staying up all night and that whiskey first thing in the morning hadn't been the best idea. It was a miracle he'd managed to last this long before going on the attack.

"Are you questioning my ability to keep my people safe?" Mica asked, deadly warning in his tone.

"Absolutely."

"Unbelievable. You can't be more than what? Four decades? And you're questioning *me*? I've ruled the Earth Court for almost a thousand years. If I couldn't keep my people safe, someone would have deposed me centuries ago," Mica said.

"It's over five decades, but whatever. You're showing your age, old man. I don't care if you've ruled for a thousand years or a thousand decades. We need to know Kaia will be safe."

Ra's answer seemed to throw Mica more than he expected and the Earth Lord ran his eyes down his body searching for something. "Five decades? How do you look so ... ageless?"

Ra rubbed absently at Bast's mark that wrapped around his upper arm, hidden by his shirt and Mica's eyes widened as he realised the answer to his question. Elemental rulers could place a magical mark on their most trusted courtiers, but it was uncommon. The magic was nothing like the rare mating bond Bast had with Hel, but it still created a permanent connection. If Ra focused hard, he could feel Bast's heart beating in his chest and his breaths filling his lungs. It also meant they could always find each other.

To his knowledge, he and Ana—Soul Tower's manager and Kaia's māmā—were the only humans to ever have a mark of this type placed on them. It had the added benefit of giving them an indeterminately longer lifespan, faster healing, and extra speed and strength. It made him a little more than human and meant he hadn't aged a day since Bast had placed the mark on him when he was thirty. He was surprised Mica hadn't figured it out earlier, given how long they'd known each other, but the passing of time felt different without mortality to confine it.

A shiver of foreign power ran over his skin, probing, and made Bast's mark on his upper arm flare with cold. Something dark flashed in Mica's eyes, his wings flaring wider as his fists clenched.

"He marked you," Mica growled.

"That is none of your concern," Ra said, echoing his earlier words. "What *is* your concern is reassuring me that your stronghold isn't going to hurt my niece."

"You should have thought of that before you extorted me into letting Helaine enter it. The stronghold wouldn't even *be* damaged otherwise. Can you even imagine what it's like to have a portion of your consciousness severed from your soul like its was? Or what it's like to have that same broken consciousness clinging to your mind for comfort? Speaking into your thoughts every hour of every day? Enough! I will not stand here and be insulted by you! I will keep Kaia safe the same way I have kept every other member of my court safe for a millennium. Just like I already told your Lord. Where is the girl? I don't have time for this," Mica growled, striding around Ra to head for the entrance to the Tower.

Fuck. This was not how this was supposed to go. He was meant to be endearing himself to Mica so he'd let him accompany Kaia and instead he'd possibly fucked up her whole leaving day. It had been a minor miracle that Mica had agreed to spend the day with them to ease her transition, especially given the time difference meant he'd left his own court after midnight. They'd planned for Mica to attend both the private family breakfast and the surprise party later that day so Kaia had a chance to connect with him.

Reaching out without thinking, he grasped Mica's biceps to halt his progress, his hand inadvertently skating across the impossibly soft feathers of his wings as he did so. Mica spun to face him, his feathers sparking with copper magic as he reacted to the perceived threat. Ra dropped to his knees before Mica had a chance to do anything they'd both regret in response.

"I'm sorry. Please don't let my words affect Kaia's last day here. I'm begging you."

Mica's nostrils flared and his magic shone even brighter for a moment before the polite mask he'd been lacking since he arrived slid down into place. "Get up. I will not be manipulated like that," Mica said, voice tight.

Ra tilted his head at the hint of discomfort in his words and fought to hide a smirk. He hadn't meant the move to be suggestive, but he could tell Mica was remembering the last time he'd been on his knees for him like this. They'd been interrupted by duty before anything could happen, but the scene had played in his fantasies for months after until he'd refused to let Mica take up any more of his mental real estate. Clearly, it had featured in Mica's memories as well.

"Please stay for the rest of the day," he said.

"Fine. But only for the girl, not for you," Mica growled, reaching down to drag him to his feet.

The electric surge Mica's touch sent through his body had him reeling, and he put a hand out for balance that landed on Mica's hard sculpted chest. What was with this insane chemistry between them?

Whatever moment they were having was interrupted by a flash of azure blue wings and the soft thump of Morrigan, the Soul Court scout captain, landing nearby. She had no reason to be there, so it was obvious she thought he needed an intervention. How long had she been watching? She was never going to let him hear the end of it.

"Greetings, Lord Mica. If you have a moment, I would like to discuss a matter with you before you head downstairs," she said.

Shooting Morrigan a grateful look for the distraction, Ra turned away from the elemental who was infuriating temptation personified.

"I'll see you down there," he muttered, not bothering to look and see if Mica deigned to respond. He needed a moment to get his errant body back under control before he could look at the Earth Lord again.

CHAPTER 2
RA

Too keyed up to take the elevators, he headed for the stairwell down to Bast's penthouse taking the steps two at a time. That meeting had not gone to plan. At all. The breakfast would be his last chance to talk Mica into letting him accompany Kaia. After that, there would be too many other dignitaries and elementals present and he'd lose his captive audience. What would it take to convince Mica to let him come with Kaia that he hadn't already tried in the previous months? The elemental's obvious exhaustion suggested the damage to the stronghold might be his best in. It hadn't occurred to him to leverage it because they'd all assumed the Earth Court's many mages would have it under control by now. He just needed to figure out how.

The scent of freshly cooked waffles and the familiar clink of plates being set on the table greeted Ra as he stepped into the penthouse. He paused to take in the scene that was so familiar and would never be quite the same again once Kaia left. Ana was busy in the kitchen slicing berries and preparing coffee. Hel and Kaia were sitting at the table already, their wings tucked carefully out of the way behind them. And Bast was just turning back from placing a plate piled high with waffles in its centre.

Ra pulled Bast into a tight hug as he approached. Things had been a little tense between them since Bast had been forced to out Ra's history with Mica to the global summit to explain the Earth Lord's bizarre behaviour. Not that anything excused the shit Mica had come out with that day when he'd told Bast to get his human under control like he was some sort of pet. Ra didn't hold it against Bast, but it had been one more tiny factor pulling them away from each other now that Bast had a mate to focus his attention on. It didn't mean they loved each other any less. It just meant their relationship, which had always been so familiar, was changing, transforming. If Ra managed to convince Mica to let him move to the Earth Court for three years with Kaia, that would only become even more true.

Ra took a moment to greet Ana, stealing a berry from the bowl and dodging out of the way laughing as she went to smack his hand. She gave him a wry smile, not fooled by his attempt to distract her from her sadness but appreciating it nonetheless.

Squeezing Hel's shoulder as he passed, he sat down next to Kaia and wrapped an arm around her, kissing the white-blonde of her hair that she'd inherited from her elemental father who'd died when she was just a baby.

"Ata mārie, Uncle Sunshine," Kaia greeted him with her mother's Māori language, eyes welling with tears and the cream and iridescent blue of her wings trembling.

He'd always loved how her colouring matched the kōtare kingfishers that perched on stray wires on the outskirts of the city, as if she was intrinsically linked to the native fauna of the city. Fuck, he'd be so sad if her wings changed to the Earth Court colours while she was training like the wings of most elementals of her power level would. They'd just have to hope her love for her Uncle Basti and the Soul Court and her deep connection to the land of Aotearoa through her Māori heritage would shine through. He didn't think Ana could handle that kind of change on top of everything else. Not after the trauma of Kaia's recent kidnapping.

Hel shot him a sympathetic look before turning toward Kaia. "I got a present for you," she said.

Kaia drew in a deep shuddering breath and attempted a smile.

"Can't have my best girl out in the world without a decent blade," Hel added, and for the first time in months, he saw a spark of excitement in Kaia's eyes.

"Helaine. You better not be arming my daughter with a lethal weapon," Ana called.

"No comment," Hel called back, winking at Kaia as she passed her a wrapped box.

Ra grinned as the girl tore into the package. Trust Hel to think of the perfect gift to distract her.

"It's just like yours," Kaia whispered, stroking the metal baton that could be twisted out to form two long blades.

Kaia withdrew the weapon from the case reverently and turned it until the words Hel had engraved on it caught the girl's attention—Kia kaha. Kia māia.—Stay strong. Be brave.

"Thank you, Auntie Hellkitten," Kaia said, throwing herself into Hel's arms with a sob. It was the first time she'd used the teasing name since she'd been taken.

"You're welcome, sweetheart. Use it well. We'll be right here waiting for you when you're ready to come back home," Hel said.

"You'll rescue a whole gaggle of baby soulweavers while I'm gone and forget all about me," Kaia said, swiping at her tears.

"Never. You're burrowed too deep in our hearts for that. We will always be there for you, baby girl," Bast said.

Ana's soft crying grew louder and Ra winced as one of the strongest women he knew strode from the room, unable to face the loss of her daughter from her life for three years. Bast went to follow her, but Hel pulled him back.

"You three eat. I'll go," she said.

Kaia stared after her mother helplessly, misery in every line of her body.

"Come on, K-bear. Why don't you try out those blades and show us what you've got," Ra said, knowing none of them would be able to eat until the two women returned.

Kaia got to her feet and moved to the nearby balcony where there was more space to move and Ra leaned into Bast's shoulder where he'd sat down next to him as they watched on.

"How'd your chat with Mica go?" Bast asked.

"About as well as you'd expect."

"Which of you is bleeding?"

Ra snorted and playfully punched his chosen brother's shoulder. "Give me a little credit."

"On a scale of one to ten, how conciliatory will I have to be when he gets here?" Bast asked.

"Thirteen, maybe? I should've kept my cool for Kaia's sake."

"She's resilient. She'll be okay," Bast said, as they watched the girl run through a series of sweeping attacks and defences she'd obsessively practised with Hel over the previous months since she'd been freed from her captivity.

"She deserves to be more than just okay. I want to see her laughing and playing tricks again. I have to try and talk Mica round one more time," Ra said.

"Can you use whatever you held over him last time when you got him to invite Hel to the council meeting?" Bast asked.

Ra winced. Bast had always trusted him with the communications and politics of the Soul Court and he'd never asked exactly what Ra had done to secure Mica's cooperation when they'd needed it. Probably because he knew he wouldn't like it.

"No. He was very clear if I kept holding that over him it would mean war between our courts," Ra said.

Bast jerked around to stare at him in surprise. "What the fuck did you do?"

"What needed to be done. You could've *died*," Ra said, refusing to back down.

Bast sighed and pulled him closer, the magical connection between them flaring brighter as he let his power flow through the black wings of his mark where it wrapped around Ra's upper arm.

"Mica was just doing what anyone else in his position would," Bast said.

"And so was I."

"Maybe try honey instead of vinegar this time?" Bast suggested.

The words startled a laugh out of Ra. "I guess he does bear a passing resemblance to a fly."

Their talk was interrupted by a firm knock at the door as Morrigan let Mica into the penthouse before disappearing back the way she'd come. Irritation rushed through Ra as the Earth Lord stiffened the moment he noticed them sitting there, Mica's eyes tracking the way Bast's arm wrapped around him.

Bast stood before whatever tension was building could result in one of them lashing out again. "Greetings, Lord Mica. Thank you again for agreeing to join us this morning. I know it must've been an early start for you."

Kaia had noticed the flash of Mica's wings and came to rejoin them at the table, bowing like the perfect elemental child, despite the fact she'd never had to do so in the Soul Court, where such formalities were seldom observed. Zee must've been coaching her.

"You honour me with your presence, Lord Mica," Kaia said.

Mica smiled down at the girl and, annoyingly, it was a genuine one. The kind of smile he used to bestow on Ra when they stayed up talking over herbal tea after the council sessions in the Tower concluded.

"It is me who is honoured to be invited, Kaia," Mica said, seemingly having recovered the diplomacy and charm he reserved for everyone except Ra.

The sound of their voices must've alerted Hel and Ana their visitor had arrived because they emerged from the hallway a moment later, greeting the Earth Lord with falsely bright voices and settling everyone at the table with food. Ana went and sat next to her daughter, the two of them whispering quietly to each other as they said the things that needed saying before she left.

Bast was sending Ra worried looks as they ate and the rest of the table was stuck in an awkward static silence that seemed to grow tighter and tighter with an invisible tension as taut as the garottes he hid in the leather bracelets around his wrists. Finally he couldn't take it any longer and Hel jerked in surprise when his voice cut across the table like a whip.

"I'm coming with her," he said, glaring at Mica in challenge as if he could force his way into the Earth Court by sheer willpower.

Ra kept his eyes locked on Mica as the Earth Lord placed his fork carefully back on his plate. His eyes flicked to Kaia before he replied.

"Why would I let you do that?" Mica asked, his tone giving nothing away.

Honey, not vinegar, Ra reminded himself.

"Because I might be able to help with the stronghold. We use technology and magic together here in a way your court doesn't." Ra knew the conciliatory offer sounded like it had been dragged from him unwillingly, but there was no hiding how desperate he was. His eyes were on Kaia as he spoke. He'd do anything for her. Even work with the elemental he now despised.

"Ra was the one who came up with the system I use to manage the sentinel souls and his scanning technology was the breakthrough in designing the shielding for the soulweavers so the children no longer succumb to soul taint. There is no one more qualified to find a technological solution to a magical problem," Bast added, sensing the crack in Mica's defences and jumping in to support his argument.

"You think I would expose my stronghold to someone like him after what he did?" Mica asked Bast.

"I think you don't have a choice. It's not getting any better. It's been months. You look like a crack addict who's—"

"Ra!" Bast cut over the top of him before he could finish the insult that would guarantee he failed.

Ra swallowed hard and then clenched his jaw, eyes back on Kaia. "I apologise," he said through gritted teeth.

Mica stared at him for a long moment and then tipped his head in acknowledgement infinitesimally. "Fine," he said, probably surprising himself more than anyone else at the table, and that was saying a lot.

"What?" Ra croaked.

"I said fine. You may accompany Kaia. Bring your technology. But you can't work for Bastion at the same time. If you insist on coming to my court, you are *mine* until you leave and this disrespect ends now. I won't tolerate you undermining me in my own court."

"Respect goes both ways," Ra shot back. What the fuck had he done? He couldn't give up now he was so close, though. "Fine. I agree to your terms," he added.

Bast shifted in his seat. "Brother..." he said, concern for him clear in his voice.

Ra looked up at him and a silent understanding passed between them. They'd spent twenty-five years being there for each other unconditionally, but now Bast had his mate to look after him and build a future with. Kaia needed him more than Bast did. Even if it meant cutting ties with the Soul Court while he was there.

"Thank you," Bast finished, even though he knew that wasn't what his brother had started to say.

"I'm counting on you to look after him for me, Hellcat," Ra said to Hel.

"Always," she promised. "Just like you'll take care of Kaia for us."

Kaia, bless her, chose that moment to let a little of her brightness back into the room. "Now that's sorted, I wanna know what my surprise is, Uncle Ra."

The strained smile Ra was wearing stretched into something more genuine as he watched Kaia bounce in her seat.

"You weren't even supposed to know there was a surprise, K-bear," he teased. "You're too sneaky for your own good."

Kaia jumped to her feet and started pulling on his arm. "Come *on*."

"How do you know your surprise isn't up here already?" Ra asked, laughing.

"Māmā, make Uncle show me," Kaia said.

Ana surreptitiously swiped at her eyes and then stood, starting to clear the table. Hel and Bast jumped in to help and before long the six of them were heading to the elevators.

"Close your eyes, scamp," Ra said as they stepped into the small space.

It got awkward quickly as four sets of wings jostled for room. Somehow Mica ended up closest to the buttons and Ra was forced to reach around him to select their floor. He didn't mean to brush up against the copper of his feathers again. He had more than enough experience with elementals in bed to know how sensitive their wings were and how rude it was to touch them uninvited.

The touch sparked a zap of energy between them. Goosebumps sprung up on his arms where his shirt sleeves were rolled up and he stifled a groan as he felt an unfamiliar power tingle through his veins from the point of contact. He was used to the cool silver fire of Bast's magic, but Mica's was a whole other level that left a deep yearning need in its wake. The Earth Lord drew in a sharp breath and both men froze at the unintended intimacy.

"Are we going to The Crypt?!" Kaia squealed, breaking the moment.

Hel laughed and put her arm around the girl. Kaia had never been allowed in the nightclub for obvious reasons, but she'd tried to sneak in there at least a dozen times throughout her childhood. He'd been planning this surprise for her since the moment they'd realised she'd have to leave.

"Happy moving day, sweetness," Hel said.

Kaia glanced up at Hel, surprise and then determination showing on her face. "Happy?" she asked.

"We're going to make it happy. You are so loved, darling girl. This is just the next exciting chapter in your story," Hel said.

Kaia glanced to her mum for reassurance and Ana pulled it together enough to smile. "Hel's right, sweetheart. Show Lord Mica how we party here."

"I'm familiar," Mica said, eyes meeting Ra's before he turned away.

They'd shared one dance together at the ball Bast had hosted during the council meetings the previous year. One kiss. One moment where their desire had almost unleashed. And then they'd both been called away by duty.

"Do you have parties in the Earth Court?" Kaia asked as the elevator doors opened.

Mica smiled. "We're planning one of the biggest parties ever in a few months."

Ra hid his surprise. That was news to him. They'd been so focused on the upcoming appointment of a new ruler for the Air Court that he hadn't heard anything about it.

"Can I come?" Kaia asked.

"Of course. I'd be honoured," Mica said, inclining his head before stepping aside to let them lead the way under the bronze plaque at the club's entrance and onto the dancefloor.

"Surprise!" a cascade of voices called out, and Kaia froze in place at the door, the electric blue of her wings trembling as she took it all in.

Ra had made sure everyone who cared for the girl was there—her friends from school, her teachers, the couriers she used to tease and harass. It was a mark of how special she was that the room was also filled with the entire ruling partnership, other than Zee who couldn't risk it, and a mix of all the peoples they'd welcomed into the city. Kaia might be hurting and broken after her captivity, but that hadn't stopped her from checking in on the children of both the vampyr and the ceptae and easing their transition into living in the city.

She may have lost her joy for a while, but she'd never lost her empathy. Now, it would be her turn to start her life somewhere new with strangers. He could only hope the residents of the Earth Court were as welcoming to Kaia as she had been to the new residents of the City of Souls. He already knew his own welcome would be non-existent, given the animosity between him and Mica.

Ra made his way to the DJ turntables and queued up the playlist of Kaia's favourite songs he'd prepared. As music filled the space and colourful lights flashed across the room, the girl found her footing and greeted her friends with hug after hug. Ignoring the urge to search the room for a certain copper-winged asshole, he fired off a series of texts to his staff to make sure his bag and the tech he would need to take to the Earth Court would be waiting on the roof for them when they were ready to leave.

He'd packed in the hopes of success, but he hadn't

realised he'd be helping with the stronghold when he did so. Now, he needed to make sure he had the right gear to deliver on his promise to Mica. Some of it he would be able to get over there, but his computer with Zee's magical upgrades was irreplaceable and Bast could spare him a drone or two for him to get started on scanning the caves before he found a local supplier. As an afterthought, he asked his people to add one of his miniature whiskey casks to the gear as well. It tasted like home and he suspected he was going to need the reminder.

"Thank you for going with her. I know living there will be hard for you," Ana murmured, coming to stand next to him and resting her arm around his shoulders as she watched her daughter flit around the room.

Ra met the eyes of one of his oldest friends and smiled. "Of course."

"You know, if things worked out for them, they could work out for you, too," Ana said.

Ra followed her gaze in time to watch the spark of Hel and Bast's magic off their wings as his best friend pulled his mate in for a kiss. He snorted at Ana's suggestion his relationship with Mica was anything like what the two shared. Mating bonds were beyond rare among elementals, and that was *not* what had been happening between them even before they'd fallen apart. The spark between them was plain old lust, nothing more. Which is why it had carried on even after any affection between them turned to loathing. He wasn't even sure humans could form a mating bond with an elemental given their lack of obvious magic. And why would anyone want to make themselves so vulnerable to a person like that? Hel could feel every one of Bast's emotions unless he actively prevented it. It sounded exhausting.

"Unlikely," he said.

"All I'm saying is don't close yourself off to possibility."

Shaking his head, Ra decided to end the ridiculous conversation by taking a trip down memory lane with his playlist. When Bast and Hel had first come to The Crypt together, he'd played a particular song, using his connection with Bast to synchronise it perfectly with the thrumming of his friend's heartbeat as he orbited around Hel. Their relationship had been fake then. Fake and fiery. But he could feel through their connection that his friend's heartbeat was still picking up the same way as he kissed her now.

As the first thrumming strains of a remixed 'Wicked Game' sounded across the club, Hel and Bast glanced over and smiled at Ra from across the room. Kaia joined them by the bar a moment later, wrapping her small arms around them both and leaning her head on Hel's arm as they pulled her into an embrace.

Ignoring the flash of copper in his peripheral vision that said a certain Earth Lord was too close, Ra headed to the dancefloor. He might not be able to let loose like he did when the club was open, but he could still lose himself in the music and the crowd of people of all genders who gravitated to him as soon as they saw him emerge from the DJ booth. They kept it G-rated for Kaia's sake, but satisfaction filled him as he threw his arms in the air and let go. This was familiar. His happy place. For the two decades since he'd established the club, he'd been known for this—generous with both his drinks and with pleasure, even if the latter hadn't featured lately.

"We need to get going," Mica growled from nearby, startling him from his reverie as the elemental glared at the people surrounding Ra.

Luckily, Kaia joined them before he could tell the Earth Lord what he thought of his statement.

"One more dance?" she asked, holding out her arm to Mica in invitation.

Mica looked surprised, but he took her arm and moved a few steps further away before bowing like the courtier he was and sweeping Kaia into a formal elemental dance that shouldn't have worked with the modern human music but somehow did anyway. Ra tried to lose himself in the song again but the cheeky girl manoeuvred them so they were back dancing right alongside each other. The edge of Mica's wing brushed against his arm sparking a full body shiver despite his best efforts to ignore him.

It all started to feel very real when he finally cut the music and he was grateful for the distraction of Kaia being swept into more hugs by her friends. Ana said her farewells to them at the elevators, unable to face watching her daughter walk through the portal and out of her life for three years.

"Keep her safe for me," Ana whispered in his ear as she held him tight, her tears soaking into his shirt.

"I promise," Ra said.

The five of them were silent as they rode the elevator up to the roof and Ra reached out to squeeze Kaia's hand in reassurance. A cool wind tugged at their clothes as they stepped out into the bright sunshine and headed to the circle of black tile that looked more ominous than it had earlier in the day.

"Stay safe, baby girl. We'll be here waiting when you're ready to come home," Bast said.

Hel pulled Kaia into a tight embrace, whispering some-thing to her.

"Thank you for taking her. Please keep her safe. You have our heart in your hands," Bast said, turning to Mica.

"I give you my word," Mica said.

"Is it too much to ask you to keep Ra safe, too?" Hel asked.

Ra rolled his eyes. Why the fuck was the prickly woman choosing now to become sentimental? "I don't need a damn thing from him."

Mica ignored the angry words. "Like I said, while he's in my court, he's mine. I will protect him the same way I protect all my people. And if he betrays me again, I will punish him the same way I would one of my own."

Ra watched Hel wince and swallow hard. The Courts were ruthless about loyalty and that threat was not idle. This was a mistake. He knew that. But it was one he had no choice but to make to look after his niece. Mica stepped away to help collect Ra's cases of tech to carry through, and Bast turned to him.

"Don't do anything stupid while you're there. I can live without you here every day, but I can't live in a world where you don't exist," Bast said.

"I can still help—" Ra started to say.

"No, brother. If you can't abide by his rules to keep *yourself* safe, do it to keep Kaia safe. No touching base with your old team here. No checking in with Morrigan on security risks. No communications with any of us that you wouldn't be happy with Mica reading."

"Fuck," Ra said, the gravity of his situation hitting him once again.

"I love you, brother."

"Love you too, bro," Ra said.

It was Hel who formed the portal this time, the searing

heat of her sparking blue magic almost comforting now in its familiarity. With a final wave, Mica stepped through the fiery gateway. Taking a deep breath, Kaia looked out over the city one more time and then followed behind. Ra's heart ached as he paused on the edge of a step that would take him further than he ever wanted to be from his chosen family.

Bast had pulled Hel into his arms and the couple were framed by the majesty of Soul Tower beneath them and the glittering cerulean of the harbour in the distance. They had each other. They would be just fine without him. He was needed elsewhere now by both the girl he loved like family and the elemental he couldn't stand. The draw to take that last step forward became overwhelming as he pictured the vulnerability in both their faces. The Earth Lord hid his a lot better, but it was still there and he wished he didn't care. Damn Mica for his magnetic pull that carried him over the threshold.

CHAPTER 3

RA

The humid heat of the Asian continent felt like a sauna after the cold wind of the City of Souls. Ugh. He did *not* need to be thinking about saunas when Mica was right there. The portal had opened unusually close to the soaring main entrance to the limestone caves that made up the sentient stronghold of the Earth Court. Portal magic was rare on the Melded Earths and the elemental rulers had taken exception to their formation anywhere near their power bases when it had come up at the global summit. Mica must've made an exception because he was travelling through it himself.

Kaia's surprised laugh sounded from nearby and Ra glanced over to see her standing near his gear where Mica was talking to an elemental with a slight build and wings the colour of oxidised copper. He recognised the elemental from previous surveillance as Wren, the Earth Court seneschal. On either side of them, lush jungle clung to the steep hillside the caves were set into.

"What's so funny K-Bear?" he asked, moving closer.

"The stronghold likes you. It got all fizzy in my mind when you stepped through," Kaia explained, smiling up at him.

As a human, Ra couldn't hear the stronghold like the elementals could, but he wasn't going to let that stop him communicating with it. Bowing low toward the entrance, he turned on the charm. "I'm fizzing, too. It's an honour to set foot in such exquisite beauty," he told the caves.

"What is *he* doing here?" Wren snapped at Mica.

Ra raised an eyebrow at the borderline rude tone, although the shitty attitude toward him wasn't exactly unexpected. It wouldn't be the first time he had to win over a tough crowd. "Hi, I'm Ra," he said, forcing his voice to stay upbeat and reaching out a hand to shake that Wren ignored.

"He's moving in while Kaia trains with us. Have the guest suite in my wing prepared," Mica said.

"My Lord, he doesn't deserve such an honour. Surely, he would be better placed with the girl in the trainee quarters, or at least in the usual guest quarters," Wren muttered, just loud enough to ensure Ra caught the words.

Ra snorted softly to himself and let his hand fall back to his side. Could the guy be any more obvious with his crush as he stared up at Mica with that obsequious obsession? In his role advising Bast, he'd kept up with all the gossip of the elemental courts. He'd heard the ponderings on why the seneschal had stayed in his position so long when most used it as a springboard to regional leadership of one of the Earth Court territories. Looked like the theories of unrequited love were spot on. Although, given the light colouring of Wren's feathers, it was possible the seneschal didn't have enough magic to be promoted elsewhere. The most powerful Earth mages all shared at least some of the shining metallic copper of Mica's wings, but Wren's had only the barest hint of that colouring on their edges.

"Do not question me, Wren. He is mine until he leaves. I need him close where I can keep an eye on him," Mica said, his eyes flicking down the length of Ra's body on those last words.

Fuck him. Ra didn't belong to anybody and that possessive crap shouldn't have him adjusting his jeans where they were becoming too tight, dammit.

"You *cannot* be serious after what he did. Whatever he's offered to get you to agree to this, I'm sure I can provide it for you," Wren said.

Ra's smirk turned into outright laughter at the thinly veiled come-on Mica seemed utterly oblivious to. "Dude, desperation isn't a good look on you. If you're so keen to claim him, why don't you piss a circle around him while you're at it?"

"Ra, behave!" Mica growled, narrowing his eyes at him. "And Wren, I already gave you your orders. I expect the suite to be ready by the time we get there. Now, where is Serena? I thought she would be here to greet Kaia and help her settle in."

Wren's eyes shifted back and forth between him and the Earth Lord like he was deciding how much to say. "She was called away unexpectedly. I can show the girl to her room."

Ra frowned at the thought of this asshole taking Kaia anywhere. And what was so urgent that the head of magical training needed to leave just as her new charge arrived? None of this was reassuring him Kaia would be safe here. Thank fuck he'd managed to convince Mica to let him come and keep an eye on her.

"Called to where?" Mica asked.

"Perhaps we can discuss this once your guests are more comfortable," Wren said.

"Wren, I give you a lot of leeway because of your centuries of service but I am losing patience. When I ask you a question, I expect an answer," Mica said, voice cold.

Wren's face flushed red with embarrassment and Ra was surprised he didn't drop to his knees in supplication. "Of course, my lord. I apologise. She is settling Kim and Jasper in the Tree City. She should return in time for the welcome dinner."

Ra could tell he was missing important context to this conversation. The Tree City was the nearest elemental city. It was home to those without enough power or status to justify a place in the stronghold, although he suspected many of the stronghold's residents also had homes there given how much easier it was to take flight from a tree than a cave for the winged elementals. Kim and Jasper must be trainees if Serena had missed their arrival to help them, but he'd thought trainees needed the proximity to the stronghold to stabilise their power as they learned. That was the whole reason Kaia was moving there after all. This was giving him a very bad feeling. He'd keep his concerns to himself for now to avoid stressing Kaia out, but he'd be quizzing Mica later for sure.

Mica's face had turned carefully neutral at his seneschal's words. "I will show Kaia to her room while you prepare the suite."

"As you wish," Wren said, gesturing to another elemental who'd appeared to collect Ra's tech gear.

"Be careful with that. It's as delicate as Wren's ego," Ra called, winking at the elemental in question, a young woman with enough copper in her wings to suggest she was going places. She stifled a laugh while Wren shot him a murderous look.

Mica growled under his breath. "Do you have a setting that isn't either flirt or aggravate?"

Kaia chose that moment to slip her hand into his and squeeze hard. Looking down at her, he could see the worry on her face. He needed to rein it in and focus on making her feel comfortable.

"I do. Protecting my family," he answered.

THE WALK through the caves and tunnels of the Earth Stronghold was eye-opening, and probably not for the reasons it usually would be. Sure, even he could sense the vast magic of the place he knew was a nexus of dozens of the ley lines crisscrossing the Earths as the source of elemental power. The limestone walls glistened with mica and the odd vein of quartz ribboned with tungsten ore that glittered under the magical illumination. It was deeply beautiful and the sense of age and calm from walking through the depths of the earth was impressive.

What he noticed most as they paused in a vast chamber that formed a crossroads, though, was the quiet. The space was lit by thousands of glowing tendrils hanging from its roof in rainbow shades and a dozen holes at various heights around its walls shone with artificial light where pathways curved out into the rest of the subterranean stronghold. It should have been bustling with elementals flying back and forth in the middle of the day like this, but the few people they passed were only those who were clearly going about a duty. No one lingered at the benches where clever mirrors let the sunshine through to creeping greenery. Conversations were hushed. The sounds of laughter and teasing he was used to from staff working in Soul Tower were absent.

The other thing that became clear as they made their way deeper was that the stronghold had, not surprisingly, not been designed for humans. The first time they reached a crossways where they needed to shift levels, he watched as Mica and Kaia spread their wings wide to coast down from the tunnel they were leaving to the cave floor and he was forced to clamber down a ladder while they waited for him. As he crossed the chamber, he noticed a pile of crumbled rockfall to their left that looked suspiciously like a tunnel collapse. Had the stronghold been destabilised enough to damage itself that way?

The next time they arrived at a chamber sporting a convergence of tunnels, there wasn't even a ladder to climb.

Mica cleared his throat awkwardly. "My apologies. We don't get many human visitors. If I'd known you were coming, we would have worked something out already. The trainee quarters are just through there," he said, gesturing to a wide tunnel to their right and above them. "Your suite will be more accessible to you. It's back the way we came on the main thoroughfares."

Leaning forward, Ra stared up across the cave wall. He was a decent rock climber, and it had enough texture that he should be able to manage it without ropes. He didn't want to be reliant on the Earth Court placing ladders for him to get to Kaia because he was certain Wren and anyone else who had it in for him would find a way to use the need against him.

Reaching out, he touched the wall, getting a feel for how well it might support him. A moment later, a noise like rockfall filled the air and he jerked his hand back as the wall started to move. A narrow staircase levered itself out from the sides of the cave to join the two tunnels he needed to navigate sending a shower of stones scattering down.

"Aren't you a clever thing?" Ra murmured to the stronghold. "Thank you."

"It's not supposed to do that without being asked," Mica said, concern in his voice.

"It really likes you Uncle Sunshine," Kaia said, smiling up at him.

"The feeling's mutual," Ra said, stroking the wall again, which warmed and thrummed beneath his fingers until he could feel the life in it.

The entrance to the trainee quarters was an inviting space hung with bright tapestries depicting the history of the Earth Court and the stages of magical learning. Ra stayed quiet as Mica played tour guide, slowing to explain each of the images to Kaia—the first stage of connection with the stronghold to stabilise a young elemental's growing power, the process of learning to channel magic safely, and finally the specialisations of each of the main types of magic that were taught.

Kaia wouldn't stay long enough to specialise, but hopefully she could carry on learning from Zee back home once she could safely control her power. The terms of her training had been spelled out by a contract between the courts and Mica had only committed to teaching her the basics of each magical specialty—defensive, offensive, and crafting and influence of the natural world. Ra was guessing the focus would be on areas more like Zee's magical engineering or uncontroversial magics like shielding and healing rather than anything that could be used to attack the Earth Court if they were at odds in the future. He hoped that wouldn't hold Kaia back from going as far as she could with her power. Even things like Mica's ability to calm and influence the predatory wyrms—earth dragons that flew beneath the earths' surface—could be used offensively, so her training would be very limited if they avoided anything dangerous.

The room Kaia was shown to was small but pleasant—just a single bed and desk—but the ensuite bathroom was a luxury he hadn't expected for her. Somehow, her bags had made it there ahead of them. He wrapped an arm around her shoulders as she took it in. It was a big change from her room in Soul Tower with its floor-to-ceiling windows looking out over the city.

"What do you think, sweetheart?" he asked.

Mica had stayed out in the hallway to give them a modicum of privacy, which was just as well given the size of the room would've had them standing nearly on top of each other.

"It's nice. It feels cosy nestled in the earth like this with the stronghold," she murmured.

The light that emanated from the walls in lieu of any light fixture flared briefly as the stronghold responded to her words.

"Ah, there you are, my lord. Welcome back. I apologise for my tardiness," a woman's voice called from nearby.

Leaving Kaia to inspect her new home, Ra stepped back into the hallway to see an elemental with sweeping wings of copper and bronze walking toward them. Her brown eyes shone with bright intelligence and the rich purple silk of her shirt matched her long dyed hair. The stronghold's light seemed to gather against the light brown of her skin and the metallic sheen of her feathers, making her almost glow. In fact, now that he had time to stop and observe, he could see the same effect was even more marked on Mica, like he was bathed in power. As if the elemental needed to be any more attractive.

He'd done his research before coming, he had co-ordinated the Soul Court's intelligence after all, so he knew this was Serena—the missing head trainer who would have primary care for Kaia's wellbeing while she was there.

"Hi there. I'm Ra," he said, extending his hand to her like he had with Wren and wondering if he was about to be spectacularly rejected again.

"My goodness! Look at you! The stronghold is positively smitten with you and is that the Soul Lord's mark you bear? How intriguing. I haven't had a chance to study soulweaving but I'd love to learn more about it. Does it feel warm or cool when it's activated? Does the mark mean you can channel some of it yourself?" Serena asked, reaching out to shake his hand with enthusiasm as the questions tumbled from her lips.

"Perhaps wait a few days before you start the inquisition, Serena," Mica said, voice dry with humour.

Ra grinned at her enthusiasm. "I'm happy to chat magic with you any time, Teach."

"And you must be Kaia!" Serena said, turning to where the girl was cautiously poking her head from the room.

"Yes, ma'am. It's a pleasure to meet you," Kaia said, bowing like she'd been taught.

"None of that! You're family while you're here. Come here," Serena said, pulling the girl into a hug.

The tension that had been ratcheting ever tighter inside him since the second he'd arrived and noticed the tell-tale signs that things weren't right here loosened a little as Kaia relaxed into the embrace. Finally, here was someone he might actually be able to trust with his niece.

"Serena has shepherded hundreds of scared teenagers into confidence with their power. I told you Kaia would be well cared for," Mica murmured. "Must you give everyone an irritating nickname, though? 'Teach'? She is an elder here and deserves more respect."

Huh. He wouldn't have guessed Serena was older than Mica. The elemental didn't look a day over twenty-five, not that any of the immortals did.

"Why? Are you jealous I haven't given you one, *Lord* Mica?" Ra asked. "Speaking of names, does the stronghold have one?"

Mica looked surprised. "Yes. Its name is Earth Stronghold," he deadpanned.

Ra rolled his eyes. "That's not a fucking name, is it baby?" he said, addressing the caves. "I'm going to call you Earthshine."

The stone floor beneath his feet warmed in response and light danced across the minerals embedded in the ceiling.

Mica looked pained. "I don't suppose you could be a little less endearing to my stronghold? It's uncomfortable."

"Why? Because you want it to hate me as much as you do?"

"Exactly that," Mica said.

"Fascinating. Are they always like this? Why did my Lord let him come?" Serena asked Kaia, mischief in her voice. She was obviously old enough to get away with the teasing.

"They used to be sweeter together, but yeah, they always look like they're about to jump each other's bones. Uncle's going to use his technology to help heal the stronghold," Kaia said.

Oof. From the mouths of children. He could've done without that truth bomb.

"I trust Serena, but I'd appreciate it if you'd keep the information about the stronghold to yourself for now, Kaia. The other trainees and staff don't need to worry about it," Mica said.

"Where *are* the other trainees?" Ra asked.

Serena and Mica shared a significant look that confirmed his suspicions that something was wrong. The space was too quiet to be the residence of a bunch of teenagers.

"The other trainees have been here longer. The younger ones are spending some time in the Tree City to study the magics that went into constructing it. The older ones are venturing further afield," Serena said.

That may have technically been the truth, but he was betting there was a lot more to the story.

"If you're available now, we will leave Kaia in your capable hands until dinner," Mica told Serena.

"My pleasure," Serena said, smiling down at the girl.

Ra did his best to hide his wave of irritation at Mica's presumption he would leave with him. "That okay with you K-bear? I'm happy to stick around."

"I'm fine, Uncle. Go."

Ra reached out and ruffled her white-blond hair. "I see how it is. Too cool for your Uncle Sunshine already."

Kaia rolled her eyes and hugged him goodbye.

Mica was already stalking ahead of him back the way they'd come when he finally pulled away. Sighing to himself, Ra jogged to catch up, ignoring the way the elemental's wings framed his ass perfectly in his tailored suit pants.

"If you coddle her, she will lose her confidence," Mica said.

"Chill. She's only twelve and we just got here."

Glancing over, Ra watched Mica's jaw tighten in the warm light emanating from the tunnel walls. "I will show you to your room and then I have things to see to until dinner. Do not venture into the tunnels without a guide. You'll get lost."

"I'm sure I'll be fine. Your stronghold's not going to let me get lost are you, Earthshine?" he asked the walls.

"Stop doing that," Mica growled.

Ra's temper flared. "No."

Mica swung around faster than Ra expected and he was pinned against the nearest wall before he had a chance to react, strong arms caging him in on either side of his head. "You are in *my* territory now. You do as *I* say."

"Yeah, no. That's not how this is going to go," Ra said, glaring up at Mica. "Especially when your orders are bullshit. I'm going to be sending drones all over your sweetheart of a stronghold. I need it to trust me so I can help it heal. You know. The whole reason you let me come."

The copper of Mica's magic flared so brightly in his wings that Ra was forced to squint and a sensation like a landslide slipped over his skin as it rushed over him.

"You gonna lose your temper with me, Lord Mica? Is this your famed diplomacy?" he taunted, which probably wasn't the brightest move to make. What could he say? The elemental brought out the worst in him.

Mica snarled and the sensation of power coming from the hand resting near his ear grew even stronger. Hot earth magic snaked around his neck and he tried to jerk away too late with nowhere to go. Had he really pushed Mica to attack so soon? He'd thought they'd last at least a few hours.

The Earth Lord pulled back a moment later, his eyes flicking down to a new weight resting on Ra's collarbones before turning away. Reaching up, Ra felt a thin strangely flexible length of a smooth warm mineral around his neck. His searching fingers found no seams or sharp edges and no obvious way to remove the construct.

"Did you just fucking *collar* me?!" Ra yelled.

CHAPTER 4
RA

"You wanted to explore. This will let me find you if you wander off," Mica said. "Come, I have places to be."

Ra planted his feet and stayed put. "You could just ask the stronghold where I was."

"Not if you leave it. This is non-negotiable."

What the fuck? The collar was extreme even given the history between them. It didn't make sense. "What aren't you telling me?" Ra asked, narrowing his eyes.

Mica glared at him. "You caught the stronghold on a good day. It's self is ... fractured ... in places. The collar will help keep you safe. The stronghold will recognise my power on you if you find yourself in a place that has forgotten who you are."

"What's this made of anyway?" Ra said, reaching up to touch the collar again.

Was that a hint of red flushing Mica's cheeks? "That's not important."

Glancing around them, Ra noticed the veins of glittering

minerals running through the tunnel walls and a sneaking suspicion settled in his gut.

"Holy shit. It's made of mica, isn't it? Why don't you just brand me like stray livestock while you're at it?" Ra asked.

"I told you, you're mine while you're here. Now come or I will carry you."

Ra took the threat seriously and forced his feet to move. The last thing he needed was to be scooped up into Mica's arms. "And what is your jealous little Wren going to think when he sees my new accessory?"

"This may be hard for you to comprehend, but not everything is about sex. Wren isn't jealous of you like that. If anything, he'll be grateful you're being monitored. It's not like I marked you like Bastion did," Mica said, tension ratcheting up in his voice on the last sentence.

Fuck, Mica was so clueless sometimes. Mostly when it came to his love life. The fact it took them a decade of flirtation to even meet was proof of that. It would almost be endearing if it wasn't going to put Ra even more at odds with the guy who could make his work here very difficult. Shaking his head, he gave up trying to explain it.

The entrance to Mica's wing of the stronghold was marked by extravagant double doors that spread wider than an elemental wingspan and over twice his height. They were made of the limestone of the caves and intricately carved into a map of the Earth Court territory that stretched across the entire Asian and Oceania continents, excluding the oceans that were the domain of Nerida, Lady of the Water Court, and the islands of Aotearoa New Zealand where the City of Souls and several other free settlements of elementals had found refuge.

The doors swung open as they approached and Ra took

in the surprisingly cosy open-plan living area that reminded him of Bast's penthouse back home in Soul Tower. They must have been on the outer edge of the cave system and higher up inside the hills that soared above it because there was a real window across from them complete with a balcony that looked out over lush green jungle. Stacked mineral rock formations made up the breakfast bar and the dining table, and soft furnishings in various shades of burnished copper made the space warm and inviting. A plush low-backed couch that could seat at least three elementals was angled to take advantage of an open fireplace that took the chill off the air of the cave system. The fire was blazing with no sign of any wood or other fuel—the perks of a home made from pure magic.

"Your room is through the wooden door and the guest bathroom is the door right next to it," Mica said, striding away from him toward one of the other doors leading off the space as if he couldn't wait to be free of the annoyance of his presence. "My rooms are through there," he added, gesturing to another impressively detailed carved door made of limestone and minerals across the other side of the room.

Ra paused as he took in the space, turning to Mica in confusion. This is not what he'd envisaged when Mica had said he'd be living in the guest suite of his wing of the stronghold. No wonder Wren had been so surprised.

"Something not to your liking?" Mica asked, warning in his tone.

"I thought you'd have like a dozen guest rooms, eight formal lounges, and a spa or something. This is your private space. Are you sure you want me here? I thought you'd put me as far away as possible," Ra said, his surprise making him more forthcoming than he'd usually be.

"I don't trust you anywhere else," Mica bit out.

"You literally have eyes in the walls and I'm pretty sure you just put the equivalent of a monitoring cuff around my neck, like humans use to track convicted criminals," Ra said.

"Well, I'm sure a human court would have convicted you for what you did to my people," Mica snarled.

Ra resisted the urge to flinch at the pain in those words. He'd done what he needed to do to protect Bast and Hel. He didn't owe Mica an explanation. "I didn't do shit to your people. I threatened *you*. We reached an understanding before it could affect anyone else."

"You held the food supply for thousands of people to ransom!"

The fact Mica believed him capable of following through on that threat showed just how doomed their 'relationship' had been. Fuck him.

"You were the deciding vote in supporting Hel's capture, knowing it would lead to her and Bast's deaths if you succeeded!" Ra snapped back.

"I didn't have any choice! The fate of millions was in the balance!" Mica said, looming over him.

"There is always a choice. You chose to betray the people who were there for you when you needed them," Ra said, losing the fight to keep his own pain hidden. "You chose to betray *us*," he added in a whisper.

"My court will always come first. If you thought any different, that's on you," Mica said, his voice almost gentle despite the uncompromising position of his words.

"Noted," Ra said, swallowing hard.

He hadn't expected otherwise, but Bast put the welfare of his people above everything as well and *he* still managed to vehemently protect and adore his mate. Not that he and Mica were mates.

Sighing, Mica reached out and brushed a stray lock of hair from his forehead before running a finger along the warm mica of the collar circling his neck. "We cannot fight like this for three years. Can we call a truce?"

Whatever answer he would've given was cut off by a sharp jolt of trembling earth beneath his feet followed by a piercing alarm coming from Mica's sat-phone.

Steel pushed aside the vulnerability in Mica's expression as he answered the phone. "Report."

Ra couldn't make out the words on the other end of the call, but he could tell it was bad.

"I'm on my way," Mica said, turning toward the balcony.

"Is it a problem with the stronghold? I need to know what we're dealing with. Take me with you," Ra said, following along behind the Earth Lord as he made his way outside.

Mica paused, an uncharacteristic uncertainty showing through. "If I take you, you must swear to tell no one what you see."

"Done," Ra said. Bast had already made him promise not to communicate with the Soul Court and who else was he going to tell?

Warmth flared in the mica around his neck and he yelped in surprise. "What?"

"My magic will constrict your vocal cords if you try and break your oath," Mica said.

"Fuck you! I keep my promises!"

"We don't have time for this. Come," Mica said, holding out his arms.

Oh shit. He hadn't thought this through. Mica was

heading outside, not back into the caves. Of course, he would have to carry him wherever they were headed.

Scoffing at his hesitation, Mica scooped him up in his arms and used his power to launch them above the jungle canopy and into the clear blue of the sky. It wasn't the first time Ra had been carried by an elemental in flight. Bast had carried him many times when they needed to get somewhere in a hurry and his friends in the City of Souls had taken him joyriding more than once, diving and barrel-rolling above the city with him in one of the specialised magical slings designed to reduce the drag of his weight and keep him safe.

This was nothing like any of those times because it was *Mica*. Ra's body was crushed tight against the Earth Lord's muscled chest, which strained with the effort of his impossibly fast wingbeats as they headed west away from both the stronghold and the nearby Tree City. The speed of Mica's magically enhanced flight turned the world into a blur around them and he forgot himself for a moment as exhilaration flowed through him. Throwing his head back, he laughed in delight.

"Aren't you even a little bit scared by this?" Mica asked, amusement in his voice that rumbled against Ra's chest where he'd instinctively turned into the Earth Lord's body.

"This isn't my first rodeo. I've even flown as a passenger in aerial acrobatic displays," Ra said.

Mica growled and clutched him closer. "You will not fly with anyone but *me* while you're here."

Ra smirked and patted the Earth Lord's chest with a placating hand, ignoring the urge to stroke and play as the elemental's enticing scent filled his every breath and the electric energy that had always strung between them sent tingles through every part of him.

"You're the boss," he said.

"I am. Don't forget it," Mica replied, spiralling into a descent.

Ra had barely noticed their surroundings as they flew, but he could see now they were somewhere just outside Granite Bay, a coastal elemental city that had a significant human population courtesy of the surrounding farmland that was a major source of food supply in the area. It was also the scene of Ra's extortion of Mica but, thankfully, the Earth Lord was too distracted to point that out.

Below them, a deep crevasse had opened in the rolling grassland like an open wound in the landscape. It stretched between two outcrops of rocks, bisecting one of the arterial roads into the city. On either side, elemental scouts stood staring into the deep rift with concern.

As they landed, a rumbling shriek echoed into the air and a huge wyrm reared up out of the riven ground. The earth dragon was a juvenile, its long eel-like body only as wide as half of Mica's wingspan. Its smooth scales were a deep mirrored silver that flashed gold and blue as they reflected the dry grass and sky. Fangs the length of his forearm stretched in its gaping maw as it swung its head toward them, blindly searching for prey. Ra frowned as he took in the copper sheen that clouded its eyes. They may be subterranean, but wyrms still usually had vision. Something had taken the poor creature's sight.

"Easy, girl," Mica crooned, gently depositing Ra back on his feet so he could approach the snapping earth dragon.

Power flashed in Mica's wings as he neared her and the wyrm settled, dropping its head to Mica's eye level. Ra held his breath as the Earth Lord reached out and placed a calming hand on the bridge of her snout, even his looming presence dwarfed by the huge dragon. A rumble below his feet had Ra stumbling back as four more wyrms breached the earth around them. Long necks writhed together as they twined around where Mica stood, like a tangled living knot, blocking him from Ra's view.

His fists clenched at his sides as he stood poised and helpless. Vehicles were backing up on the road behind them, barred from reaching the city by the deep crevasse and the dangerous predators. Knowing his worry for the powerful Earth Lord was misplaced, Ra considered what was within his control. It was second nature to help manage a crisis like this after decades on the ruling partnership back home and Mica's scouts would likely be too focused on the magical threat of the wyrms to get things moving before it became a major logistical disruption for the city.

A cursory scan of the building traffic jam revealed what he needed—a truck carrying building materials. Within moments of knocking on the window, he had the human driver smiling and proud to lend his expertise to the cause. Ignoring the thrum of power still building behind him, Ra directed the heavy truck off the road to flatten a curving path through the grassland that would let the trail of vehicles circle around the obstruction and carry on their way.

It wasn't long before Mica's scouts joined his efforts, those with magic smoothing the new makeshift road into something less likely to puncture a tyre. Without really thinking about what he was doing, Ra asked them to install a solid barrier and a series of lighted road markers so no one would come to harm in the crevasse once darkness fell. The young mage he worked with on spacing the crystal light sources was a delight, his fascination with learning to mimic human traffic signage clear in the barrage of questions he threw at Ra.

He could tell the mages were stressed by whatever it was that had happened to cause the rift but he did his best to keep things light as they worked, joking about taking their newfound roading expertise and using it to construct an aerial racetrack. Other than the curious looks they kept sending the collar around his neck, Mica's people were just as fun and respectful as his team back home. Even the looks weren't disrespectful. If anything they were pleasantly surprised.

"Thank you," Mica murmured, approaching him as the young mage waved goodbye. "The regional lead was tied up with another breach elsewhere and the scouts don't always appreciate the urgency of damage to human infrastructure. It would've been hours before we sorted this if you hadn't stepped in."

Ra glanced over at the Earth Lord, surprised to see such visible fatigue in him. "I didn't do much. They would've figured it out eventually," he said shrugging.

Mica shook his head, his eyes running down Ra's body as if he'd never seen him before. "No. You took control and delivered, and you de-escalated their stress while you did it."

"Am I allowed to ask what the fuck happened?" Ra said.

"Not here. On the flight home," Mica said, gesturing for Ra to step closer.

This time, Mica turned him away from him and wrapped his arms around his waist, resting his chin on Ra's shoulder as he used magic to take his weight and get them airborne. He wasn't sure if this was better or worse than earlier because now they were touching across the full length of their bodies, Mica's hips nestled snug against his ass.

Okay. Definitely worse. Exquisitely worse.

"Stop squirming. I'm not going to drop you, no matter how tempting it may be," Mica teased.

Ra swallowed hard and forced himself to focus on the landscape speeding past below them instead of the rhythmic surging of Mica's wingbeats. He had a new respect for his best friend. How the fuck had Bast carried Hel around like this for so long without going crazy? The man was a saint.

"So, what on the Earths happened back there?" he asked.

"You understand that the strongholds form at a complex nexus of ley lines that makes magic coalesce and infuse into a location until it becomes a kind of sentience? A bit like magical synapses forming until they become a brain," Mica said.

"Sure."

"The Earth Stronghold has a much closer resonance with the planet because of the nature of Earth magic and the fact the caves nestle so deep beneath its surface. We think even though there was no overt damage to the stronghold when the second Melding merged the vampyr reality with this one, the trauma to the planet itself damaged the stronghold's sentience. It was already vulnerable from that when the reality contagion formed in its core and what resulted was a bit like a partial lobotomy. Vital connections were destroyed and the power reserves were destabilised. We haven't been able to figure out how to untangle and reshape the ley lines to heal it without doing even more harm to the sentience."

Ra winced as he processed just how much worse the situation was than he'd thought. What Mica was saying made a lot of sense given what he knew from talking to Hel. Bast's mate had communicated directly with the planet courtesy of her unique magic while they were eliminating the contagion. She'd described the deep fractures to its essence that resulted from the forced melding of realities.

"That sucks, but what does it have to do with what happened today and why did you put a literal gag order on me about it?" Ra asked.

"The only reason I'm telling you this is so you understand what your work needs to solve. It would cause panic if it got out," Mica warned.

"I get it. I'm not going to do anything to make things worse. What are we dealing with?"

Mica dropped down to the top of a hillside that looked out over the valley where the entrance to the Earth Stronghold lay and stepped away from Ra to take in the view in the late afternoon light. It was a strangely familiar sight and after a moment Ra realised this was the view Mica had texted to him months earlier before everything had gone wrong between them. Hel had thought they were sexting, but Mica had just been sharing a photo of a stunning sunset and saying it made him think of Ra and the City of Souls.

Gesturing toward the wide vista, Mica spoke in a voice almost too soft to hear, as if afraid the distant caves might be listening. "Ley lines cross the Earths between points of magical significance like rivers of power. When a nexus like this grows unstable, blockages and dams of raw power form where they should not. Usually, the stronghold would automatically rebalance them, which is probably why the sentiences evolved in the first place, but the damage to the Earth Stronghold has broken its ability to do so."

"What happens when it can't rebalance the power?" Ra asked, but he could guess the answer.

"It has to release somewhere. Today was just a small

example of that. It's like an earth tremor releasing a fraction of the energy building between tectonic plates, except the seismic wave is a magical one and the fault lines are the hundreds of ley lines the stronghold is connected to that stretch around the Earths."

"What happens when the big one hits? A proper earthquake?"

"We cannot allow that to happen. The blast would travel the length of the ley lines and cause the same or worse damage as we're dealing with to the other three strongholds. From there it would become a cascading implosion of raw power that would be catastrophic for the function of magic on the Earths. The physical damage to the planet alone would cause the kind of loss of life we saw from the meldings."

"Fuck," Ra said, startling a bitter laugh from Mica. The meldings had killed millions.

"Yeah. Fuck."

"Why hasn't this come up at the council sessions?"

"Because I can't risk anyone finding out. The sentience is aware of every thought and feeling passing through my people's heads. It's like a symbiote dependent on each elemental that lives within its bounds and the magic they contain. I'm powerful and disciplined enough to keep my thoughts shielded, but most are not. If the reality of the situation it is causing got out, imagine what effect that would have on an already traumatised being? Imagine if part of you existed in hundreds of people, if your essence depended on the feedback loop between you and them, and every single one of them was terrified of you. If every single one of them was convinced you would destroy the world. It would be a self-fulfilling prophecy. There would be no faster way to bring on exactly the kind of devastation I am working to prevent."

He could see now why Mica hadn't wanted to get into this while they were in the caves where the sentience could overhear them. "Aren't you worried it will read this from me?" Ra asked.

"No. It can't communicate with your human mind so it can't read it either. As long as you keep your mouth shut, it won't get anything from you. And my collar around your neck will make sure nothing accidentally slips from your lips," Mica said, his eyes dropping to said lips as he spoke.

Ra let his tongue flick out to wet them just to fuck with him, smirking as Mica drew in a sharp breath. "Yeah, about the collar. Why was everyone giving it such weird looks?"

"We need to get back for Kaia's dinner," Mica said, sweeping him back into his arms and speeding back to the balcony of his chambers without another word.

Yeah, that wasn't suspicious at all. What the fuck had he got himself into?

CHAPTER 5
MICA

I missed you, the stronghold whispered into Mica's mind the second his feet touched the limestone of the balcony. *You took mate away.*

His jaw tightened at the unwelcome reminder as he carefully released the infuriating, intoxicating human in his arms, his hand hovering for a moment while he made sure Ra wouldn't stumble from the quick descent. The stronghold wasn't always so verbal, often communicating more in feelings than words. Its greeting was punctuated by a combination of neediness, love, and a hint of threat for removing Ra from its bounds.

It hadn't always been that way. Before it had been so deeply damaged, it had been a deep well of calm, much like the cave system it embodied. Now it would lash out without warning, oscillating between a youthful innocence and murderous rage fast enough to give him whiplash. As much as he would like to correct the stronghold and explain that he and Ra weren't mates and never would be because he would never act on the drive to complete the potential bond the stronghold could sense, that wasn't going to help calm the sentience. Carefully tucking all his concerns and fears out of sensing range of the stronghold, he sent it a wave of reassurance—*We're back now. We missed you, too.*

Don't leave me again. *tears* *pleading* *rockfall smashing through caves*

"Are you okay?" Ra asked him, concern in his storm-grey eyes as he ran a hand through his blond hair, setting it to rights after the flight.

Mica's gaze hitched on the movement as the man's biceps flexed and the move gave him the perfect view of Ra's muscled forearms, which were bared where he'd rolled up his sleeves. The glitter of the mica collar he'd grown around Ra's neck was a frustrating tease—the soft bronze of the mineral an exact match to his own skin tone where it sat against the much lighter pale tan of Ra's collarbone making him desperate to see the same contrast in his bed as their bodies pressed together. Magic surged inside him, reaching toward Ra, and a wave of want crashed over him that threatened to bring him to his knees where he could grasp the man's hips and...

Fuck. No.

Taking a deep breath, he forced his mind away from the temptation before him. Why did it have to be Ra? He was human. It shouldn't even be possible for there to be a mating draw between them. It must have something to do with the way Bastion's mark had changed the man over the decades. Jealousy roared through him at the thought and his fists clenched, knuckles whitening as he fought to push it down. The presence of another elemental's magic inside Ra where only *his* should be was slowly driving him crazy.

"I'm fine. I'll collect you in an hour for dinner," he

snapped, walking away before he could do something he'd regret. Like pushing the man against the wall and kissing him until his lips and cock were swollen and he was gasping for breath.

The draw to mate with someone was exceptionally rare, but it wasn't uncommon for it to be ignored. Mating bonds were invasively intimate and permanent, which was a really long time for an immortal. They also became a huge weakness if you were the kind of person who had enemies, because if your mate died, you wouldn't survive them. And there was no one with more enemies than the ruler of an elemental court. He couldn't imagine anyone he would be willing to lay himself bare to in the way a mating bond required, especially not a man who'd extorted him into complying with his demands by threatening to starve his city. That didn't make the constant instinctive driving *need* to touch Ra and make him happy relent, though.

Leaving his wing of the caves and the too-beautiful human behind, he headed to his study to catch up on the work he should've been doing before they'd been called away to deal with the latest minor ley line rupture. He wasn't surprised to see Wren there waiting for him like he often was, his seneschal jumping to his feet and bowing low as he entered the room, emotion shining in his eyes.

Was Ra right? Did Wren desire him? Surely not. They'd worked together over four centuries and nothing had ever happened between them. Sure, Mica had often used him as his plus-one to council social events to avoid the sexual machinations or awkward clinginess that inevitably arose whenever he took an actual date, but they both knew that was strictly a mutual convenience, didn't they? Mica got a hassle-free evening and Wren benefitted from the boost in status of being seen to be trusted by his lord. Everyone knew Wren attended as his assistant, not his date. Everyone except maybe Wren, if Ra was right.

"According to the scouts' reports, the damage has been managed?" Wren asked as Mica sat down at his desk.

"Yes, but I can't close the rift without destabilising the ley line even more. Have the marketing team put out a message explaining it as an unexpected wyrm migration we don't want to interfere with. Ra already organised a new temporary road, so it shouldn't inconvenience those travelling much." It was a delicate balance making sure Wren knew enough to do his job without giving away the true nature of the disturbance. The seneschal didn't have nearly enough power or control to hide his thoughts from the stronghold.

"*Ra* organised a road?" Wren spluttered.

"He was there and it helped. You know the role he performed for Lord Bastion. He has experience that is useful while he's living here," Mica said, annoyed at having to defend himself again to Wren.

"Exactly. Experience working for a rival court to undermine us. He's probably already planning how to exploit the damage as a strategic weakness," Wren argued.

"What else needs dealing with before the dinner?" Mica said. He didn't owe Wren any explanations.

Wren took the sudden change of topic as the rebuke it was and straightened in his chair, pulling out the tablet he'd been working on. "Two trainees and another half-dozen residents moved to the Tree City while you were at the Soul Court, almost all from the cave sector affected by the most recent collapse. I've taken the liberty of marking the nearby tunnels as undergoing maintenance to keep people clear now no one's living there."

Mica winced. On the one hand, he was grateful they'd taken themselves to safety. It was one less thing to worry about. On the other, the stronghold now only had around twenty percent of its usual resident population remaining and that would further upset the sentience. Reading his conflicting emotions as it listened in on their conversation, the stronghold sent him a sensation like a whining puppy asking what it had done wrong. Reaching out a hand to the nearest wall, he stroked it reassuringly like Ra had done earlier.

Just protect those remaining and I will take care of the rest, Earthshine, he murmured into its essence. Dammit. Now Ra had him using the stupid nickname, too.

"Good work. What else?" Mica said, checking his pocket watch to see how much time he had to get back to his suite and change.

"The Air Court has settled on a date for Daria's ascension as Lady. It's in two weeks. I've RSVPed for you and a plus one. Would you like me to accompany you per usual?" Wren asked.

"That won't be necessary," Mica said.

"You need to reassure people things are stabilising here. You shouldn't turn up alone," Wren pressed.

Ra hadn't even been in the stronghold a day and already his presence had upset the balance with his people. He couldn't remember the last time Wren had questioned his judgement so frequently.

"Ra will accompany me. I'm sure Lord Bastion will appreciate the visual reassurance that we haven't killed each other yet," Mica said, surprising himself with the words almost as much as his seneschal.

Wren's jaw dropped and a strangled sound emerged from him. "You're taking *him*?"

"Please see to it that he has something appropriate to wear," Mica said. It was only respect for the length of Wren's service that kept him from calling him out on his behaviour again. "Anything else?" he asked, half his mind in the study and half reaching out with his power to the collar around Ra's neck to check on him. He didn't trust the man not to get into trouble when he wasn't in his sight.

Connecting with the collar was a mistake. He could feel Ra's racing heartbeat where it pressed to his skin and warm water raining down on it. Ra was in the shower. Naked. Right that moment. Mica's cock swelled in his dusty, torn pants as he pictured it in his mind. Knowing it was wrong but unable to resist the compulsion, he opened his senses wider so he could listen in. Heat flared in his face as he heard a tell-tale moan of pleasure and the rhythmic slick of some kind of lubricant. Biting back a tortured groan, he relaxed the connection until it was a barely-there presence in the back of his mind again. Nothing could make him forget the sound of Ra's pleasure, though.

"If that's all, I need to go," he said, cutting off whatever Wren had been trying to tell him while he was too distracted to listen mid-sentence.

Striding from the room, he arrived back to his wing just in time to see Ra emerge into the living room wearing only a towel wrapped precariously around his waist with drops of water still running down his defined abs.

"Enjoy yourself?" he all but snarled, pissed off at how much of a distraction the human was proving to be.

Ra's eyes widened in surprise and a flush bloomed in his cheeks before he leaned a shoulder against the wall and looked Mica up and down with a knowing smirk, eyes lingering on the obvious bulge behind his zipper. The memory of the filthy soundtrack of Ra's moans had been playing on repeat in his mind since he'd heard it.

"Were you spying on me, Lord Mica? How dirty. I like it," Ra said.

The picture he made standing there shirtless reminded him of the texts Ra used to send when they'd been courting. Texts with teasing photos that had kept him coming back for more.

"The collar allows me to monitor you," he said, stray guilt making him at least want to ensure Ra knew how he was being watched, even if he had no intention of stopping.

Reaching up, Ra stroked a finger down the mineral and Mica could swear he felt the touch against his skin.

"Good to know. I'll make more of a performance of it next time," Ra said, before pushing off the wall and sauntering into his bedroom. His towel dropped to the floor a full second before he closed the door behind him and Mica bit back a curse.

Groaning to himself, Mica headed to the privacy of his suite to take a very cold shower. Why had he thought it would be a good idea to have Ra in his space? He knew the answer, though. He would have gone out of his skin with anxiety if the man had been any further away. With the pull of the potential mating connection between them, the next three years would be pure torture. He'd just have to hope the shielding he'd erected to keep his magic from reaching out to Ra would stop the human from realising. He didn't want to contemplate how Ra would take advantage of his weakness for him if he realised just how deep Mica's compulsion to touch and possess him ran.

The last of the sun's light had fled the living area when he returned chilled to the bone and with the comforting armour of his formal attire back in place. Ra was inspecting one of the few pieces of art on the cave walls—a stylised piano of magically spun minerals that appeared to be melting into the limestone. Mica paused in his stride, reluctant to disturb the moment. The human was dressed much more casually than him—slim black pants and a charcoal grey collared shirt that he knew would draw attention to the storm clouds of the man's eyes once he turned around. He'd rolled the sleeves up to his elbows like he always did and was sipping from a glass tumbler of whiskey, his other hand in his pocket making his pants stretch tight across his ass. The man seemed incapable of wearing a suit in the way it was designed to be worn and, annoyingly, it only made him hotter.

"Do you play?" Ra asked, apparently fully aware Mica had been standing there staring at him for the past however many minutes.

"What?" Mica asked, blinking back to himself.

"The piano. Do you play it?" he repeated.

"Not here," Mica said.

Ra rolled his eyes. "That sounds like a yes. Could you be more obtuse? Where, then?"

"Elsewhere," Mica said, not willing to open that side of himself to Ra.

The man was already under his skin and each interaction only made him burrow deeper like a thorn migrating into his flesh until it was bruised and raw. Music was too intimate. A thing he kept between him and the walls of the stronghold that absorbed the sound into its soul. He needed to make time to play again. It was one of the few things that had staved off the worst of the symptoms the stronghold was exhibiting.

"Do you wear the bow tie when you play or do you finally unbutton that collar?" Ra asked.

"Enough with the innuendo. You are the last man on the Earths I would touch," Mica growled.

"Who said you'd be the one doing the touching, *my lord?*"

Arousal shot through him, making his suffering in the icy shower earlier pointless. Pinching the bridge of his nose to ward off a rage headache, Mica took a deep breath. "I said *enough*. We are late. You will not speak to me like that in front of my people."

Ra stepped closer, challenge in his eyes and maybe a hint of the same frustrated confusion he was feeling at the way they couldn't leave each other alone. "I'm house-trained. I know how to behave in public."

Mica snorted. "No. You don't. What are you hoping to achieve with this? Do you *want* me to send you back to Bastion? All you need do is ask."

Ra shrugged, breaking eye contact. "What can I say? You bring out the worst in me. Anyway, you're not going to let me go. You need me."

Mica searched the man's face. There was something slightly off in the way he'd said the words. Like he was simultaneously smug and bitter. Reaching out with his magic to the collar that was visible where Ra had left his top three buttons undone, he felt the slight hitch in Ra's pulse.

"And you need to be needed," Mica guessed.

Bastion had needed Ra for decades, but now he had his

mate Hel. As much as Kaia might be vulnerable from the trauma she'd suffered, the last thing she needed was to become dependent on someone. That left Mica as the last-resort backup option to satisfy the gap in Ra's life left by Bastion's new relationship.

"Don't let it go to your head. I just like having the big powerful Earth Lord dependent on me after everything you did. We have a dinner to get to," Ra said, passing by close enough that his thigh brushed against Mica's primaries, sending another electric shock of desire through him.

Swallowing back a growl, Mica sent a silent request to the stronghold and smirked as Ra reached the doors and they failed to open for him.

Mate angry. Make him feel better, the stronghold whined.

Great. That was just what he needed. Relationship advice from a cave system that now had a tendency to shower rocks on people who annoyed it.

He will feel better once I feed him, Mica reassured it.

Mate-feeding good.

Frowning, Mica went to explain that was *not* what he'd meant and then thought better of it. He wouldn't get anywhere arguing with the unstable sentience.

"Are you going to let me out or have we progressed to keeping me captive?" Ra snapped, not even trying to push at the door or search for a handle. For a human, he had a surprisingly innate understanding of how the stronghold functioned.

"Ask nicely," Mica ordered.

"Fuck you. Stop playing games."

Games? Ra could talk. What the fuck did he call the constant malicious flirting? They really couldn't afford to be any later, though. People were already going to notice and the last thing he needed was for them to draw any more conclusions than they would from the fact the 'collar' he'd placed around Ra's neck wasn't unheard of as a marker of an Earth Lord's consort. He never should've formed it, and he definitely should've removed it by now. There were a thousand other tracking spells he could've used, but his magic was riding him too damn hard to make sure everyone knew Mica had a claim on Ra.

Fuck. He was so screwed.

CHAPTER 6

MICA

Stepping up to Ra's back, he leaned around him to press a hand softly to the door. The move was totally unnecessary. He could as easily have asked the doors to open with a single thought to the stronghold. Then his chest wouldn't be a breath away from the warm temptation of Ra's body, the man's sunshine scent wouldn't have filled his lungs as his jaw brushed against his collar, and he wouldn't be desperately avoiding the urge to wrap Ra in his wings and drag him down the hallway to his bed.

Neither of them stepped forward as the doors opened to reveal the sloping tunnel leading further into the caves. Ra tilted his head away from him a little, exposing the length of his pale throat and Mica let out a frustrated breath against the soft skin that had the human tensing. All he would have to do is lean forward a little and they'd be pressed together.

His hand brushed over Ra's thigh as he let it drop back to his side and the move made him sway until the last distance between them was gone. Ra was silent for once as he leaned back against him, resting his head on Mica's shoulder. Without conscious thought, Mica gripped Ra's hips and turned his face toward him like a plant to the sun, softly nuzzling the curved shell of his ear.

"My lord, forgive the intrusion but the food service is waiting for you," a voice called from nearby.

The two of them jerked apart, neither having noticed the scout approaching. Clearing his throat, Mica murmured his thanks to the elemental, who was carefully avoiding looking in their direction, and led the way toward the hall they used for more casual gatherings. He'd thought about holding the dinner in the formal chamber, given Kaia's association with a foreign court, but hadn't wanted the girl to feel overwhelmed.

Thankfully, the route from his quarters to the dining area didn't require Ra to scale any more ladders. Now he'd flown with the man in his arms, Mica wasn't sure he'd have been able to resist the urge to just carry him and the last thing they needed was any more excuses to touch.

As the scout had indicated, they passed the attendants waiting to serve the food on the way in. Mica mouthed an apology to the head chef. Their magic would keep the dishes warm, but he hoped his ill-fated run-in with Ra wouldn't leave them eating anything soggy or overcooked.

The brief surge of chattering voices silenced as the doors opened. Two dozen elementals seated at three long tables rose to their feet as he swept into the hall.

"Please be seated, this is not a formal dinner," Mica said, smiling at Kaia waiting by the seat to the right of his as he neared.

He could feel Ra's presence at his back, partially

screened from view by his wings, but he studiously avoided looking at the man to assess his reaction. Wren was waiting for him ahead, his attire as formal as Mica's, with whiskey for him on the tray in his hand. Mica nodded to his seneschal before pulling out the chair to his left and gesturing for Ra to take it.

The sound of shattering crystal had magic flaring in his wings as he snapped his attention to the disturbance. Amber liquid spread in a pool of broken glass at his feet as Wren glared at Ra, eyes trained on the mica collar around his neck.

"Good to see you, man," Ra said, winking at Wren before seating himself.

Clearing his throat, Mica raised an eyebrow at his seneschal, willing him to pull himself together, but Wren still seemed to be short-circuiting. Rather than wait for him to have the mess cleaned up so he could take his seat without draping his wings in the spilled alcohol, Mica sent a silent request to the stronghold to absorb the crystal and liquid into the floor.

The scents of lemongrass and coriander had his mouth watering as the moment passed and everyone, thankfully, turned their focus to the food rather than whatever was going on with Wren. For a while, the only sounds were the clink of spoons on pottery bowls and quiet requests to pass the rice. He hadn't realised how hungry he was until that moment, but it wasn't a surprise given he'd missed lunch and spent a huge amount of energy calming the wyrms.

"How has your first day been, Kaia?" Mica asked when his stomach finally stopped feeling like it was eating itself.

The head trainer Serena was sitting opposite them alongside the two newer trainees who Kaia would be practising with once she mastered the basics of connecting with the stronghold and channelling her power safely. They must have returned from the Tree City to visit for the dinner.

"Everyone's been super nice," Kaia said politely.

"I imagine it's very different from home," Mica said, ignoring Ra's soft snort at the understatement. He knew it took time to adjust to living in his subterranean stronghold.

"Yeah, it's so weird only having elementals around," she said.

Mica tilted his head in surprise. It hadn't occurred to him that that would be the biggest difference she noticed when everything from the surroundings to the food was so different.

"Humans don't come here much," Kim, the elemental girl opposite her, said.

"Because a stronghold is no place for them," Wren chimed in from behind him.

Mica clenched his jaw to bite back the stinging rebuke his loyal seneschal didn't deserve to receive in public. If Wren couldn't be polite to Ra, he should at least remember the girl had been raised by her human mother.

"The stronghold seems to like Ra just fine," Kaia shot back. "In fact, I think it's got a little crush on him."

A moment of panic filled Mica that the stronghold might've ignored his command not to speak of the mating draw between him and Ra to anyone, but there was no indication the girl knew there was anything more going on.

"Are there many humans in Soul Tower?" the boy Jasper asked.

"Yes. Not just humans, but vampyr and ceptae as well. The city is run by a ruling partnership with equal representation of all the species on it. Māmā and Uncle Ra have slowly been bringing in new tower staff from the new peoples to make sure that's representative, too," Kaia said.

"Is he your real Uncle? You don't look much alike," Jasper said.

Ra's rich laugh sang out from beside him, sending scatters of sunshine into the room. "Are you saying I'm too pasty white to be her Uncle?" he teased.

Kaia leaned forward to poke her tongue out at him before responding. "Uncle may be pākehā, but he's still my real uncle, just like Uncle Basti is even though we aren't related by blood."

"Kaia's mother is Māori. Pākehā means a human where we're from who was originally of European descent rather than Indigenous to Aotearoa. So, someone who hailed from what you know as Fire Court territory. We often use te reo Māori words in conversation to show our respect and value for their culture and to help keep the language a vibrant part of the city," Ra explained to the boy, who looked confused.

Mica could have told him the unfamiliar language wasn't what had Jasper looking perplexed because the translation spells that had become a permanent fixture for the elementals with all the new species on the Earths would've made the meaning clear to the boy already. Unfortunately, he was too slow to head off Jasper's unthinking comments about his real confusion.

"So, you're really half human? How are you so powerful?" Jasper asked.

Mica winced internally but Serena beat him to a reply.

"Jasper, that was rude," Serena chided.

Kaia's electric blue wings flared behind her in agitation

and she glared at the boy. "I'm not half anything. I'm all me. And I'd give anything not to have this power."

Mica shared a concerned glance with Serena as Ra got up to wrap an arm around the girl in support. Her attitude to her magic wasn't unexpected. It had been exploited and drained during her captivity and it was the reason she'd had to move away from her family. It was going to make her path to achieving control that much more difficult to achieve if she rejected it, though.

"Sorry," Jasper said, looking ashamed.

He was good kid. He just hadn't had much chance to interact with humans in his short lifetime and that wasn't his fault. Mica made a mental note to do better at finding opportunities for the peoples to meet each other.

"It's been a long day for our guests. We should let you rest, Kaia. You'll need your energy when training starts tomorrow," Mica said, standing from his place.

"Do you need someone to show you the way back to your room?" Serena asked the girl.

"Nah, the stronghold will tell me," Kaia said.

That was interesting. The stronghold didn't usually bother with casual communication with its inhabitants.

Mate's family, the stronghold said in his mind, sensing his thoughts. Along with the words came the sense of shared suffering with the girl—two hurting beings both trying to piece themselves back together.

Keep her safe, Mica sent back.

"I'll walk with you, K-bear," Ra said, ruffling her white-blonde hair.

"Don't get lost on your way back," Mica said.

I will keep mate safe, too, the stronghold interjected.

Sighing to himself, Mica watched the two outsiders head

out to the tunnels, leaning in towards each other as Ra murmured something that had Kaia giggling.

"Walk with me?" Mica asked Serena.

The head trainer inclined her head, bidding the other children farewell before following him towards his quarters. He waited until they were ensconced behind the extra shielding of his walls before speaking.

"How is she doing?" he asked, pouring a glass of the rice wine Serena preferred and handing it to her.

"Better than I expected, given the history you told me. I had wondered if she would have a negative association with the stronghold, since this is where she was taken from."

"She was in the outermost guest quarters when she was taken. Hopefully, being deeper in the caves feels sufficiently safer," Mica said.

"She is already halfway to connecting fully to the stronghold by pure instinct, which bodes well for her training. It does mean we'll have to keep a close eye on her, though. There is a level of co-dependence building there I am not comfortable with," Serena said.

The walls flared brighter for a moment as the stronghold objected to her words.

"Hush, you. I'm only trying to make sure you are both strong and healthy. That's what you want for her, too," Serena chided the sentience.

"Has she tried to use her power since she arrived?" Mica asked, thinking back to the girl's vehement statement that she wished she didn't have it at all.

"No. And none has leaked free as might be expected from someone her age. Only time will tell if that speaks to a level of control she was forced to learn alone to stay alive or a mental block we will have break through to teach her."

"But you're confident we can train her?" Mica checked.

"Absolutely."

"Thank you, Serena."

"Are we going to talk about what's going on with you and that sexy young man she arrived with now?" she teased.

Serena, at almost 300 years older than him, had become a pseudo mother-figure to him and the rest of the stronghold when his parents died and he'd taken over as lord 1,000 years earlier. Of all his extended inner circle, she and the plant-mage Elysia who was leading the agricultural recovery of the nearby lands damaged by the contagion were the only two elementals in his orbit who he counted as friends with whom he could speak freely.

"Nothing is going on between me and Ra. I won't make the mistake of sleeping with someone I can't trust again," Mica said.

"But you don't deny he's sexy. He's nothing like Aliya was," Serena said.

His dalliance with the previous Lady of Air had been an ill-advised attempt to curb her malevolent ways through a relationship. Not surprisingly, it had ended spectacularly badly when her cheating was revealed after the previous Fire Lord she'd been screwing died under suspicious circumstances and his corpse went walking down the street.

He'd been attracted to Aliya, he wouldn't have even considered a relationship otherwise, but it was nothing compared to the mating draw with Ra.

"He has the same ruthlessness," Mica said.

"No. His is different. It's protectiveness. It's not the same at all. You could use the distraction he's offering. I can see the world weighing on your shoulders," Serena said.

The doors swung open admitting the man in question

before he could explain there was definitely nothing on offer from Ra. The man could barely tolerate him.

"Is Kaia all settled in bed?" Serena asked.

"Yes. I asked the stronghold to wake me if she has a nightmare," Ra said.

"I'm closer. Let me go to her first and if she needs you then I'll call," Serena said.

Ra's brow furrowed in concern.

"Serena is excellent with children and she needs to be aware of what's happening with Kaia to safely guide her in her training," Mica said.

"I swear I will contact you if she needs you. I would never do anything that put a child at risk," Serena added.

"Okay. We can see how it goes and I'll check in with Kaia in a couple of days," Ra said. "I've been meaning to ask you, Serena, I'll need to work with a magical engineer on my scanning technology. At home I partner with ... someone ... who tweaks and refines the equipment as we go."

Ra was addressing Serena, but possessiveness swept through Mica again at his words. It was becoming a familiar feeling when the man was nearby, distracting him even from the oblique mention of Zahra, or Zee as Ra called them. The engineer had run away from their responsibilities to the Earth Court centuries earlier after a regrettable incident with a senior courtier, who Mica had soundly held accountable for his actions a little too late. He'd let Zahra go as a silent apology.

"If you need magic, you come to me and only me," Mica snapped.

He couldn't risk anyone realising just how bad things had become if Ra's experiments worked, but that wasn't what had him rejecting the request for assistance from anyone else at a cellular level. There was no way he'd be able to tolerate Ra working so closely with another mage, letting their power flow around him. It was bad enough that Bastion's magic was a constant presence through his mark.

Serena let out an almost inaudible snort of amusement at his thinly veiled jealousy.

"You can't possibly have time. And you can't stand me," Ra said, tilting his head in question in a way that bared the strong lines of his jaw now dusted with fine stubble after a long day. Mica wanted to bite his way up it, feel that roughness against more sensitive skin.

"I'll leave you two boys to it. Good night," Serena said, passing her glass to him as she left with a smirk.

"You clean up after your staff?" Ra asked in surprise as Mica took the crystalware to the sink and grabbed what he needed to wash it.

"Serena is more like family and I don't like people in my space," he explained, though why he felt it necessary he had no idea. "I will make time to ensure your technology is working. There is nothing that is a higher priority."

"Do you even have an affinity for engineering? Or any understanding of electronics? I thought you rulers of the courts were all about your offensive magics. It doesn't seem like creative types are all that welcome here," Ra said, clearly making assumptions based on whatever he thought had happened with Zahra.

"I am 1,267 years old, Ra. If I wasn't capable of every possible use of my power by now I wouldn't deserve my position, and if I wasn't capable of still learning I'd be dead. I'm sure you can teach me what I need to know."

Ra brushed up against his outer feathers as he reached

past him for a towel to dry the glass and Mica stiffened as the move sent a shiver of want through him.

"Sorry. Forgot I wasn't with Bast," Ra murmured.

Mica growled. "Brush up against him often, did you?" he asked, unable to resist curling his wings around the man so he could cage him in with hands gripped tight to the kitchen bench on either side of him.

"Wouldn't you like to know?"

CHAPTER 7

RA

Ra flirted with everyone. It was just what he did. He liked to make people feel good about themselves. He liked to find out what made them tick, what turned them on, what made their breath catch in their throat and the heat rise in their cheeks. What he was doing with Mica wasn't that, but fuck if he knew what it was or why he couldn't leave the elemental alone when he wanted nothing to do with him.

All this ran through his head when he found himself wearing the smallest towel available around his waist as he made his way back from the shower to his room the next morning. Something that was definitely *not* disappointment settled over him as he realised the wing of the stronghold was too quiet for there to be anyone else there. Of course Mica would be a boy scout and get an early start to his day.

Glancing out the window to the balcony, he saw the sun was already well risen. Okay. Maybe not so early. Between the all-nighters he'd pulled to prepare the Soul Court for his departure, and the time difference and minor catastrophe making it a very long day yesterday, he must've been more tired than he'd realised.

Pulling out his phone, he sent a text to Kaia—*Morning K-bear. You sleep okay?*

He made himself a coffee as he waited for her reply, groaning as he took his first indulgent sip. Coffee had been a rare luxury in the Soul Court where distance and the ocean's predators made shipping international goods a dangerous business. He'd grown used to the magically infused kawakawa tea they drank for an energy boost back home instead, but he'd never lost the taste for the coffee he'd mainlined in his twenties before the first Melding combined their Earth with one of winged elementals and magic.

It's almost afternoon, Uncle Missing-all-the-Sunshine, Kaia replied as he settled down to pick at the fresh fruit in the bowl at the dining table.

What are you up to? Everyone treating you okay? he asked

Serena's been taking me through some basics. Breathing exercises and stuff. It's okay. We're just having a break and then she's going to show me around a bit.

He could use a tour himself, but with Mica nowhere to be found and Wren so hostile, he was pretty sure he'd do better poking around by himself. Serena would probably welcome him along with them, but she was hardly going to be showing Kaia the parts of the stronghold that were broken and that was what he needed to see to be able to do what he'd promised Mica.

Have fun, sweetheart, he texted.

Don't get into any trouble, Kaia replied.

Putting in his earpiece, he decided to call home while he worked through the inventory of tech he'd brought with him and figured out where to start. He rang Ana first, knowing the woman would be desperate for any news.

"Kia ora, Ra. How is she? Wait. I'm putting you on speaker. Everyone's here," Ana said as he opened the case of the specialist drone he'd brought with him and carefully took it out.

A rush of homesickness hit him as Bast, Hel, and Zee all said hello.

"She's doing okay. It's a lot to get used to but her teacher seems great," Ra said once the obligatory greetings were through.

"Is she going to be safe there?" Ana asked.

That was the question, wasn't it? None of them had realised quite how dire the stronghold situation was before he came, but he'd sworn not to betray Mica's secrets once he was here. On the other hand, if anything, the stronghold seemed to like both him and Kaia. He doubted it was a threat to them specifically.

"I will make sure of it," he said.

"Have you and Mica killed each other yet?" Hel asked.

"Have you and Mica boned yet?" Zee chimed in.

Ra burst out laughing, hoping Mica hadn't chosen that moment to eavesdrop on him again through the damned collar around his neck. "Shut up," he said, but their teasing had brought the smile back to his face.

His family kept the rest of their discussion light, catching him up on various community projects back home. Bast stole the phone to talk to him in private before they said goodbye.

"Are you okay? You sound different. If it gets too much, just say the word and we'll portal you out of there," Bast said.

Was he okay? He didn't really know. He'd been so certain of his feelings before he left. So certain he understood the kind of person Mica was to act the way he had. But now he was here, he could see the pressure the Earth Lord had been under. It was the same pressure Bast and Hel had shouldered for so long—when your actions affected the lives of millions. And he was doing it all with a psychically damaged stronghold hanging in the back of his mind.

He could also see that while Mica's court might be different from back home, he had that same sense of duty and fairness that had drawn Ra to befriend Bast. When they'd been speaking about the damaged road, Mica had said his scouts didn't always understand the importance of human infrastructure, which meant the Earth Lord *did*. He might've insulted Ra's humanity when he'd lashed out at the summit, but it didn't seem like that was how he lived his life. That hurt more than it should because it confirmed his cutting words had been specifically about Ra, not his views on humanity more generally.

Bast and Hel had made their peace with the Earth Lord's actions, telling Ra many times they'd probably have made the same decision if they were flying his path. Ra's anger at the Earth Lord seemed increasingly misplaced and he didn't like where that left him, especially given what he'd done in response to Mica's actions. Guilt was becoming a constant leaden feeling in his stomach he couldn't shake. He also didn't like how he couldn't seem to control the impulse to be close to the elemental—the constant fight not to press against him skin to skin and ease all that stress for a moment.

"I'll be fine, bro. I just miss you," he said, knowing he'd taken too long to answer while lost in his thoughts.

Bast scoffed quietly. "That was stunningly unconvincing."

"Love you," Ra said, not ready to explain himself, especially where Mica might overhear.

Bast sighed. "Love you, too. Behave yourself."

Why did everyone keep telling him that?

THE NEXT WEEK settled into a rhythm of a sort. No matter how early Ra arose, Mica was already gone for the day. Ra spent his days exploring the cave system, flying the drone ahead of him through the tunnels to use the camera and mapping software to create a 3D rendering in his magically upgraded computer. It was sweaty, laborious work as he made his way to the most rundown isolated sections of the caves he could find, working his way deeper and deeper into the stronghold and often relying on his rock-climbing skills to make his way through chambers not designed for humans. He was covered in scrapes and his fingers stung. It had been a long time since he'd climbed so regularly.

Each evening, he showered in the still-empty wing of the stronghold and then met up with Kaia and the trainers for dinner, making sure his niece was happy and cared for. He was half convinced Mica wasn't even sleeping in his room, but if he'd left to go travelling, he hadn't said a word to Ra about it. Perhaps he might've caught sight of him if he'd sat in the living area and controlled the drone from there, but he wasn't certain how the elementals or the stronghold itself would respond to a robot flying through their space without him alongside it.

The stronghold continued to endear itself to him. Benches would lever themselves from the wall so he could rest when he grew weary. The limestone would warm beneath his fingers as he climbed. When he came to chambers inset with veins of mica and quartz, the stronghold would dim the glow of its walls and create magical sparkling light shows just for him.

"So clever, Earthshine," he murmured as he stood taking in the visual spectacle.

The stronghold's welcome was in sharp contrast to Mica's damn whiny seneschal, who seemed to take pleasure in making Ra's life more difficult than it needed to be. He was just lucky the caves weren't minded to follow Wren's instructions because otherwise the magical blockades that sprung up 'for his safety' whenever he tried to go somewhere that looked promising would've been insurmountable without involving Mica.

Instead, he would smile blandly until Wren moved on and then stroke the nearest wall and whisper his desire to the sentience. Wren's small magics were no match against the vast being that encompassed the rock around them.

On the seventh day since they arrived, a suit bag had appeared in his closet when he returned to his room from dinner. Unzipping it, he raised an eyebrow at the brown-on-brown ensemble. He wasn't against a good tan suit, but this was not that. There was nothing to explain its presence in his room, but he was guessing someone expected him to wear this monstrosity somewhere and that would *not* be happening.

His fingers hovered over his phone as he opened the thread of text messages to Mica. Did he really want to deal with the tension between them when he was exhausted and his cheek was stinging from a run-in with a rock wall when he was climbing? Ah, fuck it. There was no way he was wearing this thing. Resisting the urge to scroll back and reread texts from a happier time, he started typing.

Is there a reason for this garment? Its colour is an insult to dirt everywhere. I know you're the Earth Court, but this looks more like a mud court thing, he texted.

The message flicked to read, but there was no indication Mica was intending to reply and after ten minutes Ra swore under his breath and went to change for bed. Fuck him. He'd deal with it in the morning. Wearing just some low-slung grey sweatpants, he yanked his door open to go brush his teeth—because why on the Earths would a powerful Lord have an ensuite for his guests?—and barrelled naked-chest first into Mica.

Swearing, he overcorrected and almost fell before the elemental's strong hands wrapped around his arms, steadying him.

"Don't you knock?" he snapped.

Mica raised an eyebrow. "Not when the door is already opening."

"And where have you been all week?"

"Is that what has you so worked up? I don't owe you an explanation of my whereabouts. I had matters to attend to."

Now that he was paying more attention, he could see the dark circles under Mica's eyes had grown even larger and the energy in him, for lack of a better word, had dimmed. His brow furrowed in concern, despite himself. The ever-present guilt at how he'd added to Mica's stress surged forward.

"You need to take better care of yourself," he said, reaching out to brush a thumb across the darkened skin as if he could rub away the fatigue he saw there.

"As do you," Mica said, returning the gesture by running a finger softly down the scrape on his cheek.

They both froze as they realised what they'd done. Mica still didn't let him go. If anything, he'd pulled him closer.

Clearing his throat, Mica finally released him and stepped back. "What was your message about?"

"The hideous suit that inexplicably appeared in my closet," Ra said, waving his arm at the fabric he'd discarded on the ground like the trash it was.

Mica glanced at the offending garment and sighed. "Elysia, are you still there?" he called behind him.

"Yes, my lord," someone said from the kitchen.

"Of course you are," Mica muttered, too low for the other person to hear, but Ra could hear the affection in the words.

Peering around Mica, Ra watched as a smiling elemental drew nearer. Their wings were bright copper ribboned with a rich green reminiscent of the jungle surrounding the stronghold and their smile was open and calming as they approached.

"Ra, this is Elysia—a friend and the mage leading our agricultural recovery. They're also closely associated with the weavers guild."

"Nice to meet you," Ra said, holding out a hand and hoping he hadn't just insulted the weavers guild with his comment about the suit.

"Likewise. I've been desperate to meet the man who challenges Mica so well," Elysia said.

"Elysia," Mica warned, but the mage just smiled wider.

"What can I do for you, my lord?" they asked.

"Could you have someone come up with something more fitting for Ra, please? I had asked Wren to do so, but he seems to have misplaced both his fashion sense and his ability to follow instructions," Mica said.

Ah. So, that was what had happened. He could totally see Wren being behind the offensive fabric.

"Wren's been a pain in my ass, and not in a good way," he said, sparking a possessive growl from Mica that had Elysia giggling at them in a distinctly non-mage-like way.

"It's like watching a nature documentary," Elysia said, eyes flicking back and forth between them.

Ra smiled wryly and shook his head. At least someone was getting some amusement from the situation.

"I like you," he told the endearing elemental.

"I like you, too," Elysia said brightly.

"That will be all thank you, Elysia," Mica cut in. "I'll see you in the morning."

Elysia smiled and patted Mica on the shoulder. "I assume you need the replacement within the week?"

Mica inclined his head in acknowledgement and Elysia waved goodbye.

"Why am I wearing a suit in a week's time?" Ra asked. The only thing he knew of happening in a week was—

"To accompany me to Daria's ascension," Mica said.

Ra blinked. And then blinked again. "Uh ... what?"

"You will be accompanying me to the Air Court when I go," Mica said, eyes determinedly focused on his face despite all the skin he had on display.

Ra leaned on the wall and hooked his thumb in his already low-riding sweatpants, pulling them down a little further just to fuck with him. "Okay. Why? And were you going to ask me whether I wanted to go at any point?"

Mica shifted and looked away, a flush rising in his cheeks. "I assumed you would appreciate the chance to catch up with Bastion and Helaine."

"That doesn't explain why you'd take me. What am I

going as? Your assistant? I'm not an official member of your court."

"No. Not an assistant," Mica said, looking uncomfortable.

"Wait. Am I going as your *date*?"

"My plus-one. It's different," Mica grumbled.

"Right. No one is going to take one look at us attending a function, think back to the very public revelations about our 'history' with each other, and jump to any conclusions," Ra said, voice dripping sarcasm.

"I don't care what anyone decides to think about me."

"Regardless, if you want me to attend a function with you, you need to ask me first," Ra said.

Mica pinched the bridge of his nose. "Ra, would you like to attend Daria's ascension with me?"

"Oh, come on. You can do better than that. It sounds like you're doing me a favour. Why do you want me as your plus-one?"

"I don't fucking know alright?! I just ... I *can't* take anyone else," Mica snapped.

Ra blinked in surprise at the uncharacteristic outburst and then snorted. "I'm not going to be your backup because no one else can go."

"That's *not* what I said. Do you think I'm short on potential partners? I'm not. They would queue the lengths of the tunnels if they thought it would get them into my bed."

Ra bit back the growl that thought engendered. "So, why not take one of them?" Ra asked, even though everything in him rebelled at the thought.

"Because I don't *want* one of them," Mica snapped.

Which meant...

Ra swallowed hard and stared at the elemental mere

steps away from him. He had no come-back to that. "What are you doing? What are *we* doing?" he asked softly.

"Just come with me. Please," Mica said.

"Okay."

Mica nodded and turned away, striding towards his rooms and shutting the door firmly behind him as Ra watched from his doorway. What the fuck had just happened?

CHAPTER 8

MICA

Every day Ra spent in Mica's home eroded a little more of his disdain for the man and he hated it. It didn't matter that he was so caring for his niece. It didn't matter that he was so dedicated in his efforts to help diagnose the stronghold's problems. It didn't matter that he left a string of smiles on his courtiers' faces as he passed. None of that could undo the unforgivable betrayal in their past.

Despite that, despite everything that was wrong between them, every time they interacted he lost all control, either of his emotions or his body. Either one was infuriating and combined it was a recipe for disaster. When Ra cocked his head in challenge at him, it reminded him of all the times he'd done the same on their video calls before things went wrong. When he'd befriended Elysia within moments of meeting them, it reminded Mica of all the reasons he'd fallen for the man in the first place—his warmth, the charisma that hid a razor-sharp strategic mind worthy of any elemental courtier. Ra could've been the perfect complement to him if only he wasn't human with all the weakness and limited life-span that entailed. If only he hadn't sworn his admirable loyalty to another court long before they'd ever met. If only he hadn't held Mica's heart in his hands and slowly crushed it right before his eyes.

That was the litany he forced himself to run through his mind the next night as he found himself forced into proximity with the man again. He'd spent the day in the neighbouring region checking up on the elemental who ran things there and had been caught out in another disturbance from the sentience while he was there. One that had caused a landslide in an area they'd been considering extending a settlement into. The chaos of the fracturing ley line in the area had upset the local wildlife and by the time he'd helped Lachlan repair the damaged earth and calm the winged carnivorous monkeys that threatened to swarm down onto the livestock in the area, his suit was ripped and covered in dirt and his hair was a tangled mess. More and more of his time and energy were being sunk into problems like this, and the more distracted he became with that, the more freedom the ambitious members of his court had to cause trouble.

Swearing under his breath at his ridiculousness for sneaking into his own home, he'd done his best to get in and out of his rooms to shower and change without running into the human he couldn't trust himself to be near. To no avail.

Ra was leaning against the breakfast bar with his arms crossed and the achingly beautiful lines of his body on full display in his tight jeans and t-shirt when he re-emerged.

"This is a surprise. To what do I owe the 'pleasure' of your company?" Ra said before he had a chance to stride past him.

"I'm not your damn guest. These are *my* rooms," Mica muttered.

"Really? Could've fooled me. You're barely here. Are you even sleeping in your bed?" Ra said.

Before Mica could reply, a silent scream filled his mind and he jerked his head to the east as if he could see through the stronghold's walls to whatever had set it off.

What's wrong? he asked the sentience, already grabbing his phone from his pocket so he could get a report from his staff.

It rang before he could make the call and the name made his heart stop for a moment. With the stronghold almost catatonic in panic and Serena calling him, there was only one likely cause—Kaia.

"Where is she and what happened?" he asked as he answered the phone.

Ra must've sensed something from him because he snatched the phone from his grip and put it on speaker before grabbing his hand to drag him toward the exit.

"She's in Kim's room stuck in a flashback. I have the power blast contained but I'm going to have to knock her out if she can't stop projecting or she'll burn out," Serena said.

"We're on our way."

"I thought the stronghold was supposed to prevent this from happening," Ra growled as they ran through the tunnels towards the trainee quarters.

Barely slowing, Mica swept him up into his arms so they could move faster.

"It's too attached to her. To you both. It's panicking. Serena mentioned they were becoming co-dependent."

Mica was too busy trying to stabilise the dozen tiny rockfalls the stronghold was causing in the caves and keep the damage from spreading any further afield to speak further as they rushed through the tunnels. They were silent until they reached the door Serena was standing in front of. The copper of her magic glittered in a sphere that disappeared into the walls as she surrounded the bedroom with her magic to shield them all from the blast of Kaia's power.

Putting Ra down at the entryway, Mica reached out with a touch of his own magic to turn Serena's barrier transparent. What he saw there made him blanche and then rage, both his own anger and the sensation of Ra's down their connection burning through him. Kaia was slumped unconscious on the floor and disturbing images flashed from every wall, floor, and ceiling as the stronghold channelled the girl's nightmares into a visual spectacle.

"Let me in there," Ra said, voice clipped and desperate.

"I got Kim out when I first arrived but Kaia's not responding and her magic will burn you to a crisp if you try to touch her," Serena said.

Resting his hand on the nape of Ra's neck where his collar sat, Mica let his power extend from the mineral ringing his throat across every inch of Ra's body.

"He'll be fine now. Let us through," Mica said.

Serena's eyes widened in surprise at the level of protection he'd placed on the human, but she didn't waste any more time. Mica strode through the barrier as soon as he sensed it change, Ra close on his heels.

He'd realised the ward was blocking sound from escaping the room, but nothing could prepare him for the effect of stepping into the tiny room and hearing the echo of Kaia's voice ringing in the space as the memory of her torment played out in high magical definition on every rock surface surrounding them. The stronghold was just as trapped in her nightmares as she was.

"No! Please! It hurts so much. It's too much. Caelus, please stop. I can't..."

He thought there would be nothing more heart-breaking than that slow weakening of Kaia's voice until it was barely audible. He was wrong. The next second, agonised screams rocked through the air around them as they were surrounded by a view of the rock cell she'd been kept in when she was kidnapped by the Air Court and the anathema device that had been connected to her to drain her young body of magic.

The view was from Kaia's perspective, the chains holding her to the wall stretching up from her too-thin bruised wrists as the looming figure of Caelus, one of the Air Court's previous senior courtiers, leaned over her to adjust something. It was horrifying. And, even worse, he knew that in the chaos of what had followed Kaia's recovery, Caelus had never been held accountable. He suspected the second-in-command to the previous Air Lady had been trying to use Kaia's power to boost his own so he could take over if she died but, thankfully, Bastion and Ra had saved the girl before he could complete the transfer. Caelus had disappeared somewhere in the American Continents before the council could summon him to account for his crimes.

Ra had all but flown to Kaia's side when they'd entered, pulling the girl into his arms and rocking her as he tried to wake her. "K-bear. Sweetheart. It's over. You're in Kim's room in the Earth Stronghold. Feel the limestone under your fingers? Smell Mica's magic on me? You're safe here. I've got you. No one is ever going to hurt you like that again."

The human kept up a constant stream of soft reassurance as Mica reached out to the section of the stronghold's sentience present here in the room and did the same thing, gentling it with his mind.

She needs you calm. Anchor her to the present, don't chain her to the past, he told it.

The sentience responded with horror at the suggestion it was chaining her like Caelus had. *No chains. Helping*, it said. At least it was talking now.

How are you helping? Mica asked, confused.

Her magic isn't blocked anymore.

Distracted by their conversation, the images and sounds had faded from the room and Mica heard a quiet moan as Kaia shifted in Ra's arms and the constant blast of the girl's magic suddenly cut off.

"Oh thank the Earths you're awake, baby girl. You scared me," Ra said.

"I'm okay," she croaked. Ra just held her tighter.

Serena's ward dropped and the woman stepped into the room, making it a very tight squeeze between the four bodies and three sets of wings in the small space. Standing up, Ra carried the girl out into the communal space and Mica went to make them all a calming tea and call for dinner to be brought to them. He didn't think any of them could face a crowded dining hall after the evening's events. As he waited for the tea to steep, he stepped away to check in with his scouts and deal with the new damage to the stronghold. Thankfully, none of the minor collapses had been in inhabited areas.

Kaia was curled up in the corner of a couch when he returned, Ra sitting nearby with a reassuring arm around her.

"What happened Kaia?" Serena asked as Mica passed the drinks around.

"I connected to the stronghold the first day we were here, but no matter how hard I tried I couldn't purposefully channel my magic, even though I've done it so many times before," Kaia said, frustration in her voice despite the trauma she'd just been through.

"We talked about that. It takes some elementals months to master. You've barely been here a week. You are doing just fine," Serena said.

"But Kim and Jasper are so far ahead of me and I'm just *useless*," Kaia said.

"There is nothing useless about you, K-bear. You've saved Bast and Hel more than once with your magic," Ra said.

Mica had heard of the times Kaia had escaped safe-keeping and put herself in danger to help defend their city. It was impressive for one so young. It was also part of why she'd needed training so urgently.

"But that's just it! I should be able to do this already!" Kaia shouted.

Mica sighed. They should have anticipated the impatience of youth. "What did you do, Kaia?"

Ra glared at him. "Don't blame her for her trauma! It's not her fault—"

"No, he's right, Uncle. I did do something," Kaia interrupted softly.

Mica just waited patiently, knowing the girl would come out with it in her own time. She was a responsible child and she'd had to grow up too fast in her captivity. She knew she needed their help.

"I was talking to Kim and we realised that all the times I'd channelled my power since ... you know ... I had been under threat and I was really, really afraid. Serena had told us about visualisation and how magic can react to our emotional state, so we thought if I maybe imagined myself back in a stressful situation like that, it might let me channel my magic again. So, I meditated like we've been learning and focused on trying to feel the most frightened I could," Kaia explained.

"Oh, you poor child. You didn't need to do that to yourself," Serena said.

"It worked, didn't it?" Kaia snapped back, her jaw thrust forward in challenge.

"And how much control did you have?" Serena asked, voice still patient.

Kaia looked away.

"The purpose behind the meditation and acknowledging our emotions is to find a place of calm so we control our power instead of the other way around," Serena gently explained.

"But it's not working!"

"And so long as you continue to believe that, you will continue to fail," Serena said.

Kaia's face fell and tears glistened in her eyes at her teacher's words.

"I believe in you. I would not have let you come here if I didn't. You *will* master this, but there is no shortcut," Mica said, infusing as much confidence as he could in his words. Sometimes, the young just needed to know there was someone in their corner. Ra was watching him with an inscrutable expression.

"I miss home. I miss my māmā," Kaia said. And that was the crux of it. The reason she'd been so desperate to sprint to a finish line that didn't exist. Controlling and wielding the kind of power they did was something you worked on for an immortal lifetime.

Ra pulled the girl back into his lap, carefully rearranging her wings, and nestled her head under his chin. The move filled Mica with an unwelcome ache of longing.

"Shall we call Ana so you can talk to her about all this?" Ra asked, a teasing note in his voice.

Kaia flinched. "Don't even joke about that! She'd be so mad at me."

"Nah, sweetheart. She'd be so worried for you," Ra corrected.

"I don't want to make her sad again," she whispered.

"You didn't make her sad. The world did. But if you don't want her to be sad again, you need to let Serena help you stay safe."

"I will. I promise," Kaia said.

"Excellent! Must be time for dinner, then," Serena said, jumping up to grab the cart of food the two had been oblivious to.

"Serena?" Kaia called, waiting until the woman looked over to continue. "I'm sorry I didn't talk to you."

"That's okay, child. You will next time," she said.

Mica stuck around throughout dinner and the movie Ra put on afterward, grabbing one of the spare computers so he could sit at the dining table and communicate with his people to smooth the remaining chaos the stronghold's panic had caused. He could've left them to it. His power was no longer required. But something about the little found family giving each other comfort held him there. The soft laughter coming from the couch was a soothing backing track as he closed his eyes and sunk his consciousness into the sentience surrounding them so he could direct the engineers to areas where their magic would help stabilise the caves. The strong-hold was quiet but clingy in the back of his mind, constantly seeking out his reassurance.

"You coming to bed?" Ra asked, just as he finished coaching the stronghold through absorbing the last of the tell-tale rubble from its tunnels.

Mica's eyes flew open as a spear of need shot through him at the words. He glared at Ra for being the catalyst of yet another betrayal by his body.

"Fuck's sake. I didn't mean it like *that*. You look exhausted. Let's go," Ra said, jerking his head toward the exit.

It must've been later than he'd realised because the tunnels were empty as they made their way back to his wing of the caves. Without asking, Ra poured them both a glass of whiskey when they arrived and then stepped onto the balcony to stare out into the darkness of the jungle as if it might contain the answers to Kaia's pain. The humid night pressed close around them and the sounds of wildlife in the distance faded from his awareness as he focused in on the picture Ra made there—shoulders hunched and tense, feet spread as if he was poised to take off running again at a moment's notice.

Dammit. He shouldn't care what the man was feeling. Shouldn't want to wrap him in his wings to block the world away until he'd had a chance to rest. Not trusting himself to step closer, he leaned against the cave wall behind him.

"I will destroy Caelus," Mica promised. The horror of watching Caelus' exploitation and torture of Kaia hadn't left him for a single moment since they'd born witness to it.

"Not if I kill him first," Ra replied.

Mica clenched his jaw in frustration, taking a sip of his

whiskey before he started yet another argument with the man. This is exactly why they could never be together. Ra thought he was invulnerable because he'd survived at Bastion's side for so long, but the truth was that the Soul Court was so distant that he'd never faced a fraction of what the other courts were capable of. Mica was all too painfully aware of just how poisonous a viper Ra could be in the political arena, but all the traitorous schemes in the world couldn't protect him from a magical strike he would never see coming.

"He's too powerful and you have no magic to defend yourself. I will take care of it," Mica said.

"Fuck you. I bet I can kill him before you even get close," Ra snapped, turning toward him with fire in his eyes.

Mica smirked and shook his head. "You'd lose that bet." Instantly, he regretted the words. He'd only cemented the determination he could in Ra's storm-grey eyes.

"Fine. What are the stakes?" Ra growled.

"I'm not doing this with you. You are not to go after him," Mica said.

"I'm not one of your people to order around!"

"That's exactly what you are. What you agreed to," Mica growled, even though he knew better than to give an order that wouldn't be followed. Ra cared too much for Kaia to leave this in the hands of someone else.

"You and I both know how this is going down. Or are you too scared of losing and having to pay up?" Ra taunted.

This was ridiculous. What did he care if Ra got himself killed? Ignoring the sudden nausea at that thought and the spiky ball of anger in the back of his mind that was the stronghold, he set his terms. "Fine. If I kill him first, you tell me your real name."

Ra looked almost sheepish for a moment. "Seriously? Can't you pick something more arrogant and rulerish?"

The man had always been cagey about his name even after they'd had a hundred late-night phone calls where they'd talked about everything from their childhoods to their worst dates. He knew the story of how Ra came by his nickname. It was a shortening of some sort. Like how Ra called Bastion, Bast. Ra had joked that their nicknames shared an old human pantheon—deities of the Sun and Protection. He'd mentioned the word rā meant sun in the Māori language as well, which is why little Kaia called him Uncle Sunshine. The name suited him and his irreverent brightness. Ra had never given a hint of what the name he was born with was, other than to say it was one more reason he hated his estranged parents who'd died shortly after the first melding.

"No. If you insist on this foolishness, you can pay the consequences," Mica said.

Ra glared at him. "Fine. And when I win, you owe me a kiss. A proper one."

Mica's eyes widened in surprise and flicked down to Ra's lips despite himself. He swallowed back a groan as Ra's tongue flicked out to lick them. The man knew exactly what he was doing, too. Damn him.

"Done," Mica said, his voice dropping lower as he fought to keep control of himself.

It was all he could do not to haul the man into his arms when they shook on it, so he retreated from the balcony as soon as he lost the warmth of his hand against his own.

"Oh, and Ra?" he said, turning back with his hand on the door to his private rooms.

"What?"

"You are not to leave my sight when we visit the Air Court for Daria's ascension."

Ra's curses had him smiling. The human knew there was only so far he could push him and disappearing when he was Mica's plus-one at an official function would be over the line.

Good luck winning that bet when he couldn't leave Mica's side.

CHAPTER 9

RA

If Ra had thought the events of the night before would change anything, he was sorely mistaken. When he woke the next morning, the living area was just as quiet and empty as it had ever been. The limestone walls absorbing any noise he made only rubbed salt in the wound. The way Mica had sped to Kaia's rescue and sworn to destroy her attacker might have crumbled the last of Ra's resistence to the draw between them, but it clearly hadn't made any difference to Mica's feelings. Not that he was surprised. No, the only surprising thing was how badly he was falling for the elemental lord now that he couldn't make himself hate him anymore. He was right back where he'd been before it had all gone wrong—pining and avoiding even thinking the L word because it was all too impossible.

Unable to face another day of oppressive silence, Ra keyed up one of his playlists from The Crypt nightclub back home, popped in his earbuds, and headed out to the deepest, darkest section of the caves he could find. Somewhere it wouldn't be so obvious that there weren't enough people living here, and that there was one person whose very noticeable absence in particular was a constant annoyance under his skin.

The walk to the chamber that was one of the main hubs of the cave system was familiar by now, but the chamber itself still took his breath away.

Looking over the half-formed map from his previous days' efforts, he chose one of the larger tunnels heading into the depths, partly because it was easily accessible and he didn't have the patience to scramble down rock walls and partly because he felt strangely drawn toward it. It was the only passageway that wasn't already lit with softly glowing walls until he reached it and a zap like a static charge spread across his skin as he passed into the dimly lit space.

The warning shock gave him pause for a moment before warmth bloomed beneath his fingers as he trailed his hand along the stone wall of the wide tunnel. Whatever had caused it, the stronghold was fine with his presence there. Releasing the drone from his other hand, he set it to fly on autopilot a few feet behind him, following the signal from his phone as it scanned their surroundings with a grid of red light.

Lost in the meditative nature of the passages, he was caught by surprise when a voice called out to him from behind.

"Sir!"

Pausing his music, he turned to face the concerned-looking scout. "Yes?"

"Did Lord Mica give you permission to go to the council chamber?"

Huh. Is that where this tunnel led? That meant he was heading right to the source of the worst damage to the sentience. He knew the contagion that had ripped it apart had formed just outside the council chamber where Hel had been kidnapped.

"Yes, of course," he said. Mica hadn't told him he wasn't allowed anywhere in particular. That was basically permission, wasn't it?

"There's a ban on non-essential travel in this section of the tunnels. You shouldn't have been able to even get through," the scout said, looking dubious.

Huh. That must have been what that zap was. Yay for Earthshine not giving a shit about rules.

"I'm helping survey for repairs," he said, gesturing to the drone softly whirring between them.

The scout looked confused, probably because surveying was usually redundant when the caves were a sentient being. Pressing a hand to his ear with a glowing finger, the scout made contact with someone. "I have the human here inside the travel ban area," he said.

Whatever was said in reply had his brow furrowing as he flashed Ra a concerned look. "As you wish, seneschal."

Ra raised an eyebrow in question and the scout waved him on his way before heading back up out of the tunnel. A reckless smile twitched on his lips as he turned his music back on. If Wren was happy for him to be here, it probably meant he was doing something forbidden or dangerous or both. He said a silent thank you to the seneschal who definitely had it in for him. Wren's willingness to let him proceed against the scout's instincts had let him know he must be heading in the right direction. He just had no idea toward what. Maybe he'd finally make some damn progress. The sooner he fixed this for Mica, the sooner he could stop feeling so damn awful about the whole extortion thing. The guilt was a searing poker in his gut now he no longer had his anger to hide behind.

The slowly descending tunnel was wide enough that even Mica could've extended his impressive wingspan and not brushed either side. The further he went, the more crystalline minerals ribboned through the limestone, flashing like a heartbeat. His heartbeat. Smiling, he reached out once more to stroke the stronghold.

"Hey, that's my trick, Earthshine. I used to do that with Bast in the club—match the rhythm of the music to his heartbeat," Ra teased.

A vibration beneath his feet rumbled like a growl, unbalancing him for a moment and a scattering of stones dropped on his shoulders.

"Sheesh. Don't get jealous. Bast's like a brother to me, not anything else. You're as bad as Mica," Ra murmured.

The rock gave one last jolt before settling down again like nothing had happened, the flashes of light a little faster now thanks to the adrenaline that had his heart pumping harder. Shaking his head, Ra sped up until he came to a towering entryway.

The doors swung open as he approached, revealing a chamber so vast that it was open to the sky above at the peak of its curving ceiling, despite how deep within the earth he must now be. Stalactites had formed thick columns surrounding the council table in an unnaturally perfect circle.

The table itself and all its chairs appeared to have grown from solid mineral rock. Not the limestone that abounded in the cave, but glittering layers of the crystalline mica the Earth Lord was named for. Of course. The elemental lords were all about the branding after all. Reaching up, Ra touched the matching mineral collar around his neck, stroking the smooth, warm surface. A different sort of brand.

The dangling bioluminescent strands of light draping from the ceiling's surface refracted off the latticework of the table's structure to make it appear lit from within even as it sent rainbows scattering across the space. The table, the light, and the columns were the only use of the vast space. Everything else was cloaked in dramatic darkness. This was the heart of the stronghold. Its core. A womblike space from which its life had grown.

Lying down on the floor, Ra spread his arms and legs wide, staring up at the distant patch of blue sky. The light wasn't strong enough to penetrate down here, doing nothing to detract from the strands of flaring magic that were now racing in sparks of colour like fireworks in time to the music still playing in his ears.

He didn't know how long he lay there just existing with the stronghold, basking in its presence, despite the fact he couldn't communicate with it. It wasn't until the lights flashed brighter and lost rhythm with his music that he was jerked from his reverie. Pausing his playlist, he sat up cross-legged and tilted his head as he watched the change. His dance tracks had been fast-paced and heavy on the bass, matching the earlier explosive display. But now the colours shifted like flowing water, pulsing to a slower beat. A swirl of sparks skittered from the wall to illuminate the tunnel he'd just come from.

"Alright, Earthshine. Show me what you got," he murmured, pocketing his earbuds and getting to his feet.

To the right of the entryway, the tunnel that circumnavigated the outside of the chamber was blocked by a collection of rubble where it had collapsed. He knew from Bast's reports at the time that this must be where he and Mica had contained the contagion after it ripped through the stronghold, making a swathe of its essence simply cease to exist.

That wasn't where the light and the strange tug deep in his soul was taking him though. The sparks dancing across the tunnel wall were swirling around to the left, leading him to a much smaller teak door set in an intricately carved arch of stone formed to look like a wyrm twining around its edge.

For once, it didn't swing open automatically as he neared but as he reached out half mesmerised by the magic dancing through the space, the wood gave way easily. Stepping into a short curving shadowy corridor, he saw the tell-tale warm flicker of a fireplace ahead. Exquisite notes reverberated in the air. The door must have some sort of magical sound barrier because there hadn't been any sense of the music until he'd stepped through.

Tilting his head, he paused and simply listened to the haunting, intricate melody. It was a piano, or some similar elemental equivalent, being played by someone extracting raw emotion from its keys. Someone whose music was already etched in his soul from years of late phone calls and stolen absent moments. It was hope and pain, comfort and heartbreak.

It was beautiful.

As he stepped into the limestone chamber and took in the picture before him, he was as overwhelmed by the beauty of the elemental sitting at the piano as he was by the beauty of the music. Mica was leaning over the keys, lost in his playing. His wings sparked with the copper of his power where they draped behind him and magical contrails drifted through the air to coalesce around the piano, making it appear constructed of pure warmth and light. His muscled thigh was on full display, testing the bounds of his tailored pants as his foot pressed to the pedals to stretch and dampen the notes to his will. For once, the sleeves of his crisp white shirt were rolled up to the elbows and Ra watched entranced as strong hands danced across the keys, teasing forth the melodies and harmonies effortlessly.

Ra swallowed hard as he watched, fighting the urge to straddle the Earth Lord and make him dance those fingers over his skin instead. To invite him to play his body with the same enthralled dedication as he played the instrument. Forcing his gaze up further, Ra took in Mica's elegant profile —the commanding angle of his jaw with its perfectly trimmed beard he wished he wasn't desperate to feel against him, high cheekbones a sculptor would have been hard-pressed to make more attractive, and eyes closed in reverie that he longed to see turned his way so he could drown in their blue-green depths like he had before it had all gone wrong. Back when Mica used to admire his cunning instead of despising it. When he used to whisper on their phone calls that he wished the family he'd lost had had a tenth of Ra's loyalty and devotion. When he would blush at Ra's teasing flirtations instead of fume.

Bast used to ask him what it was that drew him to Mica. His chosen brother thought it was a crush. That Mica was just another conquest of many. A new challenge that appealed because Ra could mess up the too neat Earth Lord and turn his staid countenance into something softer—the attraction of opposites. And maybe that was how it had started. He liked being the only one to crack through the ruling persona Mica wore like armour.

But somewhere along the way, he'd found a thousand tiny things they had in common that together had started to feel like something more—the music they shared, the complex feelings for their families who had passed and the determined way they found new family to fill the gap, the fascination with and respectful debate of world power structures that had taught both of them so much, even when they came at the issues from different places.

Why did the Earth Lord have to be so damn honourable? Ra couldn't hold onto his anger now he understood what was behind Mica's actions and the weight of responsibility dragging at his wings. He understood hard choices. Had advised Bast to make similar ones time and again when the need for ruthlessness outweighed all other considerations. Mica had done what he thought was necessary to protect the people he was responsible for and Ra could hardly fault him for that when it was one of the things he most admired about him. If even Hel could forgive the Earth Lord, he could as well.

Not that it would make any difference after what he'd done to manipulate Mica. There was no coming back from that, but perhaps he could steal a few more memories while he was living in the stronghold. Something to look back on in the long lonely decades that loomed ahead. And he could make Mica safe before he left, just like Mica was keeping Kaia safe. If Ra found a way to heal the stronghold, the elemental would have the foundation he needed to recover. He couldn't even pretend to himself that it was about assuaging his guilt or repaying a debt. The truth was, he'd do anything for this man. The thought was terrifying.

A pause in the music jolted him from his ruminations and Ra drew in a sharp breath as Mica turned his head and stared at him, the copper ring around his pupils glowing even brighter than usual.

"How long have you been standing there?" Mica asked, his voice rasping as if he hadn't used it in days.

Ra stepped closer, unable to fight the draw between them. "I don't even know. I was lost in your playing," he admitted.

"Come here," Mica growled.

"Why?" Ra asked, already closing the distance between them. Knowing it was too late to save himself.

"Because I told you to," Mica said, reaching out to grab his wrist and pull him closer.

Caught by surprise by the move, Ra fell into his lap before he could do anything to recover. Fuck if he knew what was going on, but there was no way he was going to let this opportunity pass him by. It would hurt like hell to let Mica touch him when the elemental was sure to continue rejecting him, but he deserved the pain after what he'd done.

Shifting his weight, Ra moved until he was straddling Mica on the piano bench, his knees pressing against the sensitive inner surface of the elemental's wings and his arms looped around his neck. It still wasn't close enough. A roll of his hips aligned them perfectly so their lower bodies were pressed as close as possible, the hard ridge of Mica's erection pressing against his own in a way that made his eyes roll back in pleasure.

"Fuck. Why can't I resist you?" Mica murmured against the skin of his neck, using his teeth to nip just above the mica collar that was like a warm hug against his skin.

Ra didn't bother answering the question, too lost in his pleasure as he ground against the elemental and unwilling to say something that might break the moment. Mica growled in frustration as Ra's shirt blocked the progress of his kisses down his chest.

"Take it off," Mica ordered.

Leaning back and arching his body so he could rest against the piano without hitting the keys, Ra held Mica's gaze as he unbuttoned his shirt. The Earth Lord's large hands dropped to his hips and gripped hard enough to bruise as he worked, urging him to keep grinding against him. Ra moaned at the new shock of pleasure through him, his hands shaking almost too much to finish what he was doing. As soon as the last button slipped free, Mica was on him, pushing the fabric partway down his arms and gripping it tight with one hand behind Ra to keep his wrists trapped.

Fuck. That shouldn't feel so good. He knew Mica hated him. Knew there was no way he should make himself vulnerable to this elemental who no longer respected him. There was no future possible between them with the way he'd threatened the Earth Lord to get his way. Not for the first time, he wished he could explain the full context of his actions when he'd taken control of the city's food supply. He'd sworn to keep his silence as part of the deal, though. And he never broke a promise, especially when it could mean the difference between whether a father got to go home to his children or was lost to them forever. All that faded into background noise with Mica's magic skittering across his skin and Mica's lips sucking his nipple hard into his mouth.

Closing his eyes, Ra stopped fighting against Mica's hold and let himself sink into the sensations he was feeling. A hand cupped his jaw, tipping his head down from where it had fallen back in pleasure before grasping just tight enough onto his throat below the mica of his collar that he could feel the slight restriction on his blood flow. Moaning again as his mind floated in bliss, Ra tried to surge forward and claim Mica's mouth but the Earth Lord held him back.

"No kisses. I'm not doing that with you," Mica growled, his hand trailing down Ra's torso to tug at the button of his pants.

Ra stiffened in his hold, the words pulling him back from the fantasy he'd been wilfully losing himself in as the fractures in his damaged heart stretched wider.

"Stop," he whispered, hating himself for the weakness he could hear in his voice.

Why couldn't he have stayed angry at Mica a little longer? Long enough to be willing to take the hate-sex the Earth Lord was offering instead of feeling nauseous at the thought. Mica's hand dropped away as soon as he spoke and he couldn't help but mourn the loss.

"I thought you were all about taking your pleasure wherever you find it?" Mica asked, voice carefully neutral.

He wasn't wrong. Ra was renowned for his playboy ways and it was frankly outrageous that as long as they'd been flirting with each other, the most that had ever passed between them was a single kiss in a stolen moment. A kiss that would apparently never be repeated.

"I have standards, asshole. I don't stick my dick in just anyone, unlike some people. Will you try and control the new Air Lady with your cock like you did the last?" Ra snapped back, heartache making him cruel.

He needed to force Mica to put distance between them because fuck if he could make himself do it. Ra knew Mica regretted his relationship with the now deceased Lady of Air, Aliya. He also knew Mica never would have tried seducing her if he hadn't thought it might save the world from a little of her torture and cruelty.

"If anyone is sticking their dick somewhere, it would be me," Mica snapped, finally releasing his grip that had been holding Ra's arms behind him.

Ra rolled his eyes at Mica's posturing. "Whatever," he said, starting to shrug his shirt back on.

Before he could get it past his elbows, Mica's face dropped into a scowl and the Earth Lord reached out to grip his left biceps tight enough to make him wince.

"I can feel his magic in you. I don't like it," Mica rasped, his thumb digging into the black lines of the wings Bast's power had etched into Ra's skin as if he could wipe away the mark that bound them together if he pressed hard enough.

"Tough shit. He's my brother. And that mark will keep me alive to protect him for centuries to come," Ra said.

"You're *mine*. Not his," Mica growled.

Ra raised an eyebrow, ignoring the flare of false hope the words sparked. Mica didn't mean it. He'd kick Ra out on his ass as soon as the stronghold was better.

"For now, maybe. Let go of me," he said.

Mica's nostrils flared and the sensation of his power grew thicker in the air around them like an impending earthquake. "I can't," he admitted.

Ra blew out a breath in frustration. "Why the fuck not? You're acting like we're mates or something."

Mica glanced away, refusing to meet his eyes, and Ra's mouth dropped open in shock. "Wait. What?!"

"It doesn't matter," Mica mumbled.

Ra felt the words like a dagger to the heart. "What do you mean it doesn't matter?" he all but yelled.

"Plenty of people ignore the drive to mate with someone. Not everyone is as keen as your *brother* to bare every emotion to someone and create a walking weakness that could kill them," Mica said.

Ra frowned, still trying to process the bombshell. "I thought humans didn't have the right kind of magic for the bond."

Mica shrugged. "Bastion's magic has been running through your veins for decades. Apparently, that has altered you enough."

"Enough that you can feel the potential for a mating bond between us?" Ra checked.

"Yes."

"How common is that kind of potential?" he asked.

Mica cleared his throat. "The bond can be formed between any two elementals with sufficient magic to make it take hold."

"That's not what I asked. How common is it to feel driven to form a mating bond with someone?"

"Most elementals never feel the drive," Mica said, still sounding evasive.

Ra tilted his head and tried to read the emotions the Earth Lord was doing his best to hide from his face. "Have you ever felt it before?"

"No."

"Will you ever feel it again with someone else?"

"Unlikely."

Ra sighed, wishing he had a hand free to force Mica to look at him. "So, it's like a fated mates thing?"

Mica snorted. "There's no such thing as an inevitable fate. Like I said, most elementals ignore it. The bond is beyond invasive. It's not something most would choose to subject themselves to."

Ra nodded. "But that's why you're acting the way you do. Why you're so possessive, despite the fact you hate me."

"My instincts sometimes get the better of me. It's just one more way you're a danger to my people. I can't keep them safe when I'm distracted by you," Mica said.

Guilt was a leaden feeling inside him despite knowing Mica's distraction wasn't his fault. He didn't want to make Mica weaker.

"Bast's mark on me distracts you?"

"Incessantly," Mica said. "It's like a mosquito bite on my fucking soul that I can't scratch."

"Okay. Replace it with yours then," Ra said. Knowing it was a terrible idea. Knowing that anything deepening this connection between them would be exquisite torture, but unable to stop himself from offering this small relief to the elemental he'd been halfway in love with before they smashed it all down. The elemental he no longer hated. Leaving him right back where he'd been before it all went wrong.

"What?!" Mica asked, head finally snapping back to stare at him in incredulity.

Ra's lips quirked in a half-smile, drinking in the return of Mica's attention like it was water on the parched desert of his soul. Fuck. He was so screwed, and not in a good way.

"I don't want you bitching at me about being distracted for three years. So replace the mark if it will help," he said, giving them both the out of pretending this was insignificant.

"Always so reckless," Mica murmured. Raw possession flared in the elemental's eyes and he dragged Ra into a full-body embrace that left no space between them. "Are you sure?" Mica asked, his nose pressed into the bare skin of Ra's neck like he could breathe in his soul and keep it trapped inside his lungs if he only tried hard enough.

"Yes. Bast can replace it when I get home," Ra said, not at all sure that was true.

Mica growled and sucked hard on the delicate skin of his neck, marking him. "Over my dead body," he said.

Before Ra could reply, Mica's wings wrapped tight around them and the sensation of Mica's vast power became overwhelming as he was wrapped in a veil of softest copper. A swathe of tingling energy radiated from the point where Mica's hand still wrapped tight around his biceps stretching down past his wrist and up his neck to the indentation beneath his ear.

He'd been bleeding out on the floor of Soul Tower when Bast had placed his mark on him almost thirty years earlier and his memories of what happened before he regained consciousness with the connection in place were fuzzy at best.

This time, he could feel every grain of magic singing through his body, pushing Bast's familiar cool soulweaving power out and replacing it with something that felt like the depths of the earth, somehow both grounding and hot like its core, stoking his desire.

The connection settled with an almost painful snap and Ra instantly realised what a mistake this had been. He'd forgotten, or perhaps wilfully ignored, his conversation with Hel before she'd mated Bast when this was the only kind of connection the two of them had. She'd described it as visceral, like a part of Bast was inside her all the time, and he'd been confused because it was such a sharp contrast to his own connection to his brother, which was something he could focus on or ignore as he wished. He and Bast could sense each other's heartbeats and breaths if they tried, but their emotions only registered if they were extreme.

This new connection with Mica was totally different from the one he'd had with his brother. He should have realised the potential for a mating bond between them would have that effect on it. Mica's heartbeat was an elevated rhythm inside his chest that his own now kept time with. The two of them gasped a breath in synchrony and he could feel the thrum of Mica's desire for him as if it were his own. He could also feel the resentment and bitter anger the man still held for him like an infected wound tainting everything else.

Which meant ... Fuck!

Eyes widening, Ra scrambled to block his emotions from the connection as best he could, but one glance at the shock on Mica's face told him he'd been too late. The last thing he needed was for the Earth Lord to realise Ra didn't hate him anymore and that in the absence of that hate, the love that had been growing between them was blooming on his side at least.

He was unable to avoid feeling the chaos of Mica's emotions sweep over him, but watching them play out on his beautiful face was too much. Ra's body stiffened where he still straddled the elemental and he tilted his chin down to avoid Mica's too discerning gaze.

As his gaze locked onto his arm, he realised the Earth Lord had gone just as overboard as Bast had with Hel when he formed the new mark there. Ra now had a whole sleeve of intricate sparking copper feathers stretching from the knuckle of his ring finger up his entire arm and he was certain it extended up to that point under his ear where he'd felt Mica's power. It was not subtle and it wouldn't be hidden by his clothing unless he took to wearing gloves and a scarf. If it hadn't been for the unexpected invasive sense they now had of each other, he would have been entranced by the mesmerising way the mark shifted on his skin like the feathers were ruffling.

Anger flared inside him at what Mica had done despite the fact he'd asked for it. The elemental must have realised how his mark would take. What the fuck had he been thinking?

"Just as well you didn't kiss me. Wouldn't want to get too intimate," Ra sneered, hating that the bitterness he'd tried to hide at Mica's earlier rejection may as well be framed in neon lights now.

CHAPTER 10
MICA

What the fuck had he done when he'd placed his mark? And when had Ra stopped hating him? The tension between them over the past week had been agony but it had been mutual. At least, he'd thought it was. Now, he almost felt bad about his own mistrust of the man, but Ra deserved it. He'd never understood why Ra had gone to such extremes for a council invitation that would've been extended eventually anyway. The only explanation had been revenge fuelled by Ra's hatred of him after his choices had almost resulted in Bast's death, and now it turned out that hatred had been fleeting.

Ra had destroyed everything between them for *nothing* and that only made his own anger greater.

They'd never stood a chance. Even if things hadn't turned out the way they had, Mica would never have put the target of a lord's consort on the back of a fragile human with no magic and divided loyalties. Ra was all but defenceless in the ruthless world of elemental politics. But they could've been something better than what they were. Friends, perhaps. He shouldn't have had to lose the only brightness in his day that their communications had become. Ra had taken that from him and wasn't sure he'd ever forgive him for it.

"You could at least apologise if you're so flighty that you've moved on from your hatred already," Mica growled, pushing Ra off him gently despite the angry tension in his body.

"No," Ra said, shrugging his shirt back on and reaching down to fasten the buttons.

Mica wished he could drag his gaze away from the frustrating view of all that delicious skin being covered, but he couldn't.

"No?! Why the fuck not?" he asked, all sense of his usual staid propriety well and truly lost, just like it always was when Ra was anywhere near him.

"I don't see *you* apologising for anything," Ra said.

"I am sorry for my words at the summit. They were uncalled for. But I'm not sorry for voting for Hel's capture. If I could go back in time, I would make the same choice again," Mica said.

"And so would I," Ra whispered, turning away.

Pain stabbed him in the chest at the fresh betrayal because he could feel the truth in the words through their connection.

"Fuck you," Mica said, more gasp than statement as he shoved to his feet and fought to keep his anger and hurt in check.

Ra glanced over his shoulder at him with a sad smile. "I don't think that's a good idea," he said.

Mica took a threatening step closer, but whatever his instincts would've driven him to do in that moment was interrupted by the room suddenly turning pitch black before the walls started flashing with red light.

Attack! The stronghold screamed in his mind, the words sending him sprinting for the door.

"What's going on?" Ra asked, chasing after him.

"Something's threatening the stronghold," Mica snapped, racing for the entryway and cursing himself for spending so much time in the chamber where there was no reception for his sat-phone.

The second they emerged through the teak door, both their phones went crazy with notifications.

"Report!" Mica snapped into his phone as Ra swore softly behind him.

"A portal opened at the entry to the stronghold. The Soul Court has declared war," his second-in-command said. "Our scouts aren't a match for Lord Bastion's power. We need you here."

"Bastion's launched an assault?" Mica asked, confused.

The Captain paused a moment. "It's just him and all he's done so far is shield himself from our defence and demand your presence."

Mica slowed his pace and pinched the bridge of his nose in frustration. Dammit. Bastion would have felt the removal of his mark. He should've realised the ramifications of cutting Ra's connection to the Soul Lord but he'd been too distracted. This was exactly why he never should've let Ra come in the first place.

"Cease fire, Captain. Withdraw and do not engage unless you need to defend yourself."

"My lord, he knew what portalling here meant. The summit was clear it would be an act of war," the Captain protested.

"That was an order, not a suggestion. I'll be there soon," he said, hanging up.

Turning to Ra, he saw the man was speaking urgently into his phone. "Nah, bro. I promise I'm fine. It's just a misunderstanding."

"He wants to speak to you," Ra said, holding out the phone to him.

"Bastion," Mica said in greeting.

"What the fuck did you do to my brother?" Bastion all but shouted.

This was not how he wanted the news to get out. To be fair, he hadn't really thought that far ahead. There was no point denying it though when the evidence of his loss of control was glowing on Ra's skin in copper as they jogged back up the tunnels.

"I told you he is mine while he's here. He's fine. I merely replaced your mark with one of my own," Mica said.

Bastion spluttered and fell silent. "Bring him to me. I need to see him," he finally said.

"Of course. We'll be right there," Mica said, ignoring the fact another lord was trying to give him orders in his own damn court. Bastion had every right to be concerned when he felt his connection with Ra break.

Handing Ra's phone back to him, he swept the man up into his arms, ignoring Ra's yelp of surprise, and used his magic to speed their process through the caves.

Smash. Fight. Destroy. Protect mate. The stronghold chanted in his mind in time with his steps.

Calm yourself. He's Ra's family. His brother, Mica told the Stronghold.

I won't let him steal him, the stronghold replied, and the earth jolted beneath their feet sending them stumbling.

Sending his power out in a huge wave of pure control through the tangled broken ley lines around them, Mica took charge before the sentience could harm anyone by accident again.

Hush. I will protect him. Focus on keeping Kaia safe, he said, hoping to redirect its attention.

Mine. They're MINE, the stronghold said, before falling silent.

Dammit. He could feel the instability spreading through the sentience's presence in his mind. Putting on another burst of speed, he all but flew through the tunnels until they emerged into the late afternoon sunlight of the entryway.

Two dozen of his fighters hovered above, poised to attack, and Wren was standing in the entryway as if his slight presence could stop Bastion from gaining entry. Ignoring them all, Mica returned Ra to his feet, holding his elbow until the man regained his balance, and then stepped forward to greet the Soul Lord.

With the power of a dozen ley lines still feeding directly into him, he extended his hand and pushed it through Bastion's shielding, the process like walking through molasses. He might make allowance for the Soul Lord's panicked arrival at his doorstep, but that didn't mean he wouldn't show his strength in response. He couldn't risk being seen as weak. Bastion was powerful, but he was still young and Mica had many centuries more experience to draw from.

"Welcome, Lord Bastion," he said, offering a handclasp once he'd breached the magical protections surrounding him.

Bastion scowled at the move but dropped his shielding as he reached out to return the greeting. Hoping any threat was past, Mica signalled his Captain to return his forces to their usual positions and the skies above them cleared.

"What the fuck, bro? You can't risk starting a war over this," Ra said, brushing past him as he pulled Bastion into a tight hug despite his angry words.

"I don't suppose you could've given me some warning before you severed our connection and I assumed you'd *died*," Bastion chided, holding Ra just as tight. "Is he forcing you to do this?"

Mica growled at the suggestion he would force a mark on someone, wings flaring wide in anger.

"Woah, down boy," Ra said, pulling away from Bastion to step towards Mica and place a hand to his chest.

He wished that touch didn't calm the rage. Wished it didn't send molten hot need through his veins. Clenching his teeth, he gently gripped Ra's wrist and lowered the man's hand back to his side.

"Don't speak to me like that," he warned quietly.

Ra's gaze flicked over his shoulder where he was sure Wren was still watching. The man knew better than to be so casual in front of others.

"Sorry," Ra said.

"Can I speak to my brother alone for a moment? I'll bring him right back," Bastion said, inclining his head toward the portal.

Mica was glad Bastion was one of the few elementals who lacked the ability to communicate with the stronghold thanks to his unique soulweaving magic, because the responding torrent of emotion from the caves was murderous.

"He stays here. You may shield the conversation, though," Mica said, careful not to give away just how tenuous his hold on the situation was. If Bastion took Ra through that portal there was no telling how the stronghold would react.

Bastion held his gaze, frowning, and it was Ra who finally broke the standoff.

"I don't need to keep our conversation from Mica and I doubt I could anyway," Ra said, subconsciously touching the collar around his throat. "The magic from your mark was interfering with my work here so I had to ask Mica to swap it out. I should've called you first. I'm sorry."

Mica was impressed by how deftly Ra was navigating avoiding any of the topics he wasn't supposed to discuss. Bastion knew some of what he was there for, but with Wren and likely at least one of his scouts listening in, they couldn't risk saying much out in the open.

Bastion didn't look convinced. "And what's this?" he asked, stepping closer to Ra and touching the collar.

"A safety precaution," Mica said as Ra smirked at him.

"Did you ask him for that, too?" Bastion asked Ra.

"Nope. He's an asshole when he wants something just like you. It's a cute accessory, though. Right?" Ra said, striking a pose.

Weirdly, the words seemed to reassure Bastion, or maybe it was his friend's antics that had him laughing as he shot Mica a knowing look.

"Do you want me to make him take it off or does that hickey on your neck mean you're fine with it?" Bastion asked Ra, loud enough for him to hear.

Ra waved a hand without even looking over at him. "It's fine as it is."

Mica tilted his head, utterly confounded by the contradictory man. He would've removed the collar if Bastion had asked. The new connection between him and Ra performed much of the same function, allowing him to track the man and serving as a visual reminder Ra was under his protection. The dark obsessive drive inside him was glad it was staying, though. He was lucky Bast was too young and lived too far from the courts to know the history of such markers. Shaking his head at his own folly, he interrupted the two.

"If that is all, Lord Bastion?" Mica said.

Bastion nodded and pulled Ra into one last hug.

"You're not going to visit Kaia while you're here?" Ra asked.

"I think we've caused enough international incidents for the day. I'll wait until the agreed time."

"I can have her brought out to you," Mica offered.

Bastion shook his head. "That is generous but you and I both know your people are on a hair-trigger with how I arrived. I'll see you next week at the Air Court. If you hurt him, I'll kill you."

Mica's gaze hardened. "I will manage my court as I see fit. Stay out of it."

"The only reason I'm willing to leave him here in that state is because I can see how gone you are for him. Good luck with that," Bastion said before striding back through the portal that blinked closed as soon as he was out of sight.

"Well. That was awkward. What state? I need a whiskey," Ra said, turning back toward the stronghold entrance.

Wren, who was still standing in the middle of the thoroughfare, turned pale as anything when he took in Mica's mark climbing up Ra's arm and the bruise he'd sucked into his neck.

"Did you *mate* with him?" Wren gasped.

"What? Of course not. I just placed my mark on him." He didn't owe Wren an explanation, but he needed to shut down that rumour fast.

"But you don't place your mark on anyone, my lord," Wren said, looking hurt.

"The evidence suggests otherwise, chip," Ra said.

"I ... what? Chip?" Wren sputtered as Ra pushed past him.

"Y'know, because you're all salty and spout vinegar," Ra grinned.

Mica snorted back a laugh despite himself as he followed after the human. That one was bad even for Ra. "If you could avoid terrorising my staff I would appreciate it," Mica said, as they entered his living room.

"Where's the fun in that?" Ra asked carrying on into his bedroom.

"I thought you wanted a whiskey," Mica called, wandering over to his drinks cabinet and pondering what he was in the mood for. Something spicy and sweet like Ra's sunshine scent lingering in the air. He immediately kicked himself for the thought and was so distracted he didn't notice the man himself approaching.

"I do. But I want *my* whiskey," Ra said, two glasses of amber liquid in his hands.

"You brought your own whiskey? I have some of the best in the world right here," Mica said, taking the glass he was offered.

Ra shrugged. "I'm not saying it's better. I'm saying it's *mine*. I made it. I even made the barrels it aged in."

Mica's eyebrows raised in surprise. That he had not expected. Taking a small sip, he let the liquid sit on his tongue and savoured the flavours. It was exactly what he had been craving. Of course. "I like it."

"You don't have to say that. I drink it because it tastes like home. You don't have the same nostalgia," Ra said, taking another sip that drew Mica's gaze to his Adam's apple. He wanted to bite it.

"I don't say things I don't mean. It tastes like you," he replied.

Ra threw his head back and laughed. "I'll take it."

"What kind of barrel was it aged in?"

"Mizunara Oak. I brought a small cask with me if you want to see," Ra offered.

The Japanese oak and long storage explained the heavy spice notes and sunshiny hint of coconut he associated with Ra. Stalking after the man, he handed over his glass for a refill as he took in the smooth aged wood sitting near Ra's bed. He quickly regretted the move as Ra seated himself on the bed and leaned back on his elbow semi-reclined to finish his drink. He looked like pure temptation and Mica couldn't stop himself from stalking closer as he remembered just how good it felt when Ra had sat on his lap at the piano.

Ra raised an eyebrow in question as he paused between the man's knees where they rested on the edge of the bed. "See something else you like?"

"Like's a strong word."

The reminder of what they were to each other brought a scowl to the man's face, but it didn't last long. "How do you know the whiskey tastes like me? You've only tasted one of us."

Knocking back the rest of his whiskey in one go, he slammed the glass down on the side table and plucked Ra's from his hand to do the same before putting one knee up on the bed so he could cage the infuriating man between his hands.

"Not true. I've tasted you, too," he said, flicking out his tongue to lick the skin of Ra's chest exposed by the top buttons of his shirt. "Here. And here. And here." He punctuated each of his words with another lick or bite as he made his way up until he reached the very tip of his mark on Ra's skin just beneath his ear, knowing the magic in the copper lines would make the touches even more sensitive.

Ra arched beneath him, hunting for friction, but Mica kept his body poised out of reach above the man.

"Head a bit lower and you'll get a better taste," Ra gasped.

Mica let out a burst of sharp laughter at the teasing words. How could this man still make him laugh after everything that had passed between them? Reaching down between them, he closed his hand around the erection hiding beneath Ra's clothes and squeezed as Ra thrust up into his grip.

"Fuck. Why do I let you do this to me?" Ra asked, moaning as Mica gave the man's throbbing length another stroke.

Mica paused at the words, loosening his grip and leaning back. This was a mistake. He couldn't let himself indulge in the drive to touch Ra.

"That wasn't a request to stop," Ra snapped, sitting up and grabbing Mica's shirt in his fist before he could back away from the bed.

Mica's eyes dropped to his lips that looked so damn soft and kissable. The breath stuttered in his lungs and he could feel their shared arousal through the connection thrumming between them. Would it really be so bad to let off a little steam? Why had he let Ra manipulate him into that stupid bet? He hadn't been able to stop thinking about the man's lips in days.

His brain knew the man couldn't be trusted. Ra had betrayed him in a way that couldn't be forgiven the day he'd rung to tell him the delayed shipment of rice needed to address a massive shortage in the Tree City wouldn't be turning up unless he extended the invitation to Bast's mate to attend the ruling council. Children would've gone hungry if Ra had carried out his threat.

The problem was that his heart, his soul, and his cock didn't seem to give a shit what his brain thought. They just wanted Ra. Desperately. So, he did what he'd been doing for weeks. He avoided the problem. Avoided his own damn quarters. Turning on his heel, he strode from the room without a backward glance. He could sleep on the couch in his office. Send one of his staff to fetch fresh clothes.

Maybe if he stayed away for a few days, the new connection between them would settle down from this constant raw need to claim Ra, to protect him, from himself and everyone else.

One could only hope.

The day of Daria's ascension to become Lady of the Air Court dawned as sunny as Ra's flirtations. For once, Mica didn't bother sneaking out of his wing before the human woke. There was no point when they'd be within spitting distance of each other until they returned. Thank the Earths the ceptae had offered to portal each of the attendees to the event or he would've spent almost eighteen hours flying them there. This way, they would leave in a couple of hours and, with the time difference, arrive just before the ceremony started at sunset.

Making his way to the kitchen, he set about making some simple stuffed rice flour crêpes for breakfast. He was so focused on what he was doing, he didn't hear Ra's approach until the man groaned like he was mid-orgasm behind him.

"Fuck, that smells amazing," Ra said, moving to the coffee maker to make them both a cup.

Ra had gotten better at hiding his emotions from the connection between them, but he could still get a general sense of them. While his own feelings were still a turmoil of contradictions, Ra's had calmed. No, calmed wasn't the right word. There was still a deep hunger between them. But alongside that was something else. Acceptance, perhaps, and determination.

They worked in silence as Mica finished plating the meal, moving around each other in complete harmony as if they'd been doing this for the twenty-some years since they'd first spoken. Each time Ra accidentally brushed against his wings in the small kitchen space, they both drew in a sharp breath and then pretended they hadn't.

Mica hadn't bothered changing out of the thin cotton pants he'd worn to bed before he started cooking and he smirked in amusement at the way Ra was all but drooling over his shirtless torso.

Dammit. He wasn't supposed to be leading them down this path, but he just couldn't help himself when he was around the man.

"I don't think I've ever seen you so casually dressed, or should that be undressed?" Ra teased, as they sat down to eat.

If he thought Ra's groan when he entered the kitchen area was bad, it was nowhere near as pornographic as the one he let out when he took his first bite of the food. Mica shifted in his seat and tried to adjust himself without drawing attention. He wasn't wearing anywhere near enough clothing to hide the effect that sound was having on him.

"I'll change as soon as we're done. We need to be at the collection site in about an hour. Does your replacement suit meet your requirements?" he asked.

"Yeah, it's great. Much more me. Elysia really came through," Ra said, sounding distracted as he leaned back in his chair to drink his coffee and let his eyes scan down Mica's body again in a blatant eye-fucking.

"Are you quite finished?" Mica asked, but the words didn't sound as annoyed as he meant them to.

Ra deliberately misconstrued the question. "Mmm ... I couldn't eat another mouthful. Your eggplant is delicious."

Mica snorted at the exaggerated suggestive statement, and then he couldn't help it. He broke out in a full-on laugh. "Are you ever not ridiculous?"

Ra grinned back at him. "And miss the chance to watch you finally relax? Never."

"*Relaxed* is not how I would describe the effect of your presence."

"Is that so? What word would you use?" Ra asked, leaning closer as he rested his chin on his hand.

Well, he'd flown into that one. He needed to shut this down before he did something he'd regret. Like pulling the man onto his lap where he belonged. "Impossible," he bit out.

"Awww ... do I make everything *harder?*"

Mica rolled his eyes and stood to gather the plates. "Behave yourself. And go get dressed."

"Yes, *my Lord,*" Ra said, sarcasm dripping from his tone as he headed off to his room, but Mica's body didn't seem to get the message as bone-deep satisfaction sunk into him at the thought of Ra being part of his court and claiming Mica as his lord for real.

It didn't take him long to clean up and don one of the tuxedos he wore like armour. As he dealt with correspondence from his regional leads on his phone while he waited for Ra to reappear, he wondered what Elysia had come up with for Ra's suit that he'd seemed so enamoured of.

Knowing his friend, they'd have selected something as outrageous as they could get away with at such a formal gathering. Partly because that was their style and partly because they enjoyed upsetting the careful balance he kept around him. They had that in common with Ra.

The soft swish of the bedroom door opening had him glancing up from his phone where he was leaning against the wall and his jaw literally dropped open at the sight Ra made. Shoving his phone in his pocket, he straightened and stalked toward the too-enticing man sauntering his way.

Elysia had gone with a three-piece suit in the exact storm grey of Ra's eyes thanks to the magically enhanced fabric. For once, his shirt was actually done all the way up, but the glittering mica of his collar wrapped around the top in lieu of a bow tie in a way no one would be able to avoid noticing. The jacket looked almost painted on, drawing attention to every beautiful line of muscle, and the pants were doing all the right things for the man's assets. The waistcoat and a shorter partial kilt draping around his thighs were a contrast in black that took the outfit into just this side of edgy and gender non-conforming in a way that suited the playful, irreverent man to a tee. Elysia had used more magic to make the shoes match perfectly to the collar as if they had been carved from glittering deep brown mica.

Making his way closer like a magnet drawn to its lodestone, he was unable to stop until they were chest-to-chest in the middle of the room.

"You like?" Ra asked, tilting his head in calculating question as Mica crowded in close.

"You look ravishing, damn you," Mica growled, wrapping his wings around them and pressing his nose into the man's neck and letting himself draw in a deep breath of his intoxicating scent.

"I'd say the same, but you moved so fast when you saw me I'm not sure I even got a look," Ra teased, letting the backs of his knuckles brush against the sensitive inner surface of his feathers as he moved to place his palm over Mica's heart. "Sure you don't want to concede defeat early and give me that kiss?" he continued in a whisper.

Mica moaned against Ra's skin and bit down on his earlobe, tugging at it gently. "We don't have time for what that would lead to." Because apparently he couldn't help but be the lord of mixed messages when it came to this man.

Ra looked up at him in surprise and then whined as Mica continued his biting path down his jaw. "I mean, is this event really that important?"

Mica sighed and drew away. They both knew it was. "We need to leave or we'll be late."

The loss of physical contact was too much to bear and he placed his hand at the small of Ra's back as they made their way toward the balcony.

"What a gentleman," Ra murmured.

Mica snorted softly under his breath. If Ra could see inside his head just then he would not be saying that. Carrying the man in a way that didn't press Mica's hard length against him so he could fly them down to the portal site was an awkward manoeuvre.

"Mmm ... or maybe not?" Ra said, smirking up at him as he hefted him higher than was comfortable to avoid any inappropriate contact.

Mica recognised the ceptae waiting to portal them as Tir, the former Archivist for the elemental council before the archives were destroyed. They had a turbulent history, but

Tir seemed to have gotten past any lingering bad feelings toward him at least. Ra greeted them in their native language with a huge smile, pulling them into a hug, because of course he did. The man had no fear and seemed to be able to charm anyone. Even Mica was wary of all those rows of sharp teeth showing as the ceptae grinned right next to Ra's cheek, but the human was oblivious.

"T-bird! I missed you!" Ra cried.

"I have missed you also, Sunshine. No one calls me strange names or makes me playlists anymore," Tir replied.

"We can't have that. I'm sure the DJs at The Crypt would make you one if you asked," Ra said.

Mica eyed the angle of the sun and cleared his throat. Their little interlude had put them behind and they couldn't afford to risk offence to the new Lady of the Air Court by being late. "Perhaps you could continue this discussion after the ceremony," Mica said.

Tir inclined their head, sending a soft undulation through the tentacles draping from their scalp, and turned to form the portal. Once the liquid shadow of the rift grew large enough to step through, Mica gestured politely for the ceptae to go ahead if they wanted, conscious of the need to demonstrate through his actions the equal status of the other leaders of the new cross-species global council.

"Thank you, Lord Mica, but it's easier to close behind me if I'm the last one through," Tir said.

Ra jerked in surprise against him as he placed a hand at the small of his back again and let his wing extend behind him before guiding them both through the portal. He should've known better than to demonstrate his weakness for the man like that but his instincts were riding him hard as they headed into what was only an iota better than enemy territory. With the way the previous Air Lady had betrayed their world, and the history with little Kaia and her tormentor Caelus still on the loose, it would be a long time before any of them, especially Ra and his family, had any trust for the Air Court.

Daria, the soon-to-be Lady of Air was waiting to greet them once they stepped through, one elegant eyebrow raising as she took in who he was with. She was a study in contrast compared to the previous Lady, Aliya. Where Aliya had been tall and willowy with white hair and golden tanned skin that set off the sparkling white-gold of her wings, Daria was smaller and curvier with enough red to her curling locks to match the metallic rose-gold of her outer feathers. It wasn't until her wings swept open a little that you could see the Air Court's tell-tale white colouring on their inner surface.

"Greetings Lord Mica. Welcome. You honour me with your presence. And who is your partner?" Daria asked, disingenuously, given everyone with any interest in elemental politics knew all about Lord Bastion's human righthand man.

Before he could introduce him, Ra stepped forward with a careless grin on his lips, extending a hand. Thank the Earths he'd placed his mark on the human's left arm or it would've been painfully obvious to every person Ra greeted.

"Hi there. Ra Cooper. Congrats on the ascension. You couldn't pay me to take on that job," he said. Somehow he made it sound like a compliment when it was anything but.

The slightest of frowns marred Daria's brow as she tried to figure out if he was insulting her, but Tir joined them before she could respond and she turned to greet the ceptae instead.

"Behave yourself," Mica whispered, leaning in close to Ra's ear.

"Where's the fun in that?"

Glancing around, Mica saw the portal had deposited them directly into the large antechamber to the Air Court council room deep inside the floating crystal stronghold. The Air Stronghold's presence was a gusting wind on the edge of his consciousness, excited by the day's events but wary of so many strangers gathering inside it. Everywhere he looked, the crystal walls and floor of the space glistened in the last of the afternoon light. The magic of the stronghold allowed them to see through the many rooms surrounding them without truly seeing what was inside so that the view was mostly one of the blue sky and clouds they were suspended in.

He'd never understood the drive to waste so much power on the display of the huge floating castle that made up the stronghold, but it didn't seem to leave the air mages drained. He could only assume the shifting ley line congruence behaved differently to his own deeply anchored home. Perhaps he could ask Lady Nerida about it sometime. The Water Lady was far more likely to answer his questions on the matter and her stronghold was also one in constant motion, floating beneath the ocean's surface.

A flash of black and silver to his right drew his attention back to the people in the room as Lord Bastion and Lady Helaine came to greet them. Once the formalities were complete, Bastion turned to Ra.

"Another thing you forgot to mention, brother?" Bastion asked, fond exasperation in his tone as he pulled Ra into a tight embrace.

"Surprise! I'm here!" Ra said, making both Bastion and Helaine laugh.

Mica knew he should remove his hand from Ra's back, especially now his family was looking on and would get the wrong idea, but he couldn't make himself do it with the number of potential threats in the room. All the most powerful elemental mages in the world were here and the Soul Court had only recently been acknowledged. There was still a huge amount of prejudice against Bastion's soul-weaving and that extended to anyone he claimed as family.

"You two look cosy," Helaine observed, curious.

He was once again saved from an awkward conversation by the need to greet the rest of the dignitaries—the Water Lady Nerida, Fire Lord Tyson, Kairon as representative of the vampyr voices, and Cole who was the human representative for the Americas on the global council. Daria was dancing a fine line with her invitation list. The recent global summit had included the thirteen vampyr voices, five of the ceptae, and seven human leaders. Daria's ascension was technically about the elemental council, not the global one. But as the first of its kind since the global summit, he would've expected her to extend the invitation to all the non-elemental representatives if she wanted to show a firm commitment to the future they were trying to build.

Instead, she'd invited just enough not to cause offence, likely in an attempt to keep the more extremist of her senior mages who had thrived under Aliya's ruthless reign happy. Only time would tell whether Daria's rule would take the same tenor as her predecessor's. Daria had a reputation for violence, but so did everyone with any power in the Air Court. Aliya had seen to that by eliminating anyone more moderate who would question her methods. Whether Daria would temper her violence now she had complete control remained to be seen, but given how long it had taken for a clear contender to be chosen to ascend he suspected the internal court machinations and negotiations that must've been required for her to come out on top would influence her leadership for at least the next decade if not for centuries.

"It's good to see you, Cole. Nice to have some human company here," Ra said, clearly noticing the same thing he had about the guest list.

For his part, Cole looked stern and tense as they stood waiting for the sun to set enough for the main event. He'd been a separatist leader before the summit, and Mica suspected the last place he wanted to be was surrounded by elementals who had almost certainly hunted down and brutally tortured his people. It might've appeared logical to invite the local human leader, but it was a very definite choice, given the history of the area. Was Daria opening lines of communication or was this a thinly veiled threat to toe the line?

"I will get you home safely," Tir reassured the man, too quiet for anyone from the Air Court surrounding them to hear.

Cole nodded. "That's the only reason I turned up. You've always been a loyal ally to our people, Tir. Thank you."

As the sun set, the sky around them turned to reds and oranges. When the entire crystal stronghold was glowing the same rose gold as Daria's wings, the doors to the main council chamber swung open with a dulcet sound like a finger tracing the edge of a crystal wine glass. Daria's voice emerged from every surface as if the walls themselves had turned into a sound system, inviting them to enter.

Once the last person stepped inside, the roof shimmered in a flash of light before disappearing, drawing every eye as it left the room open to the darkening sky above. One hundred Air Court scouts and battle mages flew overhead in formation a moment later, swooping close enough that Mica could make out what each favoured for a weapon. It was a display designed to intimidate. Another choice only barely on the right side of the line between acceptable and insulting.

Sensing Ra was about to make a snide remark, Mica pulled him more tightly to his side, squeezing his hip as he pressed a kiss to his temple as an excuse to whisper a reminder. "The walls have ears."

He could feel Ra's jaw clenching in frustration against his cheek, but he kept his silence.

Thankfully, the ascension itself was brief. Daria stepped between them into the centre of the room before turning both hands palm up and lifting herself into the air using only her magic, with her wings spread wide to catch the fading light. As she slowly spiralled up into the skies, her people formed a tunnel of wings in the air through which she rose. The higher she went, the more magic she drew to her until she was a bright shining beacon high above that no one so close could look upon. The light would be visible from one edge of her territory to the other, a feat only possibly due to the stronghold magnifying her magic.

That was the only truly necessary part of the ceremony —proof the stronghold had accepted the ascendee as the new ruler. The degree to which the courts' rulers were more powerful than other elementals was vastly increased by that relationship with the stronghold sentiences. Well, except for Bastion. He was as powerful in his own right with his unique magic, which is why everyone found him so intimidating.

"Thank fuck that's over," Ra murmured once the light finally faded and servers appeared with drinks and food for the guests.

Mica didn't disagree, but he wished Ra would keep his thoughts to himself until they were back home. As he found himself drawn into the same old political conversations these things always ended in, Ra tugged himself from his grip.

"I'm going to go catch up with Bast. I'll come find you later," Ra said.

Mica's gaze sharpened on the man, not trusting him not to go hunting for Caelus in the crowds. The elemental they both wanted dead should be persona non grata at the event, but it was highly likely he was carefully hidden somewhere away from the visiting guests. No senior mage would miss this and he had been Aliya's second-in-command.

"You don't leave my sight," he reminded Ra

Ra rolled his eyes. "Yes, *daddy*. I promise I'll be back by curfew."

Lady Nerida hid her amusement behind a sip of wine. "You've got your hands full with that one," she said.

Mica was still watching Ra deftly navigate through the room with warm smiles and passing comments that left a trail of laughter in his wake. The man was as much a marvel as a liability. There weren't many humans who could not only hold their own but thrive in a situation like this.

"He is trouble personified," Mica agreed.

"He balances you well," she said, surprising him.

"That's not ... we're not together," Mica said, too distracted keeping track of Ra to pay much attention to the Water Lady.

He frowned as Ra and Bastion moved further from the crowds, finding a quiet corner to lean in close to each other and engage in an intense conversation. What were they up to? Giving his apologies to Nerida, he used the excuse of hunting out more food to dodge the people wanting his attention. Finding his own shadowed corner, he used a touch of his power to connect to the collar at Ra's throat, sinking his senses into the mineral until he could hear their whispered words.

"*You know I can't tell you that, bro,*" Ra was saying.

"*Do you have enough information to know Kaia is safe?*" Bastion asked.

Mica started making his way over to interrupt, worried what Ra might say, but his next words had him pausing in surprise.

"*Mica would kill for her. Just like I would. Cover for me while I go hunting?*" Ra asked.

"*Of course. You'll only have a short time before your absence is noted, though,*" Bastion pointed out, deftly weaving a glamour for Ra that would hide him from the guests but not bother the stronghold enough to raise the alarm—at least it didn't bother the stronghold once Mica sent a quick reassurance in response to its sudden attention. It helped that the sentience could barely sense Bastion's soul-weaving magic that was so different from the power that flowed through the ley lines.

Whatever the glamour Bastion had woven was, it couldn't interfere with the connection between Ra and him from placing his mark. He was still achingly aware of Ra's presence. He also couldn't believe Bastion was just going to let Ra go hunt down a powerful air mage with no support.

Glaring at the Soul Lord, Mica tried to pass him to follow Ra, but Bastion stood in his way.

"Let him go. He'll be fine and his prey cannot be allowed to go free," Bastion said.

"Would you start *another* war then?" Mica whispered, watching the flash of pain on the Soul Lord's face. It might not be Bastion's fault their world was invaded, but he and his mate had been the catalyst nonetheless. The Soul Lord was playing with fire by using his magic at this event.

"He was sentenced to death by the council for what he did. If Ra finds him, she can't do anything in response without admitting she's been hiding him," Bastion said. They were both careful not to use any names that might draw the attention of any listening spells.

"He is *human*. He's too fragile to go chasing such prey," Mica snapped.

A sudden sharp pain surged through the connection between him and Ra and fear froze the breath in his lungs as he blindly pushed past Bast to run in the direction Ra had disappeared. Bastion grabbed his arm before he could leave, and he snarled as he reached for his power to respond.

"Stop. I'll glamour you like I did him. The mages here can't recognise my power and you're less likely to start that war," Bastion said, words urgent.

With a sharp nod, Mica yanked his arm free and ran down the corridor as cool and unfamiliar soulweaving magic formed a moving sphere around him.

CHAPTER 12

MICA

Mica didn't have to go far to find the trouble, which spoke to just how welcome Caelus was in Daria's inner sanctum. Turning a corner, he heard a scuffle in a side room and pushed his way inside. The scene before him had a cry leaving his lips. Caelus had Ra pinned to the wall with his magic, a sickening grin twisted his face as he leaned in close to watch the man's face turn a deeper and deeper shade of red as he pulled the air from Ra's lungs with his power. It was a classic assassination technique of the Air Court.

No! Ra was *his*.

With rage burning through him, Mica flared his wings wide and reached for the familiar warmth of power flowing through the earth far below, drawing it in deep reckless waves to rip Caelus' magic from his bones, something only the rulers of the courts had enough power to do. The Air Mage screamed in agony as he staggered to face him, somehow still managing to draw his blade even as the pain must have been overwhelming as he seared such an essential part of essence away from him.

Caelus took a single step in Mica's direction before he was yanked to a stop, eyes bulging as he rocked backward. It took Mica a moment to process what had happened. Despite being half-dead and gasping for breath himself, Ra had stepped in behind the now powerless mage and was tightening a garotte around his neck.

"You don't ever get to hurt someone I love again. You don't even get to breathe the same air as him," Ra growled as he clung tight to the steel cord he must've had hidden in his leather bracelets.

Blood gushed down Caelus' chest, staining the white of his feathers as the garotte broke through skin and arteries, hastening his death. As the elemental dropped to the floor, Mica rushed forward to catch Ra in his arms before he could follow after him, holding him close as he closed his eyes and breathed in his familiar scent.

"I won our bet," Ra said, voice rasping from his near asphyxiation.

"It was a tie at best," Mica said, too relieved the man was okay to say anything more. He was going to pretend he hadn't heard Ra's final words to Caelus. It was best for both of them.

They both startled as a voice interrupted from the doorway.

"Lord Mica, how kind of you to deal with the errant criminal for me," Lady Daria said, an edge of danger to the words.

Mica turned toward her, keeping Ra tucked under his wing despite the man trying to pull free. He took a moment to inspect her face and then reached out to get a sense of what the stronghold was feeling—calm. It was not the least bit concerned about what had happened in its room, which meant neither was Daria. They'd been used as executioners. At least that would make getting out of here without fending off more attacks easier.

"You owe us," he said, making Ra stiffen in his arms in surprise.

Daria narrowed her eyes and then dipped her head in acknowledgement before leaving the way she'd come.

"What the fuck was that?" Ra asked.

"Caelus either had something on her or the other mages were blocking her from dealing with him. She let us kill him so she didn't have to deal with the fall-out," Mica said.

"Dammit. Did I just accidentally help the Air Court?" Ra asked, looking disgusted.

Mica snorted out a soft laugh and brushed a stray lock of hair from his face before smoothing down his twisted clothing. "We have to give her a chance to change things here. And it's never a bad thing to be owed a favour by someone so powerful."

"Yeah, yeah. Whatever. I just want to go home. I need to tell Kaia it's over and he can never hurt her again."

Warmth filled him at Ra referring to the Earth Court as home. Not that he wanted the man to stay once Kaia was trained. Fuck. What a mess. They were becoming more entangled every day. Forcing space between them, Mica let go of the man and headed to the door.

"News will travel quickly. We need to be seen by her court before we leave so they know she turned a blind eye and we weren't fleeing the scene. Half an hour and then we can go," he said.

Reaching out to the collar around Ra's neck, he sent a complex surge of power through the mineral there. He should've added the protections when he placed it there in the first place but he'd been stubborn, not wanting to admit how badly he needed to keep Ra safe, despite everything. Whatever happened, no one would hurt this man but him. The shielding he'd just added that would trigger if someone launched another magical attack at him would make sure of that. Ra raised an eyebrow as he felt the earth magic against his skin, but Mica didn't offer an explanation. Pulling back the second he was finished, he didn't wait for Ra to follow before heading back to the party.

It took everything in him to be able to walk away from Ra while he could still feel the air dragging back into his lungs as he recovered from Caelus' murder attempt. Grabbing a whiskey from the bar, he forced himself to do what he usually would at these things—network, manipulate, dig for information. By the time he felt Ra's presence return to the room, you couldn't tell he'd almost died before strangling someone to death only minutes earlier. Ra looked perfectly put together and everyone around him had noticed, judging by the appreciative looks he was getting. Mica suppressed the urge to stalk over there and stake his claim, knocking back his drink instead.

Ra's storm-grey eyes met his from across the room with a teasing glint as the human felt his tumultuous emotions through their connection. Turning away from him, Ra struck up a conversation with Kairon, the vampyr who'd helped heal Mica's people in the immediate aftermath of the damage to his stronghold.

He frowned at the intensity of their conversation and the easy way Kairon leaned in to grip Ra's shoulder. What were they talking about so intently? Before he could use the collar to listen in, Lord Tyson approached him and he was forced to focus on the conversation with the Fire Lord. By the time he managed to extricate himself, Ra had moved on. To the dance floor. Of course.

The way the man moved to the music was indecent but Mica felt a smug sense of satisfaction as he realised each of his admirers took one look at the collar around his neck and kept their distance. He could feel Ra's growing frustration through their connection as he was denied the physical contact he craved. It didn't take long for Ra to storm over to him and grab his hand, dragging him back onto the dance-floor fast enough that Mica was forced to murmur apologies to the elementals his wings brushed against as they passed.

"What the fuck signal is this collar sending? I thought it was a tracking thing but that doesn't explain why no one will get within arm's reach of me," Ra hissed.

He didn't know why he'd let the human manoeuvre him to their current position, but now he was there he couldn't help but pull Ra close, wrapping one arm around his waist and taking the nape of his neck in a firm grip with the other.

"It means they know to keep their hands off you," Mica growled in his ear, relishing the shiver Ra couldn't conceal as his warm breath stroked against his skin.

"Because?"

"I told you already. Because you're *mine*."

"Are you seriously going to cockblock me with this for three years?" Ra asked.

No. If he had his way no one else would ever touch Ra again. Stiffening at the impossible thoughts, Mica forced himself to loosen his hold. That was not what this was. Not what it could ever be.

"I'll remove it, but I can't do it here," Mica finally said through gritted teeth, weaving a small layer of magical shielding around them to keep his words private between them.

Ra's hand drifted up to the collar as if he was protective of it, but that couldn't be right.

"Why not?" he asked.

Because he wasn't going to leave him unshielded anywhere other than the Earth Stronghold. But that wasn't the only reason. Mica sighed. It wasn't like it wouldn't get back to Ra eventually anyway. He was sure someone had asked Lord Bastion what was going on with the collar on his best friend by now. The secret would be out the next time Ra spoke to his brother.

Letting his wings stretch out to enclose them in a screen of copper feathers to hide Ra's reaction, he focused on the tiny glimpse of his mark on Ra's throat instead of meeting the man's eyes. Unable to fight the urge, his thumb brushed against the copper lines softly as he spoke.

"Because they think it's a sign of intention. An engagement ring of sorts," Mica murmured.

Ra tried to jerk away, but Mica didn't release his hold. "What the fuck? They think you want to *marry me?*"

"Not marry. That's a human thing," Mica said.

Ra snorted and rolled his eyes. "And of course no elemental lord would be caught dead observing a human tradition. What then?"

"In the early days of my court, collars like this were given to the person the ruler intended to take as a consort. It was a sign any attack on them would not be tolerated," Mica said.

"Awww ... so you do care? It *is* a safety thing?" Ra teased, even the anger Mica could feel directed at him not enough to stop the man's natural tendency to tease and flirt.

It was a never-should-have-happened thing. And now he'd put even more power into the collar, every mage there would be certain they were together. He wished that thought didn't fill him with satisfaction.

"Someone has to keep you in check," Mica growled, pulling Ra close and swaying to the music before they drew even more attention for the way they were standing perfectly still in the middle of the dancefloor.

"You're a possessive fucker, aren't you? I can feel how much you need this on me. Your mark wasn't enough, was it? I'll let you leave it," Ra said, the false innocence in his voice setting off alarm bells.

"At what cost?" Mica asked, even though he didn't need Ra's damn permission to leave it there. It's not like the human could remove it without him.

"Well, if you're not going to let anyone else touch me, you're going to have to keep me satisfied. I'm not staying celibate for three years and I have quite the appetite," Ra said, pressing close to grind up against him.

Mica's hands tightened around Ra's body and all his blood rushed south as his cock throbbed with need. Fuck it. It's not like everyone didn't think they were intimate already. Pulling Ra behind him, he strode in the direction of one of the small rooms he knew surrounded the council chambers. They were designed for taking private calls and bilateral negotiations—layered with soundproofing and privacy spells that would keep the noises he was going to force from Ra's lips from anyone else's ears.

"If you don't want this, tell me now," he said as he

slammed the door closed behind them and pinned Ra against it.

Ra groaned as Mica sucked another mark onto his neck, grinding against him. "Are you sure you can stand to touch me for this long?"

Guilt surged in Mica for a moment as he sensed the pain behind that question, but it wasn't his damn fault Ra had chosen extortion over the connection they'd shared. He'd been ignoring the fact that Ra seemed to have gotten over his hatred of him because he just couldn't return the sentiment. When the human forgot to keep his emotions to himself, there was a disturbing affection and yearning underpinning their every interaction. The potential for a mating bond between them meant the yearning was a two-way street, but the affection was decidedly one-sided. Mica wanted Ra. Maybe in the early hours of the morning he could even admit he needed him. But he couldn't feel affection for him after what he'd done.

Mica made himself pull away for a moment to focus on his words. "If we do this, it's just sex. Nothing more."

Ra shrugged. "Fine by me. That's all I was asking for."

But Mica could feel the evasiveness in the words. Feel the way Ra was bracing himself for the pain a meaningless fuck would cause when he wanted more.

"Dammit. I don't want to hurt you," he whispered. Because despite everything it was true. Ra might have been happy to hurt him with his actions, but Mica would never do that if he had any choice in the matter. He couldn't.

Ra looked surprised and then annoyed. "Stop snooping in my emotions and you'll be fine," he snapped, grabbing a fistful of Mica's hair and pulling him into a filthy kiss that was all tongue and clashing teeth and raw desire.

Groaning, Mica took back control because it was the only way he could do this. He wasn't going to risk his own pleasure with the man. He knew his limits and the drive to mate was overwhelming. This was just a way to keep his collar around Ra's neck. To make sure the irritating human behaved himself and stayed safe.

A brush of his magic along the seams of Ra's elemental tailoring had his clothing falling down to the floor, leaving him utterly naked before him. Fuck the man was beautiful. The light golden tan of his skin almost glowed in the ethereal light of the crystal room.

Ra's surprised laugh at his sudden state of undress was interrupted by a gasp as Mica trailed biting kisses down his chest until he could suck each of his nipples into his mouth, working them with his tongue. Mica slid his hands down to the man's ass, kneading the muscles there as he fought for the control not to take this further than could go and keep his heart safe.

Ra's head thumped back against the door and his body strained toward him as he lost himself to the pleasure of Mica's kisses trailing further and further down his body. The deep groove of Ra's adonis belt was a siren call to his tongue as he sank to his knees and traced a wet path across warm skin. Nuzzling into the join between his groin and thigh, Mica drew in a deep breath of his scent.

When Ra responded by gripping tight to the upper edge of his flared oversensitive wings and stroking down firmly, he was lost. Feral. Unable to do anything but surrender to the need between them. Reaching up to grasp the throbbing steel of Ra's erection, Mica pulled the head of his cock into his mouth, moaning again at the burst of salty pre-cum against his tongue. Sucking him deep, Mica swallowed him down to the root in one long, slow move that had Ra cursing and babbling as he gripped Mica's hair in shaking fingers.

"Fuck, Mica. Don't stop. Please," he gasped, hips pumping his shaft into Mica's mouth as he lost any control of himself.

He could feel the intensity of Ra's arousal through their connection and a dark sense of satisfaction settled in him as he used every noise, every spark of excitement he could sense, to drive Ra wild. He worked him fast and hard with no mercy. Driving his pleasure higher and higher until his cries were echoing off the crystal walls.

Sensing Ra's impending climax, he slid his hand down further, stroking over the sensitive skin behind Ra's balls until he could press a single finger against the hole he was desperate to feel around his cock. That light touch alone was enough to set Ra off and he pushed forward into his mouth one last time, screaming Mica's name as he came deep in his throat. As Mica swallowed every drop, the tightening of his throat around Ra's cock had him convulsing in drawn-out waves of pleasure until the human slumped against the wall with trembling legs.

"Fucking hell. It's always the quiet ones. Give me a minute to find the reset switch for my muscles and I'll return the favour," Ra said, eyes closed and body lax as he finally released his hold on Mica's wing that had been driving him half crazy with the need to claim.

"No," Mica said, running a hand through his hair to fix it up as he got back to his feet.

"No?" Ra asked, incredulous, as his eyes tracked down to the very clear bulge in his pants.

Not bothering to explain himself, he picked up Ra's shirt from the pile on the floor and silently started redressing him.

Still drunk from the intensity of his orgasm, Ra actually let him. Mica said a silent thank you to Elysia for the magicked garments that made this so much easier even as he internally shook his head in disgust at himself that they'd been so overcome he'd never even bothered removing Ra's shoes. It wasn't until the last item was in place and he was buttoning Ra's jacket that the man shook off the daze he was in.

"What the fuck just happened?" Ra asked.

"You came."

"No shit. Why aren't you letting me return the favour?"

"Because I don't trust you," Mica said. It was only part of the truth. The bigger problem was that he didn't trust himself.

The sensation of Ra's emotions that had been a pleasant tease in the back of his mind shut off suddenly. For a human, he was surprisingly good at blocking his side of the connection. At least for short periods. He guessed Ra must've had lots of practice with Bastion, which pissed him off even more.

Ra shoved him hard as his hands dropped from the last button, pushing him away.

"Fuck you, Mica."

"We did that already," Mica said, knowing it would only fan the flames of Ra's bitter rage. It was for the best. They couldn't keep doing this.

Twisting in place, Ra yanked open the door they'd entered through. They hadn't got more than a single step into the room. At least their toxic exchange had taken care of his erection before he had to re-emerge into the party. Ra made a beeline for the portal area, his friend Tir noticing from across the room and moving to join him.

Catching Tir's eye, Mica gestured for them to wait while

he said the necessary farewells. By the time he was finished, he was surprised Ra's fuming glare hadn't burned a hole through his wings. He'd almost reached the two people waiting for him when an anguished scream rent the air and a flash of white dropped from the still open ceiling straight toward Ra.

"Murderer! I will end you!" the elemental shouted, the tell-tale buzz of gathering magic speaking to her abilities as a mage as she pulled a short sword glowing with gold light from her back.

Copper power flowed down his hands like lightning as he flung a shield around Ra and Tir that would fry their attacker to a crisp if she made the mistake of flying into it. If he could've gotten away with an offensive magic in the heart of Daria's stronghold in front of so many people he would've, but the new Air Lady was still an unknown and he couldn't be sure how she would react. To her credit, Daria was only a touch slower than him in responding. The attacker disappeared behind a solid golden sphere of the Air Lady's magic that quickly floated through a hole the crystal stronghold opened in its wall before it was cut off from view.

"My apologies, Lord Mica. Lucia can be a vengeful bitch," Daria said.

It wasn't him she should be apologising to, but one glance at the Air Court soldiers had him holding his tongue on that. They were poised to attack at the slightest provocation, their eyes trained on the man their fellow courtier had named a murderer.

"Who is she?" Mica asked, although he could guess.

"She was Caelus's sister. I will deal with her," Daria said, ignoring the murmur of voices as the crowd realised just who had been murdered.

"Deal with her how?" Mica asked.

"That is not your concern," Daria replied, confirming his suspicions Lucia would likely fly free by morning.

He'd have to warn his scouts to keep an eye out for her. Ra was in her sights and he didn't think the elemental was going to let this go.

CHAPTER 13
RA

Ra had always gone after what he wanted, unapologetically. He didn't do regrets. Until now. Sex with Mica had been almost transcendent. Right up until he'd been cut off at the knees. That asshole. How could he feel used when he was the only one who'd got any pleasure from it?

When they returned to the Earth Stronghold, Mica didn't give him more than a glance before stalking off to his office or wherever it was he went when he was hiding from their shared living arrangement. Sometimes he wondered if Mica was sleeping there because the silence in the living area was relentlessly stifling.

And the worst part was that he *still* couldn't hate Mica anymore. His heart still skipped a beat when he thought of the bitter Earth Lord. The what-ifs were torture, and he'd never been a what-if guy. What if he'd found a way around the oath he'd sworn to his contact here? What if he'd tried diplomacy one more time before breaking out the big guns with that threat that sat between him and Mica like a poison tainting every word they spoke and every point they touched? What if he just apologised? Begged for forgiveness?

He knew nothing he said would sway Mica, though, and it would just lead to questions he'd sworn not to answer. It was too late to salvage now. Too many lies and hurts lay between them. All he could do was spend his time here balancing the scales in his own mind at least in the hopes he could assuage his guilt. If he could make Mica safe, take away the tension that never left the elemental's eyes and know that he'd left Mica's life better than he'd found it, it would be enough. It would have to be. Because Mica's actions at the Air Court showed he would never forgive him.

Mica might've stepped in to save him when Caelus attacked and held him like he owned him on the dancefloor, but that was driven purely by the potential mating bond between them and the connection forged by Mica's mark. Ra could feel some of Mica's emotions when he forgot to block them and what he'd felt throughout was heartbreaking. Mica resented the instinctive urge to protect him and was disgusted with himself for wanting Ra. Worst of all was the guilt on Mica's end because he saw the desire between them as a betrayal of his loyalty to his own people.

Enough. He wasn't going to wallow in this misery. Pushing aside the guilt and the knot of tension that was his awareness of Mica in the back of his mind, Ra got to work processing his scans of the Earth Stronghold, losing himself in the familiar lines of code. He stayed up so late his eyelids felt like lead weights were dragging at them, but something wasn't working and he was determined to find it. The scan didn't look complete and the code wasn't behaving as it should. Where the presence of the ley lines should have become sharper and more accurate as he progressed, they were instead remaining frustrating blurs that disappeared as soon as he looked at them.

He must've lost his battle with sleep at some point because he woke lying on the couch the next morning, groaning at the ache in his head from too long hunched over his screen. As he sat up, he looked down at himself in confusion. There was a soft copper blanket draped over his body and someone had taken his shoes off and placed them to the side so he could stretch himself out fully on the comfort of the cushions. There was only one person who would've been in the living room to do it and the ache in his heart grew a little deeper as he felt the familiar twinge of resentment down their connection. Mica's actions had been sweet, but the emotions they sparked were not.

Shaking his head as if it might shake the Earth Lord's presence from it, he staggered to the bathroom and turned the shower on hot and hard. As he waited for it to get to temperature, he flicked Kaia a quick message. If anything could drag him from this pity party he had going on it would be the niece of his heart, and he had an appointment he needed to keep.

Hey, K-bear. Let's do something today. Just you and me, he texted. He probably should've told her what was going on, but he didn't want to stress her out before he had to.

Her response was waiting when he stepped out. *Yes! I'll find you as soon as I finish my meditation practice.*

Perfect. Now he just needed to figure out how to get them where they were going.

Glancing in the mirror as he finished getting ready, Ra paused and took in the sight he made. He had another deep bruise on his neck from Mica's mouth peeking out above the collar that had drawn so much attention at the Air Court.

Ha! If only they knew how Mica really felt about him they wouldn't have given it a second glance because they would've seen it for the lie it was. He couldn't help but trace the lines of Mica's mark on his skin, the copper tattooed feathers seeming to shift beneath his fingers as he traced them from his ear all the way down to his fingers. A self-deprecating smirk crossed his face as he felt a surge of arousal and possessiveness through the connection. Apparently, Mica could feel when he touched his mark. Locking his own emotions away as much as he could, he quickly went back to dressing. He was too fragile that morning to deal with any more of Mica's disgust in him.

Kaia was waiting in the living area when he emerged, and she threw herself into his arms with a laugh, clinging to him tight.

"Love you, Uncle Sunshine," she said as if she could sense the sadness in him.

"Love you too, sweetness. How'd you get in?" he asked.

"Earthshine opened the door right up for me. It's worried about you," Kaia said, concern in her eyes.

Ra sighed. The stronghold should not be letting people into Mica's quarters like that, no matter who they were, and he wished it had a little more sense than to worry Kaia when she was already dealing with so much. "I'm fine, baby girl. But I'm always up for a fun day out with you."

They used to do this in the City of Souls—taking off together for a day where they each ignored their responsibilities for just a little bit and ventured wherever their urges took them. They hadn't done it since the girl had been held captive and it was past time he rectified that.

"Yes! Can we go to the Tree City? Kim says it's beautiful but no one's had time to take me," Kaia said, bouncing up and down with the electric blue and cream of her feathers rustling out in excitement.

Ra smiled. How serendipitous. The only problem now was that he really didn't want to ask Mica to take him and the irritating lord had ordered him not to fly with anyone else. Of course, what Mica didn't know couldn't hurt him. Either that or the masochistic part of him just really wanted to see what the Earth Lord would do when he found out. Mica was sexy as anything when he got all angry and possessive. Not that he should be encouraging that.

When an unexpected knock at the door interrupted them, Ra decided fate had intervened to help them. Elysia, the elemental he'd been texting on and off after they supplied him with such a stunning suit, was standing there searching out Mica. Elysia had all Ra's sunshine, but without the side of bitterness he was suffering from. They were just an all-round genuine and bubbly elemental who spent their days making things grow, which was exceedingly rare. They were also the answer to Ra's problems for the morning.

"He's not here. I think he's hiding from me," Ra said with a smirk. "Want to help me draw him out?"

Kaia giggled from behind him and Elysia laughed with her.

"Sounds fun. What's the plan?" Elysia said.

"Kaia and I want to go explore the Tree City, but I need a ride and Mica isn't likely to give me one," Ra said.

Elysia smiled and gestured toward the balcony. "It will be my pleasure. Although if you're hoping to play hide and seek with your lord, he's not going to have any trouble finding you with that beacon of power down your arm and the collar round your throat," Elysia teased.

Ra rolled his eyes. Mica was not his anything. "At least then I'd see him," he muttered.

The green in Elysia's wings flared a sparkling emerald as they reached the sunlit balcony and drew on their power. The nearby vines climbing up the cliff-face outside stretched toward the plant mage and Elysia drew a complicated pattern in the air that had them forming one of the passenger slings Ra was used to back home, which weren't as common here because of how few humans there were in the area. The magic would mean Elysia could carry him suspended below them instead of in their arms.

"Worried Mica's going to get jealous if you hold me?" Ra teased.

Elysia threw their head back and laughed, the sound joyous and carefree as it carried across the jungle. "Absolutely. We have been friends long enough that I know where his boundaries are. He'd be all formal and grumpy with me for at least a year if I touched you like that and then I'd be sad."

"Stop trying to get Elysia in trouble, Uncle Sunshine," Kaia chided.

Ra ruffled her hair and turned toward the now complete sling lying on the ground. "Okay, K-bear. Just for you."

The air was warm and humid in the morning light but not as sweltering as it would be later in the day as the three of them winged their way the short distance toward the nearby city. Kaia peppered Elysia with questions about the sling they'd fashioned with their power as they flew and Ra was proud of the way the girl could articulate the fundamentals of how the magic functioned so much more coherently than before they'd come here already. He was even prouder when she had a go herself at weaving when they landed on the outskirts of the city at Elysia's urging.

"You've come so far, Kai," he said as she managed to control multiple vines to start weaving the sling for several seconds before losing track of them.

Kaia sighed as she looked down at the tangled greenery. "Not far enough."

"You are a credit to your teachers, Kaia. It took me months to even get the plants to listen to me. You've only been here weeks and they're willing to weave!" Elysia said, sparking a much happier look on the girl's face.

"Thanks, Elysia," she said softly.

"As much as I would love to explore with you, I need to leave you two here. I really do need to find Lord Mica. Although I suspect following you around might be a faster way to do it. Flick me a text if you need a ride back but I suspect someone might've found you and dragged you back himself by then," Elysia said, eyes twinkling as they clasped Ra's hand in farewell.

Ra wrapped an arm around Kaia as the two of them took in their surroundings. They were standing on one of the outer platforms suspended around the soaring trunks of the huge magically enhanced trees in the area. Bright flowers bloomed in the canopy, sending rich scents into the air, and the chatter of local birdlife was audible, despite the busy thronging of elementals coming and going nearby. There were three wide swing bridges leading off from where they stood. Those to their left and right seemed to head to quieter residential areas and the one ahead of them led into the busiest part they could make out, where the flash of various coloured wings was constant as elementals came and went.

He was a little surprised the elementals even bothered

with bridges, but as he guided Kaia down one of the quieter bridges to the east, he quickly saw why. For those with less magic, they provided a way to transport goods in carts around the city, and for the very young living there, it provided a way to move about without getting into trouble in the crowded airspace that was filled with all the hazards of a jungle created to catch on unsuspecting wings and feathers.

Ra kept them circling east as he checked his sat-phone.

"Where are we going, Uncle?" Kaia asked, head craning as she took it all in.

"I have a surprise visitor for you," he said, finally spotting a ladder that would get them down to the forest floor. "Race you to the ground!" he cried out, leaping for the rungs as Kaia's head snapped round in surprise.

"Uncle," she laughed, launching herself into the air as he placed hands and feet on the outside supports of the ladder so he could slide down it like a firepole.

She beat him, of course, wings raised high as she dropped to the ground like an eagle launching at its prey.

"No fair," he teased. "Let's make it a foot race instead. First one to that frangipani tree wins!"

Kaia chased after him breathless and laughing. "That's not any fairer! Your legs are like twice as long as mine and I've got all the drag of my wings!"

He was too busy watching where he was going as they careened through the jungle to notice the vine twisting up to loop around his ankle and trip him just short of their destination.

"Ha! Got you!" Kaia said, racing past him to touch the rough bark of the tree.

"Did you just use magic to *cheat*?" Ra cried, grinning so

hard his cheeks ached. It had been too long since he'd just had fun, and even longer since Kaia had.

"You never said magic wasn't allowed," Kaia shot back at him, waving a hand to free him from the plant.

The two of them collapsed back against the tree, panting side-by-side, staring up at the shifting green of the canopy above.

"Who's visiting?" Kaia asked. "And did you ask permission first?"

The girl was too clever for her own good. "Sometimes it's better to ask forgiveness than permission," Ra said.

"I hope that doesn't mean you're about to spark an international incident. Again," Kairon said, emerging from the jungle like a shadow.

"Kairon!" Kaia cried happily, jumping up to hug the vampyr.

"It's good to see you, little one," Kairon said. "How have you been?"

Kaia sighed. "Oh. *That's* what this is about. I should've known it wasn't just a visit to say hi."

Ra came over and wrapped an arm around the girl, tipping up her chin. "Hey, none of that. Kairon was keen for any excuse to come."

"Why? Is he avoiding Lady Nerida again?" Kaia asked.

Ra let out a burst of laughter as he watched his vampyr friend give the girl a wry grin.

"Why are you teasing me when it was Ra who set all this up and kept it a secret?" Kairon complained.

Kaia laughed. "Okay, Mr Vampyr. Do your healy thing and make my brain all better," she said.

Ra wished it were that simple. Kairon had been working with Kaia for months before she left, so they knew it wasn't.

"I wish brains were as straightforward to heal as bodies, but sadly it takes time and effort to get all those chemicals and synapses shifting aim so they don't sabotage you," Kairon said, squeezing her shoulder. "Ra said you had another episode?"

Kaia nodded and sat down on a limestone outcrop of rock, pulling at a weed in the dirt. "Yeah. It was my own fault, though. I was trying to stress myself out to access my magic."

"And did it work?" Kairon asked.

Kaia sighed. "Kind of, but not really. I've made some progress with the magic now I've talked to Serena about it, but..."

"But the nightmares are worse now you've made yourself relive all that trauma again?" Kairon asked, kindness in his voice.

"Yeah," Kaia said as Ra forced himself to stand back and not intervene. He'd had no idea her nightmares were getting bad again. "It doesn't help that people here can be really awful about folks back home either," she added in a quiet voice.

"Who? What have they been saying?" Ra snapped. No one was allowed to make his niece feel sad.

"It doesn't matter who. And just the usual. Necromancy is evil, so I must be a terrible person if my uncle's a necromancer. Blah, blah, blah," Kaia said.

Ra frowned. "You know that's not true."

Kaia rolled her eyes. "Duh. I told them they're ignorant if they think that. Soulweaving is beautiful. Uncle Basti's power is a gift from those who passed before us and he used it to protect the entire world, so I don't know what they're complaining about."

Ra frowned. It wasn't surprising people still had such a negative view of soulweaving, but it was concerning they felt comfortable enough to bother Kaia about it inside the stronghold. The global summit meant there was now an edict in place to protect the rare soulweaving children from the kind of horrible prejudice that had been so damaging in the past, but attitudes like that showed just how far they still had to go.

"I couldn't have said it better myself. Bast mentioned you're meditating as part of your training?" Kairon said, steering them back on track. It was just as well, given the longer he stayed here, the greater the chance he'd be discovered.

"Yeah," Kaia said.

"Okay, I'm going to talk you through a guided meditation and weave some of my power through it that will reinforce the effects each time you do it. I want you to spend ten minutes at the end of each of your training sessions every day on this. It will help redirect the power of those emotions and memories in your mind so you have control over them instead of the other way around," Kairon said.

Ra sat back silently as Kaia closed her eyes to focus and Kairon continued to speak softly. He couldn't help with this. He was just grateful the vampyr's magic could do something. It made him wonder what Kairon might be able to do for the damaged stronghold if he had more time there. He knew from speaking to the vampyr back home that Mica had already declined the offer of further help, though. Probably a combination of the elementals not trusting the vampyr who had only recently come to the Melded Earths and Mica's instinctive need to keep the seriousness of the situation under wraps so they didn't inadvertently trigger the apocalypse they were trying to avoid. There was no point protecting the secret if it meant the stronghold would never be healed, though.

"Thanks, K," Ra said when the vampyr finished his healing and stood to bid them farewell. Kaia was still sitting with her eyes closed on the other side of the small clearing as she slowly brought herself out of the trance she'd been in.

"I'm just glad I can help. It's lucky we spoke when we did, because something here had been creating the wrong kinds of pathways in her brain. It's a bit like wearing away at a small stream bed until the river diverts and causes a flood. I've reinforced the stopbanks now and, if she keeps practising, the river will run deeper until it can't be pushed off course so easily."

"Look at you rocking the water analogies. Got a certain red-haired, tattooed elemental on your mind?" Ra teased. He didn't know what was going on between the vampyr and the Water Lady, but it was volatile whatever it was.

Kairon winced and cleared his throat. "You're lucky you're cute or I wouldn't be taking that from you. What about you? I saw the way Lord Mica dragged you off that dancefloor and those hickeys on your neck are delightful. Reliving your teenage years?"

"Okay, I deserved that. I won't ask you about Nerida if you don't ask about him," Ra said.

Kairon smiled and shook his head. "Nice try. I'm not living with Lady Nerida and she hasn't put a collar around my throat. Also, Bast asked me to check in."

Ra sighed. "It's under control, okay?" It wasn't. Not even slightly. He was standing at the bottom of a cliff staring up at a landslide about to bury him whole.

"Just look after yourself. Protect your heart," Kairon said, looking worried as he gave him one last hug before disappearing back into the shadows of the jungle the way he'd come. Tir would find the vampyr somewhere further away from the city to portal him back home to the Soul Court.

Ra didn't tell him it was far too late to protect his heart. It had been too late since the first time he'd stayed on a video conference with the Earth Lord for hours after their business was concluded so many years earlier.

Ra startled as Kaia's arm wrapped around his waist and the girl leaned into his side. Cursing to himself, he forced his mind back on his surroundings. They weren't protected here. He needed to keep his wits about him.

"Feeling better?" he asked.

"Much," Kaia replied.

"It would be best if you didn't mention this to anyone back at the stronghold."

Kaia snorted. "Yeah, I got that. Can we go explore now?" she asked, pulling him back toward the ladder.

CHAPTER 14
RA

The two of them spent the rest of the morning wandering the Tree City. It was a marvel of elemental architecture—residences and shops grown right out of the tree trunks in twisting shapes of beauty. They stopped for lunch at an outdoor market of street vendors, finding a spot on the edge of the platform to sit and eat staring out into the chaos of plants that made up the canopy. Thanks to the magic of the elementals who maintained the space, the greenery was far thicker and more varied than would naturally occur but somehow still let the sun filter through. Flowering plants created a riot of colour where they twisted around nearby branches.

For the first time since they'd arrived, Ra could see the bustling hive of elemental activity he'd expected to find in the stronghold. The constant flashes of colour from the wings of people coming and going was a sharp contrast to the tense quiet movements of Mica's staff who remained in the caves.

A group of younger elementals laughing and teasing each other near them made him smile.

"What do people do for fun around here?" Ra leaned over to ask them, hoping he wasn't about to face the same kind of vitriol Wren threw his way every time they spoke.

These elementals were much more like Elysia though, greeting them both warmly.

"The outer platforms like these host dance parties at night," said an elemental, who'd introduced herself as Esme, her eyes drifting over his body with appreciation. "I've never danced with a human. You want to stick around and play?"

Ra returned her smile as Kaia made a noise of faux disgust. "How do you always find someone to flirt with wherever we go?" she muttered with fond exasperation.

"I'd love to, but I need to head back to the stronghold this afternoon. Do you ever dance there?" he asked Esme.

"Nah. It's too formal. Lord Mica's millennial celebration will be there, but I'm sure the real party will shift here once the official stuff is done," she said.

Ra had almost forgotten the party Mica had mentioned to celebrate 1,000 years of his rule. He wondered who was organising it. Probably Wren if people were already writing it off as boring. The seneschal had no idea how to have fun.

Kaia's brow had furrowed at the exchange. "Do you visit the stronghold much?" she asked.

The group of elementals shifted in their seats and exchanged glances that were difficult to read. "We used to when Lord Mica hosted meals or activities for us, but it's been a while. It's easier to do that kind of thing out here."

It wasn't difficult to read between the lines. They didn't mean easier, they meant safer.

"No wonder the stronghold's so lonely," Kaia said, voice sad. "You're all abandoning it."

"It's not like that. We'd still go there if we were invited," one of the other elementals said, a man Ra guessed to be somewhere late in his first century, with wings that were a rich brown tipped in copper.

"Is an invitation required?" Ra asked, curious.

More guilty looks passed between the elementals. That would be a no then. The stronghold was always open to Mica's people.

Kaia still looked upset at the way the stronghold had been left alone when it was hurting and he could tell this meant a lot to her. As he thought back to the way the caves had put on such a stunning light display to the music Mica had played and even to the music in his earphones, an idea sparked in his mind.

"I used to run a nightclub back home. If I set up a dance party at the stronghold, would you folks be able to spread the word and get people there?" he asked.

They looked sceptical. "Yeah, that would be awesome, but would Lord Mica let you do that?"

"Let me worry about Mica," Ra said.

Esme smirked. "Yeah, you seem like you could talk a man into just about anything. We've got to get back to work but give me your number and we'll make it happen if you tell me the time and place."

Exchanging phone numbers with Esme, they waved farewell to the group and went to return their dishes to the food vendor.

"Thank you for doing that, Uncle. Earthshine would be so happy to have all those people and music to keep it company," Kaia said.

"My pleasure, baby girl. What shall we do now? Fancy a milkshake from that stall over there?"

"Nah. I'm okay, thanks. Lord Mica always brings me a

hot chocolate for afternoon tea and I don't want to spoil my appetite. Do you think he'll come find us soon?"

Wait. Mica did what?

"What do you mean Mica brings you hot chocolate?" Ra asked.

Kaia looked at him like he was crazy. "What about that sentence didn't you understand, Uncle?"

"The bit where the stuffy Earth Lord I never see any sign of for days is having afternoon tea with my niece every day."

Kaia looked surprised. "Oh. Well, he is. He lets me talk about back home when I'm feeling homesick. And he asks about what it was like to have the ceptae and vampyr in school with us and things like that."

Ra's eyes narrowed in concern. "What kind of questions exactly?"

Kaia rolled her eyes. "I grew up surrounded by the ruling partnership, Ra. You know I've had training on how to avoid questions that might become a security risk for māmā and Uncle Basti. He was just being nice. And maybe trying to learn a bit more about the new peoples on the Earths, given he doesn't get to talk to them every day like we did."

"Why haven't you mentioned this before?" Ra asked. They ate dinner together every day and exchanged a constant stream of texts.

"You both get weird if I talk about the other to you. I didn't want to make it worse. But you must be doing okay if he's going to let you organise a dance party, right?" Kaia asked.

"Oh, sweetheart," Ra said, pulling her into a hug. "Please don't hide anything from me just to make me feel better."

Kaia looked up at him with suspicion. She'd known him from birth, after all, so she was well familiar with the kinds of trouble he got up to. "You *are* going to ask Lord Mica's permission before you organise this thing, right?" she asked.

Ra grinned down at her. "Do you want to bring back the stronghold's whānau or not? Like with this trip, sometimes it's better to ask forgiveness, K-bear. If there's any trouble, I'll make sure it's only me who gets the blame."

"*Uncle!* That is *not* reassuring," Kaia cried, shoving at him even as she smiled in exasperation.

Ra laughed and was about to suggest another race when a deep voice that sent a shiver through every cell in his body called out from behind them.

"What is not reassuring? What are you planning now?" Mica asked.

Ra turned to face the Earth Lord. Mica had caught up to them at a garden of sorts hidden in the canopy, a series of platforms of different heights and sizes that were covered in exotic botanicals and trickling fountains. Leaning against the nearest tree, he cocked an eyebrow.

"Took you long enough to find us," he said, ignoring the questions he didn't want to answer and hoping Kaia didn't give the game away before he'd even started playing.

"I was very clear that you were not to fly with anyone but me. Explain yourself," Mica snapped, stepping forward like he was going to pin him against the rough bark.

Sadly, he aborted the move and kept a few paces between them when his eyes flicked to Kaia, who was watching them like they were a tennis match, eyes bouncing back and forth between them.

"It's my fault, Lord Mica. I wanted to come see the Tree City with him," Kaia cut in.

Mica's eyes softened a little as he turned his attention to

the girl. "This is not your fault, Kaia. He didn't even text me to ask if I had time to take him."

"Would you have come?" Ra asked.

Mica clenched his jaw. "I was busy and outside of phone reception or I would've dragged you home hours ago, but that is not the point."

"It's entirely the point. Unless I'm a prisoner, you can't just expect me to stay put because you're too busy to take me for a ride," Ra said, smirking as Mica's pupils dilated at the subtle innuendo.

It was quickly followed by a flash of anger through their connection before Mica locked it down. Apparently, the Earth Lord didn't like the thought of anyone else taking him for a ride.

"I expect you to follow a direct order," Mica said.

"It seemed more like a wishful statement than an order."

"I don't trust you to wander around unattended. For all I know you're inciting my people to betray me again. You're lucky I trust Elysia implicitly. Next time you leave the stronghold without me, I will send you home. Understood?" Mica growled.

Ra couldn't have stopped the stabbing pain and guilt Mica's words sparked from travelling down their connection if he tried. The elemental would never trust him again. Rightfully so, given he'd used his temporary freedom to meet with Kairon. Something Mica would absolutely see as a betrayal as the vampyr was a leader in his own right and associated with a rival court. Kairon should not have been in the city without seeking permission from Mica first, but neither of them had wanted to risk their request being denied when Kaia's wellbeing hung in the balance. He just hoped Elysia didn't catch any trouble for it if Mica figured out what had happened.

Seeking comfort, Kaia shifted closer and leaned into him, squeezing his hand tight.

"Yeah, I get it," Ra said, voice flat as he looked away.

The short flight back to the stronghold was another exercise in torture as Mica once again eschewed using a sling like Elysia had in favour of carrying him in his arms. The physical contact made their connection thrum brighter, making it impossible to hide the hints of emotion slipping through. The only plus side, if you could call it that, was that Ra knew he wasn't alone in having to fight the insane attraction between them.

Kaia was quiet on the return journey and veered off to the entrance closest to the trainees' quarters with a wave when they got back rather than following them down to land on Mica's balcony.

As Mica pulled away from him, his sleeve pulled up and Ra couldn't help but reach out to grab the thin colourful bracelet wrapped around his wrist. It was woven of silk threads of copper and the blue-green of Mica's eyes with a single strand of tan leather wrapped between them that spoke to Kaia's increasing skill. She'd obviously used a touch of magic to get the colours right, something she wouldn't have been able to do a year ago.

"Kaia gave it to me," Mica explained, holding still as he inspected it.

"I know. You should be honoured," Ra said. Dammit. As if he needed another reason to love the elemental. Why did Mica have to remind him he had a heart after all by supporting Kaia so empathetically?

Mica raised a brow in question. "How so?"

"She only makes them for people she considers whānau —family," Ra said, gesturing to the twisting tan leather on his wrist that Kaia had made for him years before, which nestled against the other more deadly leather cuffs that hid his garottes.

"The leather matches the one on mine," Mica observed.

Ra sighed. "She can be a right little matchmaker. You should've seen her when she was adopting Hel into our family. She made her *four*." He paused for a moment, looking down at where he was still touching the warmth of Mica's wrist. "Thank you for reaching out to her. It means a lot to her."

"Just to her?" Mica asked softly, reaching to tip his chin up with a single finger so he was forced to make eye contact.

Jerking his face away, Ra pushed past the elemental to head inside. "Fucking hell, Mica. Enough with the mixed messages. You were clear you don't trust me as far as you can throw me, so stop pretending you care."

"Ra! Come back here. We're not done with this conversation," Mica snapped, following him into the living area.

Ra spun back toward him at the entrance to his bedroom. "What conversation? The one where you try and make this damn connection even more unbearable?"

"No. The one where you explain what you were thinking leaving the stronghold without me, and exactly what you and Kaia got up to for five hours," Mica said.

Ra reared back, the whiplash of Mica's words catching him out despite the fact he should've learned to brace for it by now. "You tell me. You're the one that put a monitoring collar on me."

Mica frowned. "I was too busy to check it."

"Sounds like a you problem."

Ra smiled as Mica's fists clenched by his sides and his wings trembled with suppressed annoyance. At least he could still get under the Earth Lord's skin.

"Fine. Give me an update on your work, then. Have you made any progress or are you too distracted swanning about?" Mica said.

Ra snorted, stalking over to pour himself a whiskey. He was too sober for this conversation. Without even thinking he poured one for Mica too and then kicked himself for the instinctive need to care for the elemental. He was so fucked.

"I've scanned as much as I can with the drones, but there are key parts of the stronghold I can't access because they're blocked by rockfall. I need to find a way to get to them. I also need to talk to a magical engineer soon about tweaking the integrations in my computer. It was originally set up primarily to function with Bast's soulweaving, even though it was created with more standard elemental magic. The calibration is a bit off, which is stopping the map I'm building of the ley lines from focusing and flexing the way it needs to," Ra said.

"Why do you even need a map? I can sense where all the ley lines run," Mica said, but the question seemed genuine rather than antagonistic for once.

"Unless you've got an eidetic memory, even you will struggle to recall the exact shifting locations of every ley line running through here. The map will display a real-time three-dimensional depiction of them so you can assess where the problems are coming up. Then we can model the effects of different treatments until we find one that gets them untangled and running back where they need to be," Ra explained, wandering over to his computer and sitting down on the couch so he could bring up the half-complete map to show Mica what he meant.

Mica came up behind him and leaned in close, peering at the screen. The warm breath on Ra's neck and the familiar scent of the elemental had him squeezing his eyes shut for a moment to suppress a surge of lust before he regained control.

"You can see the minor ley lines are blue and the major ones are copper. Once we get the calibration right they'll stop jumping around so much, but these dark patches here and here are where I'm missing vital data that correspond with key nexus points," Ra continued.

Through their connection, Ra felt Mica's power flare behind him—a point of warm reassurance.

"If you leave the computer with me, I think I can fix your calibration issue," Mica said as his magic flowed past Ra's skin into the machine sitting on his lap, leaving a trail of goosebumps behind it.

"Do you want to talk to the original engineer?" Ra asked, carefully avoiding using Zee's name.

Mica huffed a laugh that tickled against his neck. "I taught Zahra most of what they know about engineering. I'm sure I'll be fine without their assistance."

Ra rolled his eyes at the arrogance. "Okay, sure. But don't you think it's possible they learned some new things since they've been gone? Especially about human technology? Wouldn't it be faster to just get over yourself enough to have a little conversation and accept some help?"

"I don't need an outsider's help to keep my people safe," Mica growled in his ear.

He guessed that was the answer to his pondering on whether Mica might reconsider letting Kairon help as well.

"It'll take you twice as long, but whatever," Ra said.

"Do you have a plan for the black spots?" Mica asked.

"I thought if I secured some scanning tech that didn't have any external moving parts, then Earthshine might be willing to absorb it through the rockfall like the way it absorbed that glass on our first night here," Ra said.

There was a brief pause where he could feel Mica checking in with the stronghold through their connection. "Yes. It will do that for you. It would do a lot for you," Mica said, sounding chagrined at the thought.

This was where it was going to get tricky. Bracing himself, Ra did his best to try and keep his emotions to himself and his voice casual. "Good. I've found something that might work in Granite Bay. I just need to head over there and check I can modify it the way I need to before we pick it up."

"I will take you tomorrow," Mica said.

Ra hid a wince. "Yeah, about that. You can't come with me. It's with one of my Soul Court contacts and he'll freak if he thinks you know about him."

Mica went dangerously still behind him and he wished he could turn to keep an eye on him, but something told him he'd be better off staying put.

"Is it *him*?" Mica asked, voice low and dangerous.

Fuck. He couldn't lie his way out of this. Mica would sense the deception. "Yeah," he whispered, confirming it was the person who'd enabled him to extort Mica's food supply the previous year.

"Absolutely not. Find your tech somewhere else and give me your contact's name while you're at it so I can finally rid myself of the traitor you've been hiding from me," Mica snarled.

"That is *not* fucking happening. And the alternative to this tech is me building something from scratch, which will take at least another month. Come on, it's not like you're losing anything by letting me do this. You don't know who he is anyway," Ra said.

He'd never felt such rage from Mica, but it was quickly shut down until there was so little sensation through the connection he almost couldn't tell it was there.

"Fine. But I am taking you to the city and you're not going more than a minute's flight from me," Mica said.

"Deal. But you have to swear not to try and identify him. No following me. No setting your people after him," he said.

"You are in no position to make that kind of demand."

Ra shrugged. "Do you want to heal the stronghold or not?"

Mica grabbed his jaw and twisted him until he was staring up at the beautiful rage-filled elemental. "I will leave him be this time only because Earthshine's damage is escalating and I spent the entire morning locked away dealing with it, but I will be listening to every word you say through your collar," he growled, searching his eyes for any sign of betrayal.

It was the best he was going to get and it was enough to keep the oath he'd sworn to Saryn not to betray his identity to the Earth Lord. Mica wouldn't recognise his contact's voice and all he needed to do was confirm the tech could take his upgrades and handle the pressure of being buried deep in rock without compromising the external seal, so it should be fine. He'd be in and out in five minutes and Saryn was a sneaky bastard at the best of times. He wouldn't give himself away, even if he didn't know they had an eavesdropper.

What was the worst that could happen?

CHAPTER 15

MICA

It took Ra a couple of days to set up the meet with whoever the asshole was who had facilitated holding the Earth Court's food supply for ransom. Days where Mica grew more and more suspicious of the man. He might not be spending any time in Ra's vicinity, but the stronghold was reporting on his movements. Where before the human had been busy navigating the tunnels with his drone, now he seemed to have launched a charm offensive on the people of his court, drawing them into conversation and laughter that made the stronghold send him giddy fractured emotions and images. Ra popped up all over the caves, working alongside his staff in their endeavours. He was also constantly on his phone messaging someone. What was he up to?

No matter how many times he tried to get a sense of the impulses behind the man's deception through their connection, Mica could only feel determination and a cheeky irreverence that said trouble was coming. Did he get off on betraying Mica? Is that why whatever he was hiding was making him excited?

Wren's arrival in his office had him looking up from the correspondence he hadn't been able to focus on. His seneschal looked flustered, feathers rustling and cheeks red as his eyes glittered with annoyance.

"The human is overstepping my lord. He needs to be dealt with before he undermines you," Wren said, as soon as he had his attention.

"What did he do now?" Mica asked, reaching out to the stronghold, which had been suspiciously quiet for the last hour and feeling something akin to a giggle like someone was tickling it, which was ridiculous.

"Somehow he roped in a few of our lower-level mages and Serena and the trainees to redecorate the amphitheatre. It looks like a damn nightclub," Wren said.

The amphitheatre had fallen into disuse with the exodus of his people to the Tree City. Mica could feel a happy thrum from the stronghold as it responded to the direction of the elementals helping Ra create sweeping lines of light and bioluminescence in the space along with glittering irregular panels of colour from the minerals and metals that made up its body. Images of the changed space flashed in his mind, including the words Earthshrine emblazoned into the wall in tungsten steel over the main entrance.

"What is he playing at?" Mica murmured to himself.

"He's been pumping our people for intel and I have reason to believe he's still in contact with the Soul Court spy network," Wren said.

"Explain," Mica said, voice clipped.

"There are several hours he was unaccounted for during his trip to the Tree City. I tried to have our intelligence team trace his messages, but he has soulwoven magical protections on them."

Mica frowned. He'd gently quizzed Kaia about their field trip the other day and she'd mentioned spending some time in the jungle itself away from the main population centre. It was suspicious. As was the fact Ra was still relying on Bastion's magical protections. He should've checked the man's phone earlier.

"What is he trying to learn from my staff?"

"It's hard to say. His questions seem innocuous, but that's how spies operate. He's been asking around about who's moved to the Tree City and why. I believe he's laying the groundwork to undermine your rule and claim there is a safety issue here. A skilled manipulator would use the split in our population to sow discord," Wren said.

Wren's assessment was nothing more than supposition but in combination with the fact Ra himself had admitted he was still working with at least one of his old contacts, the one he was getting the tech from, Mica was losing what little trust he'd had left for the man. His spiralling thoughts were interrupted by the buzz of his phone.

You free to give me a ride this afternoon? Ra texted.

Despite everything, his mind still went straight into the gutter at the words, his cock swelling in his pants at the thought of the human riding him in other ways. Their potential mating connection was a damn hazard.

Yes. Be on the balcony at three, he shot back, ignoring his traitorous body and already planning how he could get around his promise to the man to figure out what he was up to. He'd said he'd leave the contact alone this time, but once Ra's meeting was complete was another matter.

Mmm I love it when you get bossy, Ra replied.

"I'll be in Granite Bay this afternoon. Please reschedule my meetings," Mica told Wren, ignoring that last message.

"Would you like me to accompany you, my lord?"

"That won't be necessary."

"I need to check in with our suppliers there anyway. It's no trouble," Wren said, busy on his tablet.

"I said no, Wren."

Wren looked up, surprised by the warning in his tone. "Are you taking *him*? Didn't you hear what I was just telling you?"

Mica shoved to his feet, knowing he needed to get out of there before he took out days of anger on his unsuspecting seneschal. In the back of his mind, the stronghold rumbled its displeasure at the insult to the man it was so enamoured of. "You forget yourself, Wren. Again. Next time I will place you on involuntary leave."

Wren swallowed hard and lowered his eyes submissively to the ground, but the flush in his face suggested he was reining in just as much anger. "I apologise my lord. There won't be a next time."

"If you are at a loose end this afternoon, the southern food stores need to be inventoried," Mica said.

Both of them knew it wasn't a suggestion. His staid seneschal was unpredictable where Ra was concerned and he wasn't going to risk having to deal with Wren's insubordination if he got it in his head Mica needed protecting.

By the time he was heading to his quarters to meet Ra, he was in a foul mood. He couldn't let Wren's accusations rest and his memory kept replaying the conversations he'd had with Ra, wondering which he was going to report back to Bastion when he was free of the collar keeping him gagged.

The man in question was leaning against the outside wall of the balcony when he arrived. He was dressed in a tight long-sleeved black tee and cargo pants reminiscent of the military. It was just another reminder that this man was more dangerous than he seemed.

"Who pissed in your coffee? You're even more wound up than usual," Ra said, pushing off the rockface.

Mica's jaw tightened and he yanked the man into his arms more roughly than he intended as he prepared to take them airborne. "Let's just get this over with."

"This meeting really bothers you, doesn't it? He's helping us. He's working *for* you this time," Ra said, as Mica used more power than usual to speed them into the air until the world was a blur around them.

Mica gritted his teeth against the hint of hurt he could feel underneath Ra's words.

"Why do you have Bastion's magic shielding your phone?" he asked, sliding a hand up to grasp the back of Ra's neck.

"Because I don't betray my people and you wouldn't be able to resist poking through it, as you've just proven by even asking," Ra snapped.

"You just betray me," Mica shot back.

His words threw them into silence as he strained his wingbeats faster just to distract himself with the comforting burn in his muscles.

"I'm sorry I hurt you," Ra said.

"Your apology is meaningless, given you said you'd make the same choice again if given the chance."

The brush of Ra's fingers against his cheek did nothing to soothe his hurt, but it did stoke the flames that burned between them brighter. Reaching up to fist his hair, Mica bit down on the sensitive skin of Ra's neck, knowing it would bruise.

A whine left the man as he mouthed at him, but it was quickly followed by a soft "No."

"What?" Mica asked.

"I can't do this toxic hate-foreplay thing with you again. I don't hate you. It hurts too much," Ra said, looking away as Mica's wingbeats stuttered.

"Good," Mica said, even as the ache in his chest escalated until he felt like he was having a heart attack. He stopped his sensual assault on the man regardless.

"You can put me down in that park down there," Ra said.

Mica blinked in surprise. Had he really been so distracted by the man in his arms that he hadn't noticed them coming up on the city? The tightly packed elemental structures, sweeping copper bridgeways and glistening waters of the harbour in the distance said that was exactly what happened.

Dropping down onto the fragrant ground cover wafting scents of lemon into the air, Mica kept Ra in his arms a moment longer, halting his move to pull away. "I will know if you move more than a minute away from me," he warned.

"I get it. I'm not going far."

Reaching up, Mica brushed his fingers against the mineral collar circling Ra's neck and imbued it with a touch more power until he knew it would be almost uncomfortably warm against the man's skin. "I'll be listening to everything."

Ra snorted and managed to extricate himself from his grip. "Kinky."

Rage filled him and he backed Ra up against one of the trees screening the green space from the buildings around them, pinning him to the rough bark. "If there is even a hint of anything sexual in what you're about to do with him all bets are off. I'll come for you," he growled.

Ra smirked up at him and shook his head in fake amusement. The hurt lingering in the connection told a different story of what he was feeling. "I'm trying to heal your home, not get my rocks off."

"Go," Mica said, stepping away before he gave into the urge to mark the man any more than he already had so this traitor would know to keep away.

Reaching into his pockets, Ra pulled on a pair of black gloves before wrapping a black bandanna around his neck. When he was finished, there was no hint of either Mica's collar or his mark on his skin.

"What are you doing?" Mica growled.

"I don't want to scare him off. Can you put a light shield on me so he can't sense your power signature?"

Mica's fists clenched. Everything in him rebelled against hiding his claim on Ra, which is the only reason he ended up doing it. He couldn't let instinct control him. Drawing on his power, he deftly wove a form of glamour around the man that made him seem purely human. Ra's scent subtly changed as the magic snapped into place. He didn't realise how much Ra smelled like home until the notes of earth magic and the stronghold left him.

"You've got half an hour," he said, turning away.

Ra slipped silently out into the city like the highly-trained soldier it was so easy to forget he was. Letting his magic shift out from him, Mica erected a shield around the park that would ensure he'd remain undisturbed and unseen before settling down on a nearby limestone bench to eavesdrop.

His promise not to try and identify Ra's contact kept him from using his other senses to spy on the man, but he closed his eyes anyway to focus on what he could hear. He would memorise the traitor's voice so he'd know him if they ever met in person.

"*Hey man, good to see you,*" Ra said.

"*It's been too long, Sunshine,*" the man replied, the nickname turning Mica even more murderous. This guy was more than just a spy contact to speak to Ra that way.

Their conversation quickly turned to technical specifications and scanning capability that Mica couldn't follow, but he didn't lose focus for so much as a second. His patience was rewarded when he felt a surge of adrenaline and discomfort from Ra through their connection at the man's next words. The emotions were quickly shut down, suggesting Ra was worried about what Mica was reading from him.

"*The Air Court is sniffing around again. Not as bad as last time.*"

"*Is your family safe?*" Ra asked him, concern clear in his voice.

"*Yeah, the protections you set up are still holding. They won't be taken again.*"

Interesting. If Ra had helped save this man's family that might explain why he'd been willing to betray his own court. Explain, but not excuse.

"*Is it Daria? What do they want?*" Ra asked.

"*I'm not sure if it's sanctioned or not. Might be someone trying to get in her good graces. They're trying to find someone to scuttle the rice transports again. Thought you'd want to know.*"

Mica frowned in confusion. What was he talking about? It was Ra who'd threatened to destroy the supplies in transit last time. Ra had arranged to have the magical vessels shifted outside of the neutral coastal area and into Lady Nerida's territory, so Mica had no way to defend them without admitting his weakness to the Water Lady. It had made more sense to agree to Ra's demands than to lose face with the other court. Plus he'd had no way to be sure he could get control of the transports fast enough to prevent their destruction if Ra thought he was going after them.

"*You're not going to let that happen though, right?*" Ra asked.

"*Of course not! Now my family's safe I would never even contemplate it. I wouldn't have even shifted the transports for you if I thought there was any chance you'd actually destroy them. I'm loyal to my lord, even if he would never believe that now. The only reason I helped you was because you saved me from betraying him. I hate that my weakness was a chink in his armour.*"

"*You weren't weak. You were doing the best you could with your family held for ransom. I just happened to have the right people in the right place to help,*" Ra said.

"*And I will be grateful for that every day of my life.*"

Mica sat in place, stunned as the conversation ended and the only sounds coming through the collar were the background noise of the city's streets. Everything he thought he knew about what Ra had done shifted on its axis. He was still sitting like that minutes later when Ra appeared in front of him holding a large stainless steel briefcase in one hand.

Looking up at Ra, all he could do was stare at the beautiful man.

"Heard all that did you?" Ra asked finally, voice cautious.

"Aliya was going to destroy my transports," Mica said, eyes trained on the storm-grey of Ra's.

"Yes," Ra said.

"You took control instead," he continued.

"Yep."

"Why did you do it?" Mica asked. "Was it just an opportunity for leverage?"

"You know it wasn't just that," Ra whispered.

"*Why?*" Mica asked again.

"Because I couldn't let that bitch hurt you."

"Why didn't you just tell me that? All this time I thought you betrayed me, betrayed *us*," Mica said, not bothering to hide his pain from the man.

"It was easier to stay away if you hated me. Even believing you'd betrayed me first, I don't know that I could've otherwise. Plus, I swore not to say anything to you about what happened and I never break my word. My contact is a good man. He has a family who depend on him. Children. He doesn't deserve how you would have to punish him if what he did got out."

Not how he would punish him. How he would *have to*. Ra understood the ruthless demands of being a ruler of an elemental court and that Mica would make different choices if it wouldn't put the greater good at risk. The world narrowed to Ra's beautiful face and reality faded around him as everything he thought he knew was proved wrong.

Ra fell to his knees in front of him, tears flowing down his cheeks. He'd never seen the man cry before. Not once.

"I'm sorry. I was so angry at you and so scared for Bast and Hel and I used the opportunity to lash out at you even while I was helping you, but I *never* would've hurt your people. I swear," Ra said.

"You let me believe you would," Mica said, struggling to process what this meant for them.

"And I've never been so heartbroken as when you fell for it," Ra whispered.

Mica blinked wetness from his eyes and hauled the man onto his lap, hauled his *mate* onto his lap, burying his nose in the juncture between neck and shoulder and clinging to him like he might disappear if he loosened his grip the slightest bit. He was done with denying the intense connection between them. Even if they never completed the bond, even if they never got past the ways they'd hurt each other, Ra would always be his mate. The answer to the question of his soul. His to protect. Just like he was Ra's.

"I'm sorry, too. I knew you better than that. *Know* you better than that. I should've realised there was something more going on," Mica said.

"You were run ragged and trying to prevent the end of the world on top of all the damage to your home. I get it. You were a little distracted," Ra said.

It was just like Ra to try and lighten the mood with his teasing understatement. His mate had always been a ray of sunshine in the darkness. Movement in the stillness. Music in the silence.

"Forgive me for believing that of you. Please," Mica begged, voice cracking. Despite everything, he couldn't bear the thought that his disdain had hurt his mate, was still hurting his mate.

"I forgave you weeks ago," Ra admitted. "Can you ever forgive me?"

Tipping up Ra's chin, he kissed him, relishing the contrast of soft lips and rough stubble as he teased his tongue inside the man's mouth. "I can, but it's going to take time to get back to what we were," Mica said when he could finally drag himself away.

"But you're willing to try?" Ra asked.

Mica gripped his neck and kissed him hard. "There's no

trying about it. I'm not giving up until the tears are a distant memory and we trust each other like we always should have."

"Because of the mating drive?" Ra asked.

"No. Because you're everything I've ever needed in one infuriating, intoxicating, imperfect package."

Ra leaned forward and pressed their foreheads together. "Back at ya."

"No more secrets between us from now," Mica said, his hands caressing up and down Ra's spine for the pure joy of touching him.

Ra nodded. "No more secrets."

The moment was broken by the vibration of Ra's phone against his leg. Leaning back, Mica traced absent-minded patterns on the man's muscled thighs as Ra checked the message, doing his best not to sneak a look at the phone. He'd said they would rebuild the trust between them and he meant it.

"It's killing you not to ask who's messaging me, isn't it?" Ra teased.

"I trust you that much at least," Mica said.

Taking pity on him, Ra tilted the phone so he could see.

Earthshrine opening night is a go, Sunshine! See you soon!

"Who's Esme?" Mica asked.

"Why? Are you jealous?"

"No. You're mine. If she needs that to be spelled out to her, I'm happy to get the stronghold to add some more words to the wall of my amphitheatre you've been defiling," Mica said, pulling Ra's hips forward until he could grind up into him.

Ra's laughter was cut off by a low groan of pleasure as

Mica changed their angle so his erection was pressed against the man.

"You knew about that?" Ra asked.

"Of course."

"I wanted it to be a surprise."

"If it makes you feel better, everything about you has been a surprise to me," Mica murmured, sliding his hands under Ra's shirt so he could trace the grooves of his sculpted muscles.

"Take me home," Ra pleaded. "I need to feel your skin on mine and I need more time than a quickie in the park."

Growling his agreement, Mica scooped the man up into his arms and launched them up into the skies above the city. The speed of their ascent had Ra laughing in delight and he couldn't help but play a little, sliding into a series of barrel rolls and aerial manoeuvres only possible because of his magic.

"I've changed my mind. Why don't we just get naked up here," Ra gasped, his delight at the thrill of their flight coming through loud and clear.

CHAPTER 16

RA

Damn cockblocking court members. Thanks to a poorly timed urgent call, Mica was forced to stop with the aerial acrobatics and they were speeding back to the stronghold as fast as his magic could accelerate them.

"Get him out of the communal spaces. Take him to my office. The last thing we need is more gossip," Mica was instructing his seneschal.

Ra couldn't hear the reply, but whatever it was had Mica's free arm tightening around him in frustration.

"Then take him to the Glade and call Serena for help. I'll be there in five minutes," Mica said, hanging up.

"What's wrong?" Ra asked as soon as he was enveloped in both Mica's arms again.

"While we were out, Earthshine had another episode that reached outside of this region into the one immediately to the west. The regional lead there is difficult. He fancies himself as my replacement if I'm ever killed. Now, he's shown up at the stronghold loudly demanding answers and spouting off about the ley lines being out of control."

That wasn't good. If Mica's people thought they could sense weakness in him, things would get messy fast. Court politics were known for their ruthlessness for a reason. Ra had spent the first decade of his friendship with Bast helping fend off assassins from the other courts. With the level of chaos created by recent events, it wasn't surprising unrest was building.

"He sounds like a dick," Ra said.

Mica barked a laugh at his assessment and Ra felt him relax a little through the bond. A deep satisfaction filled him that he could have that effect on his mate. Ah fuck. When had he started thinking of Mica as that? He was so screwed. If only they could hurry up and get to the literal part of that instead of the figurative one.

"Lachlan is all of three days older than me and seems to think that makes him entitled to something."

Ra scoffed. Surely elementals got over that kind of age difference after 1,200 or more years?

Mica dropped them down to the glade he'd mentioned in an impressive show of control. The clearing was nestled in the jungle just past a side entrance to the stronghold and Ra wished he could take some time to get a better look at it. On the far side, the native limestone formed a natural hot spring filled with steaming mineral water. The space looked like it would be a popular spot, but right now there was no one there except for this Lachlan asshole and Wren.

Their descent was fast enough that he was forced to cling to Mica for a breath to regain his balance as he slid down Mica's body from where he'd had his legs wrapped around the elemental's waist. Wren's quickly stifled noise of distress when he caught sight of them had him smirking. The seneschal really needed to get over his crush already.

He was surprised when Mica didn't immediately turn to deal with the two waiting men, taking the time to tilt up his chin and brush a kiss to his lips that quickly turned deeper than either of them intended. Lachlan's throat clearing in annoyance at the display barely registered because there was no space in his body to feel anything except the heat of Mica's tongue stroking against his. It was only once they parted that he realised he'd left his back exposed to two elementals who would likely sooner drop him from a height than speak to him. What did that say about how much he trusted Mica now? He didn't want to think about it.

"My lord, you have more important things to focus on than your human toy," Lachlan said, his irritation clear.

Mica pressed his lips one more time to Ra's before turning to face his subordinate. "Speak like that about him again and I will strip you of your position and demote you back to scout duty. I would've thought *you* had more important things to focus on than flying here when your region is damaged and in need of your attention."

Lachlan sputtered and Wren cut in.

"I think Lachlan only meant there was some urgency in his need to speak to you, my lord," Wren said, glaring at Ra. "Perhaps the human could make his way back to the stronghold so we can talk openly."

Ra took pleasure in making the lives of posturing assholes like these two difficult, but now was not the time. It would just make Mica's job more difficult and that was the last thing he wanted to do. Not that he was worried at all about the Earth Lord's ability to fend off any challenge if it came. Besides, he had a pop-up nightclub to organise.

"I'll leave you to it. Come find me when you're done," he said.

Leaning over, he unbuttoned the top of Mica's shirt a little further and pressed a kiss to the skin beneath his throat.

"Tease," Mica murmured in response, but Ra could feel his tension reduce a little through their connection.

The surrounding shadows were deepening as evening approached and the humid heat was bordering on oppressive, but there was something about the lush greenery that relaxed him as he headed back to the stronghold on foot. As enjoyable as it was being carried in Mica's muscled arms, cocooned in his power, there was something to be said for moving under his own steam.

His good mood faded when he stepped into the cave mouth and noticed the tense wings and fearful faces of the few elementals around him. A chill rippled through him as the sunshine disappeared from view, despite the air still being warm. Reaching out, he placed his hand on the stone walls reassuringly. He might not be able to talk to the stronghold, but he knew the poor thing must be in pain again. It only made him more determined to follow through on his plans for that night. The stronghold needed music and company and it needed them yesterday. He'd just have to hope the latest troubles didn't drive folks away.

"I'm glad to be home, Earthshine. I missed you," he murmured to the walls, stroking the limestone.

"Uncle!" Kaia's voice called from ahead of him just before a bundle of wings and worry barrelled into him.

"What's up K-bear?" he asked, as he carried her toward Mica's quarters and some privacy.

"Earthshine's so broken and I just want to take its pain

away, but nothing I do makes any difference," she whispered, breath catching in a sob.

"Sometimes you just have to keep reaching out and hope it makes a difference," Ra said.

"Just like you all did with me?" Kaia asked.

"Did it help?" Ra asked back.

"It didn't help the pain, but it reminded me I wasn't alone."

"And that's what we'll do with our Earthshine too until we can figure out how to heal it. How are you feeling now?" Ra asked as he stepped through the door to Mica's wing of the stronghold and headed for the couch. He didn't have the benefit of magic to carry Kaia's weight and she was damn heavy. He was pretty sure she'd grown at least a few inches in height since they arrived, and likely wingspan as well.

"The meditation is helping me. Sometimes the stronghold joins its consciousness to mine while I'm doing it so I hope maybe it's helping Earthshine as well," she said.

Ra hid his frown and made a mental note to check with Mica whether that was dangerous. Not wanting to upset the caves by asking more about the situation, he changed the subject instead.

"Are you excited for tonight?" he asked.

Knowing Kaia needed the chance to connect with people just as much as the stronghold did, they'd arranged for the first hour to be all ages before the children would head home and the night would, with any luck, turn much more R-rated.

Kaia slid off his lap onto the couch and beamed at him. "Yes! I can't wait! Elysia made me a special outfit and everything. Will you use one of your playlists from back home? Please?"

Ra smiled down at the girl. He hadn't had time to sort his DJ set, what with everything else going on, and he doubted anyone here had been to one of his sessions before. He may as well give him and Kaia another reminder of home by playing something familiar.

"Anything for you, sweetheart."

Leaving Kaia inside to work on her studies, he stepped onto the balcony and pulled out his phone. He had a lot of calls to make to ensure tonight went off without a hitch. Esme had advertised the night across the Tree City and Granite Bay but if the people here were anything to go by, the elementals would need some reassurance things were in hand.

Like most courts, the Earth Court had its own social media platforms to connect on. Once he'd checked in with everyone helping to promote the event, he recruited Kaia and her friends to come take some teaser photos with him. If the cute images of the young elemental mages decorating the caves and having fun didn't convince everyone it was perfectly safe, he didn't know what would.

Mica didn't appear again until right before they were due to start. Ra had ensconced himself in the DJ booth with an eager Kaia beside him acting as translator for the stronghold so it could see the visuals of what they were trying to achieve through her mind. He'd left his own DJ gear back home, but Esme had come through with some great equipment for him. Everything was ready to go when he felt a warm presence at his back, impossibly soft copper wings filling his vision as they wrapped around him.

A shiver travelled down his spine as Mica kissed the back of his neck and he leaned back into the embrace, reaching an arm back to hold Mica's head close. Focusing on their connection, he tried to get a sense of what the Earth Lord was feeling, but he wasn't letting a lot through.

"Everything okay?" he murmured.

"It is now. I can't thank you enough for bringing my people home to comfort the stronghold like this," Mica replied, nipping at his skin as Mica's hands traced a fiery path exploring his body. "Lachlan lost all his leverage once everyone started arriving and some of the damage healed on its own as the Earthshine stabilised."

"He's a liability," Ra said.

"Yes. But I don't want to think about him right now," Mica said, pulling away a little to take in the scene.

The DJ booth was set partway up the amphitheatre and, below them, the dance floor was starting to fill with excited bodies, mostly families at this stage. While the space was technically part of the stronghold, it was high up on its outer edge and only half was covered by the soaring cave walls. The rest was open to the night sky where stars were just starting to emerge in the darkness. The older children were chasing each other in a game of aerial tag in and out of the space while various adult elementals watched on either from the dancefloor below or from the layers of limestone benches marching up the walls.

Turning on his microphone, Ra called out to the gathered crowd. "Who's ready to dance?"

The children all screamed excitedly but the adults weren't there yet. That was okay. They would be soon. At least the slight scepticism he'd seen in their faces had disappeared once Mica joined him.

"Tonight you get something a little bit special courtesy of my niece Kaia over there. We're bringing one of my sets from

The Crypt to your very own pop-up Club Earthshrine. So, let's make some noise!"

Not waiting to see if the audience warmed up, Ra started a dance track with a thumping beat. Thanks to their rehearsal earlier in the day, the stronghold knew just what to do. Not only did every surface become a stunning light display as it channelled raw power through the various minerals and bioluminescent growths surrounding them, but the rock itself became the speaker system. Music came from every direction, wrapping them in sound and light just like Mica had wrapped him in his wings.

The children went wild dancing both on the ground and in the air, and their families weren't far behind.

"Sweetheart, this is incredible," Mica murmured in his ear, stunned.

"It's all our Earthshine. I just nudged things in the right direction," Ra said.

"You and I both know you did far more than that. Can you leave the booth?" Mica asked.

Twisting so he could face Mica, Ra smiled up at him. "Fuck yeah, I can. The next tracks are all queued up already. Let's go."

Grabbing Mica and Kaia's hands before the Earth Lord got any ideas about scooping him up into his arms again, Ra pulled them both down to the dancefloor with him. As he let the rhythm move through him and threw his hands in the air, he noticed the flutter of wings in his peripheral vision as more elementals landed to join them now their lord was there. Laughing, he twirled Kaia around and flashed Mica another grin as the elemental was inundated by children begging for a dance and teens slinking closer just to be near him.

He could feel the niggling frustration of Mica's thwarted desire for him growing in the back of his mind, but nothing showed through to anyone else as the Earth Lord patiently and enthusiastically danced with his people in his own formal way. Ra wasn't the slightest bit surprised when less than a minute after they finally convinced Kaia and the last of the children it was time for bed, he was hauled into his mate's strong arms. Mica's wings flashed with the copper of his power as he moved, leaving sparks like fireflies drifting in the air behind him.

"You dance like sin and feel like pure sex," Mica groaned in his ear as Ra shifted until his back was pressed tight to Mica's chest and he could grind himself against the Earth Lord.

Twisting his head, he nipped at Mica's throat. "You need to behave until we wrap this up unless you really want to put on a show for your court," Ra said.

Mica huffed a laugh against his skin. "I am quite certain it's you who needs to behave. Why did you make this event so damn long?"

Ra's face ached from how much he was smiling. He'd always wanted to make the staid Earth Lord lose control. Wondered what it would be like when Mica finally admitted he could have a little fun and still be in charge.

"It's only three more hours," he teased.

"Are you going to torture me like this the whole time?" Mica growled, enveloping Ra in his wings again until he was screened from view so he could let his hands roam free over his body.

"Hold that thought. I need to go queue up the next songs," Ra said, laughing again at Mica's grumbling complaint as he pulled free.

The Earth Lord was immediately pulled into a conversation with a group of elementals he assumed were fairly senior by the amount of metallic copper flashing in their wings. Trust Mica to find a way to end up working when he should be having fun. He'd have to go and distract him again once he was done. Tonight was not for politics.

Holding a headphone to one ear, he got to work sorting the thrumming beats he wanted to drive Mica crazy with, murmuring to the stronghold as he worked.

"You're doing so amazing, Earthshine. You're a natural. Love the way you're matching the light colours to the lyrics and hitting those beat drops."

The rock ledge he was leaning against warmed under his hip in response and he gave it a gentle pat, wishing he could hear the stronghold's voice in his mind like the elementals around him could.

"If you think this is going to endear him to you, you're wrong," Wren's snide voice said from nearby. "He's too old to fall for lewd dancing and a flashy event. His people always come first to him and no elemental courtier would risk having a weak human so close to the seat of power. You'd be dead in a week. He's going to have his fun and then he's going to ditch you. And I'll be here to pick up the pieces."

Ra rolled his eyes, but Wren's words sent a niggling discomfort through him. What were they to each other really? Mica's statement about the mate bond replayed in his mind—*not everyone is as keen as your brother to bare every emotion to someone and create a walking weakness that could kill them.* He didn't need Mica to form a mate bond between them, though. He just wanted the chance to love him a little. To help him heal.

Would Mica be able to stop himself from forming a mate

bond when he could barely keep his hands off Ra even when he'd hated him, though? The last thing he wanted to do was create a vulnerability for Mica's enemies to exploit. If they did form that kind of bond, Mica would die if someone killed Ra.

They'd just have to be careful.

"He's had several hundred years to make a move on you if that's what he wanted. If you think he's going to go running to you, you're welcome to have a go at him now. See what response you get," Ra shot back, waving a hand toward where Mica was standing.

"I am going to *end* you. And I'm going to make it so my lord pulls the trigger," Wren growled, a murderous glint in his eyes.

The stone beneath their feet rumbled and jerked in response, but Ra was quick to reassure the stronghold. "It's okay, Earthshine. He's full of shit. And if he's not, we can smash him later when he signs his own death warrant going after me," Ra said, faking a confidence he didn't feel.

The last thing they needed was for the stronghold to panic and hurt the crowds here. They were supposed to be reassuring everyone it was safe and rebuilding the connection between the caves and the people.

"You won't be protected forever," Wren warned.

"Fuck off, Wren. You're undermining your own lord by upsetting the stronghold like that," Ra said, turning his back on the bitter seneschal.

CHAPTER 17

RA

By the time Ra turned around, Wren had disappeared. All his instincts were screaming that the seneschal's threats were real, but there wasn't much he could do about it just then. So instead of worrying, he finished up what he was doing and went to find Mica.

"What did Wren want?" Mica asked him as he slipped an arm around Mica's waist, purposefully brushing the backs of his knuckles against the elemental's sensitive feathers as he did so.

Ra shrugged and looked up at the Earth Lord with a wicked smirk. "To stake some sort of claim on you. Which means I need to show everyone here that you're *mine*."

Placing both hands around Mica's neck, he pulled him into a filthy kiss before running a firm grip down his muscled shoulders until he was stroking along the upper ridges of his wings. Mica moaned and his eyes rolled back in his head, as Ra pushed in close and let him feel just how hard he was.

"Fuck. Ra," Mica gasped, shifting so they could both get the friction they were craving.

"That's the idea."

"If you keep that up we will not be staying here," Mica said, nuzzling under his ear as he laved at his skin.

"Let's play a game then. Whoever lasts longest without dragging the other out the door gets to pick what position we end tonight in," Ra said.

"How does that help?" Mica asked, moaning softly again as Ra's wandering hands stroked over his chest. "I want to do *everything* with you."

Ra grinned. "You don't want to go all bossy Earth Lord on me and tell me what to do?"

"I don't care. I just want you."

The heaving crowd of people around them faded away from notice as Ra lost himself in the sensations of dancing with Mica. The Earth Lord couldn't seem to help but keep his wings wrapped tight around him, leaving them both dripping with sweat in the already humid space and ensuring no one could see what their lord was getting up to. Pun absolutely intended. If someone had told him a month ago he'd be frotting in public with Mica like this, or at all, he'd have laughed them out of Soul Tower.

By the time the final song was playing, they were barely moving to the beat, too busy devouring each other's mouths. He'd never been more grateful that he'd arranged for Esme to shut things down. The bass was still fading when he grabbed Mica's hand in his and headed to the exit, waving off the catcalls from his new friends among the court as they left.

Too impatient to wait, Mica swept him up in his arms and sped them through the tunnels in a blur of magic. Ra laughed as his head spun at the change in pace until he found himself shoved up against the door to Mica's rooms. The Earth Lord hitched his legs around his waist and sucked on his neck hard, renewing the bruise there he'd never let fade.

"You forfeited the game," Mica pointed out as he started unbuttoning Ra's shirt. "Damn these human closures are annoying. I'm having an elemental wardrobe tailored for you so I never have to deal with this unreasonable delay again."

Ra threw his head back with another breathless laugh. "It only adds a few seconds. You can cope," he said, running his fingers along the collar of Mica's shirt until he found the magical seam that had it dropping to the floor.

They both groaned as they could finally press their bare skin together. Toeing his shoes off, Ra pushed Mica back enough to fumble at his belt and fly until he could shove his pants off. Okay, maybe human tailoring was a little annoying. Looking up, he forgot to breathe as he took in the sight of an entirely naked Earth Lord standing before him. Wings flared and trembling, thick erection standing proud against his stomach, and those hands. Those perfect, achingly strong musician's hands that could create beauty as easily as they could weave dangerous magic.

"Touch me. Please," Ra whispered.

Stepping forward, Mica cupped his jaw, brushing his fingers across his lips. "You're so beautiful like this. All passion and need."

Ra sucked one of Mica's fingers into his mouth and wrapped his tongue around it, not breaking eye contact.

"Fuck, Sunshine," Mica said, pulling Ra with him as backed up until his legs were pressed against the arm of the couch.

Pressing in close, Ra reached down and wrapped a hand around both their lengths, stroking them together. "You won fair and square. What's it going to be, my lord?" he asked.

He cocked his head in confusion as Mica reached an arm behind him and the familiar feeling of the Earth Lord's power surrounded them. A moment later a bottle of olive oil from the kitchen shot across the room into Mica's hand.

Shaking with laughter, Ra raised an eyebrow. "Or we could go find a bed and some actual lube?"

"Not a fucking chance. I'm not taking another step until I feel you inside me," Mica growled, shoving the oil into Ra's hands and turning to bend over the couch.

Ra's mouth dropped open in shock as he took in the picture of the powerful lord splayed out before him, wings draped elegantly to the floor and muscled back arched. "What..."

Mica looked back at him over his shoulder, pupils blown with desire but amusement showing through. "Did you need a hand?"

"No, I just didn't think you'd trust me enough to..." Fuck. Why couldn't he even finish his sentences? His brain had checked out when every bit of blood flew south. No way would he ever reject this offer though. Uncapping the oil, he slicked his fingers before leaning over to carefully place the bottle on a nearby table. His hands were shaking so badly he was surprised he didn't knock the whole thing onto the floor.

Running his clean hand over the enticing softness of Mica's feathers, he gently traced the other down the tight muscles of his ass until he could brush a teasing finger against Mica's hole.

Mica's breaths were coming in sharp pants as he spoke. "I trust you with this. And it's easier this way. Less likely to bond you by accident. Fuck. I need you, baby."

Maybe Mica's words implied he still didn't trust him in other ways, but he'd take what he could get. He couldn't have ignored Mica's plea if his life depended on it. As his first finger breached Mica's body and he felt the tight warm heat clenching down on him, his focus narrowed only to the pleasure of the man before him. A kind of trance descended on him as he stroked and stretched Mica, every sense directed at drawing out more of those intoxicating moans and shudders. This was how they were meant to be. How they always should have been. Entwined together, making each other soar instead of dragging each other down.

Mica's gasps grew more desperate as he massaged the exact spot inside his mate that was keeping his wings straining wide with tension instead of draping on the floor.

"Get inside me before you make me come like this," Mica gritted out.

The words brought Ra back to earth and he became keenly aware of the throbbing ache in his neglected cock. "Of course you'd be bossy even like this. I *am* inside you," he pointed out, even as he reached for the oil again, the move making his fingers twist inside Mica and drawing out another moan from the elemental.

Gently pulling his fingers free, he poured more of the oil on his shaft, making sure he was slick. No way was he going to hurt his mate. Not more than he wanted to be anyway.

"Need you!" Mica said, reaching back to pull at his hip.

As he lined himself up, he leaned forward and pressed a kiss to Mica's spine right at the sensitive join where the bottom of his wings met his body. Holding Mica's hips tight so he could take total control of their movements, he slid forward inch by inch kissing each vertebrae on the way up.

"Fuck, you feel amazing," he groaned, as warm heat enveloped his cock and Mica's body seemed to be sucking him in, welcoming him.

The strain of Mica's muscles beneath him as he fought to push back on him was so hot Ra was worried this would be over before it even began. Reaching up, he gripped the upper edge of Mica's wing and used the leverage to slide the rest of the way in. Their shared pleasure was overwhelming as he paused, pressed as close and as deep inside his lover as he could, both of them able to sense what the other was feeling through their connection. He would live inside this man if he could. He wanted to crawl inside Mica's skin and curl up safe in his heart and that thought was as terrifying as it was disturbing.

"Move," Mica ordered, voice strained.

He fucked Mica like he'd danced with him—bodies working together in perfect harmony, hips rolling in time to their accelerating heartbeats instead of music. Every thrust shaking with need.

It wasn't enough. Wasn't quite right.

Pulling out, he ignored Mica's cry of complaint as he somehow managed to manhandle the elemental and his huge wings into spinning around and falling back onto the couch.

"Needed to see your face," he gasped in explanation to Mica's silent question.

He was on Mica in less than a second, lifting one of his knees so he could carefully slide back inside him. Back home. The thrum of Mica's magic was a constant around them, copper sparking in his wings. Ra could feel the effort it was taking Mica to keep it contained. To stop it reaching for him to tie them together forever.

Mica fisted a hand in his hair and pulled him close, crushing their lips together, as he began to move again. And now it was right. Now it was perfect. Mica's blue-green eyes on his. Mica's kisses trailing down his neck. Mica's cock rutting against his abs as they pressed as close as two people could possibly be.

They came together, orgasms rushing through them like a landslide and the world whiting out as they succumbed to this driving need between them.

When his awareness finally drifted back to the room, Ra found himself nestled on Mica's chest, his head tucked beneath the elemental's chin and his body covered in the soft warmth of his wings. He squirmed a little as Mica's hand rubbed softly down his mark on Ra's arm.

"Tickles," he murmured, pressing a kiss to Mica's collarbone.

"It's late and we're going to be stuck together if we don't get up and shower," Mica said, shifting underneath him.

Oh yeah. Mica couldn't be that comfortable with his wings squashed into the low back of the couch.

Uncertainty returned as he stood and watched Mica get back to his feet. They both paused, unsure of what was next for them.

"Good night, sweetheart," Mica said finally, brushing a kiss to his lips. And then he headed to his room.

Ra stood staring at the door he'd gone through. Mica had left it open when he usually would have shut it but with no invitation to follow him. Like he wanted to show something had changed but wasn't ready to take that next step. Sighing, Ra headed in the opposite direction toward his own shower and bed. Mica lived and breathed court politics and, apparently, that extended to communicating through ridiculous subtleties in their love life as well. Or maybe that should just be sex life, given Mica's withdrawal? He was too tired to figure it out. They could talk about it in the morning.

Sleep was hard to find that night. Even when he caved

and wrapped himself tight in his covers and hugged a pillow to his chest he still felt a constant tug in his chest to go find Mica and slip into bed with him. Dammit. He'd slept alone for fifty years, one night with the Earth Lord shouldn't have changed that. The restlessness he could feel from Mica in the back of his mind through their connection wasn't helping either.

Sometime at ass o'clock in the morning when there was still no sign of the sunlight peeking through his window, he gave up and headed to the dining table to poke at the new toys he'd bought from Saryn. The fine electrical work of adding the receptors they needed to integrate with elemental magic finally distracted him enough that he was caught by surprise when a steaming cup of coffee was placed by his elbow.

Glancing up, he took a moment to admire the strength and intelligence in Mica's face as he looked over his shoulder at the nearly complete scanners.

"When will you have them working?" Mica asked.

Ra's eyes narrowed. "Good morning, love. Did you sleep well?" he said in a falsely sweet voice.

Honestly, the man was infuriating with the way he kept defaulting to his Earth Lord persona. Surely they were past that.

Mica's eyes flicked to his and then dropped to his lips before clearing his throat. "I've slept better."

"And whose fault is that? Maybe if you hadn't slunk off like I was a one-night hook-up we both would've got some actual rest."

Okay, he might be more bitter about that than he'd thought. He'd meant to have a calm mature conversation about it.

Mica sighed and leaned down to brush a kiss to his lips. "I told you I needed time. I can't trust my own judgement with you when the draw to mate is riding me so hard. I'm not going to rush into anything."

Blowing out a frustrated breath, Ra forced himself to move on. Mica was right. There was no rush.

"The scanners just need the same surveillance spell on them that my drones have. Can you do it?" Ra asked, turning his attention back to the tech so he could reseal the body of the scanner. He'd been modelling the electrics off the drone sitting nearby, so hopefully Mica could do the same with the spell.

"Of course," Mica said, and immediately Ra could feel the warmth of his power surrounding them as it rolled out across the collection of scanners on the table.

Mica's mark on his arm tingled as the magic amplified through the points they were touching and he shivered at the strange pleasure of feeling a piece of the Earth Lord under his skin.

"That should do it," Mica said not long later.

"Awesome. If I bring up the map showing the black spots where we need more data, could you have Earthshine absorb the scanners into the rock and send them to the right areas? We can move them closer if that's easier. It might be worth leaving them there to monitor things over time as well," Ra said.

Mica tilted his head and his eyes grew distant as he communicated with the stronghold. Not for the first time, Ra wished he could talk to the caves himself.

His question was answered when the first scanner sank straight through the table and into the floor, leaving no trace behind. One after another, Mica and the stronghold shifted them where they needed to be. He was barely aware of the time passing as they worked together. For once, they were both trying to achieve the same goal and it felt so natural to problem solve and talk back and forth as they filled in the rest of the ley line mapping he'd been missing before redistributing the scanners to key points of power throughout the cave system. At some point, Mica had pulled a stool up next to his, but he'd positioned it so his legs were straddling either side of Ra and his chin was resting on his shoulder as they manipulated the model on his screen to check what was needed.

It wasn't until his stomach growled loud enough to be heard over the whir of the laptop fan that Mica pulled away and glanced outside toward the balcony.

"It's after midday. I need to feed you," Mica said, standing up and stretching his wings wide as he cracked his neck before heading to the kitchen.

Ra stayed focused on the images on the screen as the comforting sounds of cooking drifted in the space. Finally, he leaned back as he made the final tweaks to his code.

"I think this is as good as it's going to get. The scanners are picking up most of the major ley line fluctuations and at least you can see the points where something's not right," Ra said.

"Now we just need to figure out how to fix it," Mica said, reaching past him to set the computer aside and replacing it with a bowl of steaming shakshuka.

Ra's groan was almost pornographic as he took his first mouthful. "This tastes amazing. Thank you."

"It's a dish from my childhood. Comfort food," Mica said, squeezing his thigh briefly with his free hand.

"If you need help figuring out ways to heal the damage

now we can see where it is and what it looks like, Kairon might have some ideas. He made a difference with Kaia. The vampyr have techniques to use their healing magic to reinforce different neural pathways in the brain. My theory is the ley lines here might respond in a similar way for the stronghold," Ra said.

Mica shook his head. "No. I appreciate the suggestion, but I can't bring in outsiders when the stronghold is already so vulnerable. I know the Soul Court is on good terms with the vampyr, but the rest of us are not so close to them. I can't take the risk, given what's at stake, and even inviting him here to consult would worsen the difficulties I have with some of my senior courtiers right now. The memories of the early days after the Melding when they clashed with the vampyr are too strong. I could easily fend off any challenge, but the conflict would sow more discord and fear. I can't afford to alienate my people."

Annoyance and guilt fought for precedence in him as he forced himself to take a breath before replying. This kind of untrusting attitude was exactly what was holding back the Melded Earths from achieving a more stable peace, but also he hadn't appreciated the finer points of Mica's challenges from the regional leads when he'd arranged to meet Kairon in the Tree City before. He didn't think anyone had noticed the vampyr's presence, but he would hate it if the way he'd gone about that made trouble for Mica. He didn't regret it, because Kaia was finally thriving in her magic lessons, but he might've arranged to have Kaia go to the vampyr instead of the other way around if he'd realised the state of things here.

It was on the tip of his tongue to come clean to Mica about what he'd done, but this thing between them was so new and fragile he couldn't make himself do it. What if it destroyed what little trust Mica had regained for him?

"What are you going to do then?" Ra asked.

"I'll consult with the elemental healers here. I'm sure they can figure something out."

"If they're all as closed-minded about other peoples helping, are they even going to look at my modelling, given it's based on human tech?" Ra asked, unable to keep the bitterness from his tone.

Maybe he'd been foolish to think anything could grow between them. The elemental courts were not like home. There weren't even any other humans living in the area.

"They will because I'll tell them to," Mica said, reaching out to wrap an arm around him and press a kiss to his temple as he sensed his anger.

"You can't force people to innovate in the way this kind of hybrid magic/technology fix needs to work. If they don't respect it, they won't try to use it. All this work will have been pointless," Ra said.

"The technology is helping diagnose, but that doesn't mean we will need it to solve the problem," Mica said.

Ra snorted. "And how's your purely elemental magic fix been working out for you for the last six months?"

"Can we not fight, please?" Mica said, nuzzling under his ear and nipping at the skin there.

"You can't just distract me with sex every time we disagree now we've fucked," Ra said, tilting his head to give Mica better access and reaching up to grab his head and pull him closer.

Mica huffed a laugh against his skin. "Are you sure about that?"

"No."

Ra moaned as Mica continued to press achingly light butterfly kisses to every bit of skin he could reach.

"Kiss me properly," Ra begged, twisting to face the Earth Lord.

"That reminds me, you never paid up on our bet. What's your real name?" Mica said, smiling as he kept up his sensual assault and refused to press their lips together.

"You didn't win that bet! I killed Caelus," Ra said.

"You bet you'd kill him before I even got close. I was in the same room saving your ass, if you recall."

Ra was losing track of the conversation as Mica's hands started wandering. "Not close enough," he gasped, flipping around so he could straddle the Earth Lord in his seat.

"I'll get it out of you one day," Mica murmured, finally giving in and kissing him properly.

CHAPTER 18

RA

After succumbing to their desires against the wall near the dining table, Mica disappeared off to speak with the healers. At this rate, they'd have fucked against every surface in the living area before they even got near an actual bed. He'd offered to accompany Mica and talk the mages through what the model was doing, but Mica said he needed to warm them up first. The fact Mica had taken the computer with him suggested he might not even bother calling in Ra if he thought they could make progress without him.

Feeling more homesick than he had for weeks, Ra went and found Kaia so they could video call their friends and family back in the Soul Court. Even Kaia's giggles as they spoke to Zee and her māmā didn't help much, because the whole time he wanted to be asking the Soul Court's magical engineer for their thoughts on healing the stronghold, but there was no way Mica would be okay with that.

Wren's sneering face and whispered threats when he passed the seneschal in the tunnels on the way back was just the icing on a shit sandwich. He still couldn't shake the guilt about not telling Mica about Kairon's visit, either.

The one light in the cave's darkness was the way most of Mica's people now stopped to chat with him as he passed, many telling him what an amazing time they'd had at the dance party. One of the subcommittees of Mica's upcoming millennial celebrations even reached out to him to help plan the music side of things. He could only assume they'd hidden that request from Wren. It was almost like being back in the Soul Court as he laughed and joked with some of the younger elementals while they figured out how to scale up what he'd done in the pop-up club to the much bigger event. People would be coming from around the world to show their respect to the Earth Lord for 1,000 years of unusually responsible rule.

Mica was nowhere to be found when he finally stumbled back into their wing of the stronghold sometime late that night. He thought about following the ever-present tug in his chest to find the Earth Lord and force him to rest, but he wasn't sure what welcome he'd get. Especially if he interrupted the mages trying to come up with a solution.

Instead, he downed a whiskey and slunk off to bed, sleeping even worse than he had the previous night.

When he staggered into the living area late the next morning, Mica was sitting at the dining table working.

"Morning," Mica said, glancing up with a smile.

Ra paused next to him for a kiss before going to grab them both a coffee. "You look happier than yesterday," he observed.

"We think we have something that will shift the ley lines back where they need to go. We're going to give it a go this afternoon when the children are all out on a field trip so we don't have to worry so much if something goes awry," Mica said.

"Want me to take a look at your plan?" Ra asked, handing Mica his drink before leaning back against the breakfast bar to take a much-needed sip of caffeine. He didn't know how he was going to deal with the lack of coffee if he had to return to the Soul Court one day.

"No offense, sweetheart, but you don't have the magical knowledge to make an assessment and the final plan won't be ready until lunchtime anyway. We'll be fine," Mica said.

Ra took a deep breath and counted to five slowly in his head before he responded. Mica was 1,200 years old, he reminded himself. It wasn't surprising it would take him a little while to overcome his preconceived ideas.

"I've been working with the Soul Court mages for over two decades. I have as good an understanding of elemental magic as someone who doesn't wield it can have. I also have way more experience with different ways of working it with technology than your people do. Let me help," he said.

"And I have *centuries* more experience than you in keeping the stronghold thriving. I told you we have a solution already. It's not necessary," Mica said.

Ra tilted his head, wondering why the man was being so stubborn. "Did your mages refuse to work with me?" he guessed.

"Not all of them," Mica said, looking away.

Which probably just meant Elysia and Serena had stuck up for him. They were the only powerful mages he'd spent any time with.

"Isn't the whole point of your stupidly ruthless elemental politics that you have complete control over your court? Why do you care what they think when it could make a difference to our Earthshine?"

"I told you. Navigating this is as much about keeping the confidence of my senior courtiers as it is about healing the damage. Our magics are an ecosystem that supports the stronghold. I need us all pulling in the same direction, not fractured by arguing over your involvement, or we won't succeed. Plus it makes Earthshine unstable when we discuss you."

"Because your mages are being pig-headed assholes," Ra snapped.

"It's not your call. They're not going to let us fail. The stronghold is the core of everything that makes the Earth Court what it is. It's their home," Mica said.

Ra stiffened. "And it's not mine?" he asked quietly. He knew he hadn't been there long, but he'd thought things had shifted between them. Mica's hesitation was all he needed to see. "Don't answer that. I don't think I want to know."

"It's complicated. You're still a member of a rival court. If it will make you feel better, you can monitor the changes through your scanners while we work," Mica offered.

If it would make him feel better. Not if it would help, because Mica still couldn't see that he wasn't a useless human. He wasn't going to abandon Mica or Earthshine when so much was on the line, though. Whether he could stand to stick around afterward as his heart was chipped away one broken shard at a time by Mica's distrust was another matter.

THE LOCATION the mages had picked for their working was over the nexus most damaged by the broken ley lines, which happened to be the same glade they'd landed in the other day. Below their feet, deep underground, was a series of tunnels that had collapsed in the immediate aftermath of Bast and Hel healing the reality contagion that had threatened the world.

He'd set up his computer as far from the elementals as possible, hooking into the static scanners they'd positioned throughout Earthshine to keep an eye on how the ley lines were shifting.

"Why is *he* here, my lord?" Wren asked from nearby.

"Why are *you* here? Aren't you like the babiest of mages?" Ra snapped back. Not his most mature moment but he was fuming at the elementals' refusal to work with him when it could be the difference in succeeding.

"Enough. You're both here because I want you to be," Mica said as if that should be the end of it. As if Ra was just another one of his staff.

Whatever. He had more important things to focus on. Like monitoring the stronghold to keep his mate safe during whatever they had planned so he could tear him a new one in private once they were done.

"Mica, I don't think this location is going to be the best for whatever you're planning. It is showing the most damage generally, but it's not the most volatile and, looking at the flows from this point, I think you could end up increasing the imbalance if you direct too much power here," he said.

"That is *Lord* Mica to you, human," Lachlan growled from where he was standing near Wren.

Oh great. They were forming a little anti-Ra clique. He rolled his eyes at the posturing. He didn't know when the regional lead had shown up again but he really could have done without his aggravating presence making this even harder.

"Ra is more accustomed to reading the models he's looking at. Maybe we should double-check our working," Elysia chimed in.

"Do I tell you how to grow your plants, Elysia?" the dry voice of the head Mage healer Garett asked, condescension clear in his tone.

None of the elementals looked over forty, but Ra imagined Garett as a grumpy old curmudgeon nonetheless. When you lived forever it was hard for new blood and fresh ideas to get a foothold in the leadership. He'd thought Mica had better judgement than that, but apparently whatever internal politics were at play meant they were stuck with this guy with a stick up his ass.

"If you give me the details on how much power is going where, I could run some scenarios to see how the ley lines might respond," Ra offered through gritted teeth. He wouldn't let his temper put the stronghold at risk. He had to try and get them to see sense.

Mica met his gaze and shook his head. "Thank you, Ra, but we don't have time. We only have a limited window to do this working before the ley line shifts again. Then we'll have to wait at least another week."

Something wasn't right here and he really didn't like it. Wren had been deep in conversation with Garett and Lachlan when they arrived and they'd stopped talking the second he stepped into the glade. He couldn't help but feel like they'd delayed starting until it would be too late to slow things down when they'd left it until this afternoon as well.

They could easily have sent the kids off earlier in the day so they had more time.

As the mages gathered their magic and the earth beneath their feet began to thrum with power, Ra's worry only deepened. He could see the nexus below them swelling with power through his scanners until it overflowed out to the crisscrossing ley lines that fed into it, but he couldn't see what they were hoping to achieve by doing it. This was just reinforcing the existing flows, not shifting or reconnecting them. As powerful as the elementals surrounding him were, there also wasn't nearly enough magic being used to make any real difference to something as vast and complex as the stronghold's sentience.

"Mica, I don't think..." Ra started to say.

His words were cut off by a huge earth tremor and a deafening roar that got louder and louder until he stumbled as the earth through the glade was riven in two, a jagged chasm spreading open only metres from where he stood. Heat blasted his face like a furnace as magma was forced up near the surface from how deep the damage went.

What the fuck had just happened?

Mica and Elysia fell to the ground from where they'd been hovering mid-air as the other mages turned accusing eyes his way. He barely paid them any mind because Mica all but collapsed when he landed, clutching his head.

"What's wrong? Are you okay?" Ra cried, running to where Mica had dropped to one knee.

"He's fighting to calm the stronghold after you sabotaged it," Garett sneered, shoving Ra away from Mica.

"What the fuck are you talking about? I told you *not* to do whatever it was you just did!"

Mica staggered to his feet and turned to the mage with a

frown. "Ra doesn't have any magic. He couldn't have done this."

"Look at the source of the damage, my lord. You'll find it's one of *his* scanners that you let him sink into the stronghold like a cancer," Garett said.

Mica's frown deepened as he turned his head toward the stronghold and held a glowing hand out that sent copper power sheeting across the broken earth.

"He's right. The rift came from your sensor," Mica said, turning to him.

Ra's mouth dropped open, but before he could defend himself, Wren chimed in. Of course.

"Our spies recently gave me footage of Ra meeting with a vampyr leader in the Tree City several days ago. I was waiting until we'd completed this working to bring it to your attention. I apologise, my lord. If I'd realised how dangerous he was I would've acted sooner," Wren said, handing Mica a tablet that presumably contained the footage.

Mica turned to him with hurt in his eyes.

"It's not what you think. He was there helping Kaia," Ra said.

"So, why didn't you tell me?" Mica asked.

"Because you wouldn't have believed it was innocent!"

"Perhaps we could get to the bottom of this if Ra provided access to his message records so we could see what was communicated," Lachlan offered, voice falsely conciliatory.

Ra glared at the elemental. "You know I can't do that. It has all my Soul Court contacts in it."

"So you admit you're still working for a rival court then?" Lachlan asked.

Fuck. He'd been well and truly screwed over. He should've guessed Wren would be planning something.

"Mica, come on. You know I wouldn't do this. What benefit do I get from a random hole in the ground?" he said, waving at the chasm.

"It extends all the way into Lady Nerida's territory. We'll be lucky if she doesn't see the damage as an act of war," Mica said, voice tight.

Ra turned to Garett and Wren, incredulous. "Really? You hated me so much you would risk starting a war over it? What the fuck were you thinking? You need to fix this."

A flicker of uncertainty showed in Garett's face, but it was quickly squashed. Maybe they hadn't meant things to go this far, but it was too late for him to own up to whatever they'd done to cause this now without facing severe repercussions. Wren, on the other hand, didn't look the slightest bit regretful.

"My lord, you need to act decisively to show what happens when someone betrays you," Wren said.

Turning to Mica, Ra watched him with concern. Not for himself, but for the strain he could feel his mate was under trying to stabilise the extensive rift in the landscape while keeping the stronghold from panicking and dealing with this insidious crap from his people. The Earth Lord throbbed with raw power as he tried to contain the worst of the damage this plan had set in motion.

"Ask Earthshine what happened. It will tell you this wasn't me," Ra said, striving to stay calm so Mica wouldn't think his fear came from guilt.

"The stronghold is incoherent right now, Ra," Elysia explained quietly when Mica didn't immediately reply.

"Let me deal with him for you while you focus on what

matters," Garett said to Mica, and Ra's eyes narrowed as he felt the collar around his neck grow hot like it was responding to a magical attack against him.

Mica was staring at him like he was a stranger, but before he could say anything more, a rumbling scream like the earth had found a voice echoed in the air and broken hunks of molten rock started flying from the chasm, pelting around them like burning hail. Wren and Garett cowered under the worst of it, the head mage quickly shifting his focus to shielding himself instead of whatever the collar had blocked him from doing to Ra with his magic.

"The stronghold is protecting you," Elysia said, vines of greenery extending from their hands to shelter them and Mica from the ricocheting missiles.

"Because I didn't do anything to hurt it," Ra snapped, voice pleading for Mica to understand as the Earth Lord stood there, still silent.

The falling rocks continued to multiply, growing so numerous that he lost sight of Mica, Elysia, and everyone else, but not a single one hit him. However panicked Earthshine was, it was still being careful not to harm him. What the fuck was he going to do?

Scanning his surroundings, he noticed there was a clear passageway deeper into the jungle, away from the elementals threatening him. It wasn't in his nature to run when he'd done nothing wrong, but, in this case, removing himself from the situation might be the only way to get the stronghold to calm down so Mica could deal with the international incident and keep his people safe. Also, he wasn't sure he could face seeing the look of betrayal on Mica's face for a single second longer. He needed space.

Turning his back on the man who held his breaking heart

in his hands, he jogged through the swirling blizzard of rock. Once he'd started running, he couldn't stop, because if he stopped he'd have to face just how much this hurt. He kept running even after he passed the edges of the stronghold's awareness and the chaos of magic around him gave way to eerily quiet jungle. Kept running until his lungs ached and his legs were shaking with fatigue. Until darkness fell and he couldn't go any further without tripping and doing Garett's job for him.

When he finally stumbled to a halt, he had no idea where he was. Grassy plains stretched to his right in a landscape riven with volcanic boulders. Putting his hands on his knees, he fought to catch his breath.

"I love it when my prey runs itself to ground."

It took him longer than it should to place the female voice speaking from the shadows but in his defence, the only time he'd heard it before she'd been screaming for vengeance against him—Lucia, the sister of the elemental he'd killed.

CHAPTER 19

MICA

Fuck. Panic filled Mica as he felt Ra moving further and further away from him, but there was nothing he could do. Every drop of his power was being spent keeping the ley line from splitting any further and interweaving his defences with Elysia's against the falling rock and whatever other foul play was no doubt about to be attempted. What little attention he had spare was focused on trying to calm the stronghold enough to figure out what the fuck had happened.

He knew he should've used more reassuring words when he'd spoken to Ra, but, with his mind split in three directions, all he'd been capable of was responding to direct questions and stating facts. It was fact that the damage had come from one of the buried scanners, but given Mica had imbued them with the necessary magic himself, he was certain whatever had caused it happened after he and Ra had finished with them.

It was telling that three of his senior courtiers were all trying to pressure some kind of response from him on this.

He had no doubt one or all of them were responsible. Only time would tell if they'd realised how fragile the stronghold was before they'd acted. Were they only trying to drive a wedge between him and Ra, or were they trying to start a war? Had they known how much damage this would cause?

A tremor through his consciousness heralded another series of tunnels collapsing through the stronghold's panic. From the flashes of images he was getting from Earthshine, he didn't think anyone had been hurt, but some of his people were now trapped within the caves while the limestone rumbled in fear and anger around them.

Earthshine, it's okay. I won't let them hurt him and we will try again and help you heal, he told the stronghold.

Traitors! I will swallow them and grind their bones to dust! the caves screamed back.

Complete sentences were progress at least.

I need you to stabilise the rift so I can deal with them, Mica said, sending a wave of calm he wasn't feeling toward the sentience along with a hint of his own murderous thoughts towards anyone trying to harm his mate so the stronghold knew it wasn't alone.

The pressure in the back of his mind finally eased a little as the stronghold hyper-focused on the task he'd given it now it was reassured he wasn't about to attack Ra.

Elysia had kept their shielding strong as he worked, and with the sentience not slapping at his subconscious and the wounded ley line staunched for now, he could finally turn to his friend.

"I don't like this. Only some of these falling rocks were from Earthshine. The rest reek of mage craft," Elysia said.

Mica nodded. Raising one hand, he drew deep on his vast power that was magnified a thousand-fold by his connection to the sentience, even as damaged as it was. Copper magic flashed from his body in three perfectly spinning blades that temporarily severed the other mages' connection to their power. Igneous rock pattered to the ground like rain until, finally, silence fell.

Closing his hand into a fist and twisting, he forced the three men to kneel before him, knowing his eyes were flashing with raw power and rage. How dare they try and harm his mate? How dare they harm his land and his people?

"Explain yourselves. Now," Mica growled, as he pulled out his phone to call for his enforcers to bring the magic-blocking shackles they used when powerful mages went rogue.

It was Wren who broke first, babbling words so fast he could barely follow as the other two glared at the seneschal.

"It was just supposed to be a small rockfall on the outer edge of the caves. No one should've been hurt. Just enough to get you to send the human home or kill him."

A deadly calm settled over Mica. "Just enough to kill my mate?"

Wren's face turned white as a sheet and he opened and closed his mouth several times before his strangled voice asked "Your *what?*"

"I have a good guess at Wren and Lachlan's motivation, but yours is more puzzling, Garett. You are supposed to be a healer, but you've broken open the stronghold's wounds that had barely closed over," Mica said.

"You betrayed us the moment you asked a *necromancer* for help. Death magic is anathema. You learned that as a child the same as me. We could all see the way things were heading with Ra. You already had his necromancy tech defiling the stronghold. It wouldn't be long before his so-called brother started showing up and you reached out to the vampyr who are just as abhorrent. You needed to be reminded of what the human's true nature is," Garett said.

Fucking hell. All this over an outdated prejudice? The Soul Court had saved their land from destruction over and over again. He'd known it would take time for people to get over their aversion to soulweaving, especially with Bastion raising its profile with the way he was adopting the few soul-weaving elemental children in the world, but he'd thought his closest circle could at least appreciate what Bastion had done for them. Instead, they seemed determined to become an isolationist outpost while the rest of the world moved toward peace.

He should've paid more attention when Kaia pointed out how strange it was that only elementals resided in the stronghold and Tree City. That was on him. He should've done more to encourage his people to reach out to the other species they now co-existed with. That didn't excuse his courtiers' betrayal, though. They had almost brought about the catastrophe he'd spent months working to avoid and their actions would definitely draw the problem to the attention of the other courts.

A flash of wings on the edge of the glade heralded the arrival of five of his enforcers, all covered in a thin layer of limestone dust that made them almost ghostly in appearance.

"These three are guilty of treason. Cuff them and take them to the cells," Mica said.

The enforcers' eyes widened and flicked between him and the three elementals still kneeling. It had been centuries since they'd been faced with a crime of this nature and he'd likely be dealing with the repercussions of three of his trusted circle betraying him for decades to come. Before he could say anything more, a sudden draw on his magic had his head jerking toward the direction Ra had disappeared.

The remote magical defences in his mate's collar had been activated and he could feel them flickering under an assault it wouldn't be able to hold against for long.

Lachlan's mouth twisted in a smirk. "He ran right where we directed him. We win no matter what you do to us. When Bastion learns you let him die, you'll be at war with both the Soul and Water Courts. No necromancers or vampyr will come here in peace again and the Earth Court can finally be rid of their taint."

"You'd better hope for your sake that's not true," Mica growled, throwing himself into the air.

The last thing he heard before he was speeding across the jungle canopy was Elysia's reassurance they would handle the tunnel collapse and the traitors. If Ra was hurt or killed, Elysia would have to hide them somewhere until he'd calmed because he would exact every injury on them a thousand times over.

Pushing the limits of his power, he accelerated his flight to a speed he'd seldom attempted, his magic ripping through him like a magnitude 10.0 earthquake and his muscles straining. Ra's presence was a shining beacon pulling him forward. A target every atom of his being was focused on reaching. Even so, he felt the shielding embedded in the collar flicker and collapse just as he hurtled to the ground hard enough to send a shockwave echoing out that formed a crater where he'd landed.

He'd aimed his body like an arrow, hitting the hovering gold and white feathered form of Ra's attacker mid-air and taking her to the earth with him where his power was greatest. His booted feet crushed her ribs with a satisfying series of cracks as he pinned her down.

Nearby, the too still, too pale form of Ra's body was lax where he lay sprawled in a nest of earth that cushioned him from the chaos around him. Mica's vision went red and he became nothing but rage as he felt the tenuous grip Ra held to life. Earth magic sprung to his call, slamming into the weakly fluttering heart of the elemental lying beneath him and stopping it forever. Without a backward glance, he scooped Ra's unconscious body up into his arms and somehow flew even faster back to the stronghold than he'd arrived.

Time was of the essence and there was no way he would risk his mate's death if he could help it. He had no pride to swallow as he used his earpiece to call Bastion as he flew. Nothing was more important than the man in his arms.

"He's dying. I need Kairon here now," Mica all but yelled into the mic as he landed on the balcony, not even bothering to wait for Bastion to speak. He couldn't risk calling his own healers until he figured out how deep Garett's betrayal went and whether anyone else was working with him.

For once, the stronghold was a focused presence in his mind working quietly with Elysia in the background so it didn't distract him from the danger to his mate. As if it could sense that distracting him now would mean a disaster they would never recover from. Through their connection, he could feel the shifting rock and the patter of running feet as the tunnel collapse was repaired, but he ignored it all.

Reaching deep into the depths of the earth, he spun his magic through Ra's body, urging his blood to keep flowing, his stuttering breaths to continue. Unlike Caelus, Lucia hadn't just cut off the oxygen from around Ra's face. She'd dragged it from every blood cell in his veins while her power tore through bone and sinew. The only reason Ra was even still breathing at all was because there had been less than a second from when the collar's shielding collapsed until Mica arrived and their connection was reinforcing his tenuous grip on life.

Sinking down to his knees, he cradled Ra's head in his lap, gently stroking a lock of blond hair from his face with shaking fingers.

"Hold on, my love. Don't you dare fucking die on me," he rasped.

It was a measure of how distracted he was that he didn't even notice the portal forming at his back. The first he knew that company had arrived was the looming presence of the black-winged soulweaver over his shoulder.

"I was all set to rip you a new one, but I think you're probably doing that yourself already," Bastion said, the chilling sensation of his power filling the air as he worked to hold Ra's soul with the living.

Ignoring the soulweaver, Mica glanced behind him and breathed a sigh of relief as Kairon stepped through the portal.

"Hurry, please," he begged the vampyr.

Worry in every line of his face, Kairon sped to where he was kneeling with a speed even Mica would have trouble matching on foot. The flash of a blade appeared and was gone before he could react as Kairon sliced open his palm before letting the blood-red of his healing magic coat Ra's body until he was surrounded by a throbbing sphere of power.

After long minutes, Kairon finally broke the silence.

"He's stable now, but his recovery will take time. You can release your magic from him. It might interfere otherwise," Kairon said, brushing against his wings as he crouched down and stretched out a hand over Ra's chest.

Everything in Mica screamed not to trust his mate to anyone else, but he shut it down. If he'd listened to Ra and called Kairon for help in the first place, none of this might've happened. Ra trusted Kairon, so he would too. Reeling his magic back under his skin, he kept his senses alert for any deterioration in his mate, but the vampyr magic seemed to be working.

None of them spoke a word as Kairon continued to work and Mica didn't shift away a single inch. He couldn't. The stronghold had locked the doors to his wing, responding to his own fear there may be more traitors in his ranks. He was grateful for the chance to block the rest of the world from his mind and ignore the chaos this unannounced visit from Bastion would cause in his court.

Stroking his thumbs along Ra's gorgeous cheekbones over and over, he sat otherwise perfectly still on the hard, cold stone. Some of the tension left him when Ra's breathing improved enough that he could feel his exhalations against his fingers where they brushed against his lips.

Finally, Kairon straightened, swaying slightly, as the red of his power faded. "It's safe to move him now."

"When will he wake?" Mica asked as he stood with Ra cradled close to his chest.

"It's hard to say. He heals faster than a human because of his bond to you, but not as fast as you or I would, or as fast as he would if you were mated," Kairon said.

"We're not leaving until we're sure he's fine," Bastion said, breaking his silence.

Mica nodded, barely paying any attention to the other lord. "You two can take Ra's room and the guest room over there," he said waving toward the doors off the living area.

"Won't Ra need his room?" Bastion asked, a teasing note to his voice now the immediate danger had passed.

Mica growled. "Ra will be in *my* room where he belongs."

Fuck. His fear for Ra had made him lose all his filters. Glaring across at Bastion, he raised an eyebrow in silent question. Was the Soul Lord going to make an issue of this?

"It took me a while to see it, but I'm not going to stand between my brother and his mate," Bastion said.

Of all the elemental rulers, Bastion was the only one who would really understand this drive to bond he was feeling because he was the only one who'd succumbed to a mate bond himself.

"I do have *some* control. We're not mated," Mica muttered. But he wished they were. Ra might've healed already if he'd been brave enough to form the bond.

"Yet," Bastion added with a smirk. "Take my brother to your room and let him rest. Then we have things to discuss."

Mica headed for his rooms, the stronghold opening doors for him along the way until he could place Ra gently down on his bed where he should've been all along. Rage threatened to overtake him again as his mate's body remained limp and unresponsive as he carefully undressed him down to his t-shirt and boxers before tucking him under the grey silk comforter. Had he realised he'd decorated his room in the exact colour of Ra's eyes before? No. He just hoped Ra would wake soon to tease him mercilessly about it.

Leaning forward, he brushed a kiss to his mate's forehead before silently making his way out of the room. The stronghold dimmed its glow as he went, ensuring Ra could sleep undisturbed.

As he re-entered the room, his first stop was the cask of Ra's whiskey by his drinks cabinet where he poured five generous measures.

"Are you expecting company or are you planning to line those up and shoot them all back yourself?" Bastion asked.

Serena and Elysia's arrival that he'd sensed through the stronghold meant he didn't need to bother answering.

"What the fuck happened?" Bastion asked once everyone was seated.

The time for secrets was past. There was no way to explain the shitshow of an afternoon without explaining the damage to the stronghold and what it meant. Even if he'd been able to weave a glamour over the rift that extended from the stronghold out to the coast and beyond, he couldn't do anything about the damage he could sense extending into Lady Nerida's territory in the ocean.

Fuck. Nerida.

As if his thoughts had conjured it, his phone rang with the distinctive ringtone he allocated to the other courts' rulers.

"I can explain," he said in lieu of a greeting, putting the phone on speaker.

"I should fucking well hope so. I thought we were at least close enough that you'd tell me if we were at war in person," Nerida snapped.

Sighing, Mica pinched the bridge of his nose and took a long sip of whiskey. "We're not at war."

"Greetings, Lady Nerida," Bastion chimed in.

"Hello, sweet Water Lady," Kairon added.

There was silence down the line and Mica winced.

Maybe whatever antagonism was happening between Nerida and the vampyr would distract her from the damage to her court?

"You've got two minutes to explain what the fuck is going on and why you're cosying up to another court and *that* vampyr just as your magic invaded my territory," Nerida said, voice low and dangerous.

It took longer than two minutes, but thankfully Nerida seemed to regain some patience after he launched an explanation of the cause and nature of the damage to his stronghold.

"We knew it wouldn't be plain sailing when we initiated the global summit," Nerida said grudgingly after he explained the prejudice behind his people's betrayal. "I assume they will be made an example of."

"I will go even further than that. If you want them, I will hand them over to you for justice in recompense," Mica said.

Bastion jerked in surprise and stared at him. It was a big call. Nerida was bloodthirsty in her punishments. Usually, the courts would refuse to hand over a courtier in that way, regardless of the crime, but his people had knowingly betrayed him and the Earth Court in a way that could incite a war. As they'd discussed the magical damage to the ley lines, Nerida had shared an image of the effects on her stronghold. The Water Court that usually floated suspended in the ocean wherever she and the ley lines saw fit was now trapped static in a huge whirlpool; the only thing keeping it intact was the combined vast magics of her and her stronghold. It was a disaster in the making.

"You would forego taking revenge for what they did to your human?" Nerida asked, surprise in her voice.

Mica growled in distress despite himself before cutting it

off. This was bigger than his possessiveness and he knew Ra would never forgive him for starting a war in his name. "Yes. To demonstrate my commitment to peace between us," he said.

"And what of your stronghold? I can feel the instability from here," Nerida said.

"If the Soul Court is willing to assist, I will do what Ra suggested in the first place and have them help design a solution. I'm confident we can do it," Mica said, carefully avoiding mentioning that he would be including the vampyr Nerida couldn't stand as well.

Kairon met his gaze over the coffee table and nodded his assent to the unspoken request.

"I'm glad to see you're finally admitting I was right all along," a croaky voice said from nearby.

CHAPTER 20

MICA

Mica had been so distracted by navigating the conversation with Nerida that he hadn't noticed Ra waking. Ignoring everyone, Mica jumped to his feet and sped across the room, pausing with his hand raised to touch Ra's cheek before dropping it.

"My love, I am so sorry. I never should've let you think I didn't trust you. I never should've let you out of my sight," Mica said.

"Did you really think I hurt Earthshine?" Ra whispered.

"Not for a second," Mica said.

Ra nodded but looked doubtful. "And you *do* trust me?" he asked.

"Without reservation."

"What changed?"

"I could feel everything through the connection. You weren't guilty or worried for yourself. You were worried for me, for Earthshine. Even with accusations and the earth itself flying at you, your focus was on protecting me. I only wish I could say the same," Mica said.

Ra snorted and rolled his eyes. "Please. You literally stopped the earth from splitting apart under my feet and a war starting that would have affected me and everyone I love. You protected me just fine."

"I should've listened to you. I swear I will do better."

"Good, because I dreamed what might be a solution to our problem while I was out. I think you need Zee to come help," Ra said.

Mica paused. He had no real problem with Zahra, but it would be another hard pill for the more traditional members of his court to swallow.

I shared his dream. We need the engineer, the stronghold spoke into his mind.

This was it. The moment at which he could start to change the way his court functioned to move into the future. The moment he could demonstrate to his mate that he trusted him with more than words.

"Okay," Mica said, smiling a little as Ra's mouth dropped open in surprise.

"Just like that?" he asked.

"Just like that."

He could feel the tiny seed of hope his words planted in the earth of their relationship through his connection to Ra. He wished it was stronger though. Wished the seed was already a deeply rooted tree and his awareness of Ra's emotions had the full depth of a mating bond.

"You want more," Ra whispered, surprise and something else in his voice. Something wary.

"I want it all with you. I love you," Mica admitted, uncaring of their audience. It's not like anyone there didn't know Ra was his mate.

"Are you crazy?! I just almost *died*. If we mated, that could've killed you," Ra snapped.

Mica smiled and pulled the trembling human into his arms, wrapping him in his wings and kissing his temple. "Or you would've accessed my power and taken care of Lucia yourself. Come sit, darling. I'll get you a drink."

"You don't know I would be able to access your power just because Hel and Bast can access each other's," Ra grumbled as he let himself be manoeuvred onto the couch.

It was true. They didn't know for sure what would happen when an elemental and a human mated. The bonds were so rare that he was only aware of three others and, other than Bastion, they were elemental couples who shared a court, so there was no way to know if they were sharing powers or simply boosting each other's magic.

"I think it's likely you would," Bastion said, sounding thoughtful. "It's not that humans are totally magicless after all and Mica's mark on you accelerated your healing. The mating bond would just extend that exponentially."

"Could we maybe focus on the matter at hand, instead of my love life?" Ra asked, exasperated.

That was okay. Ra might not trust his intentions but Mica would show him he was serious. Almost losing his mate had made him realise how soul-deep his need for Ra was. He was all in now and nothing was going to stand in his way of making Ra his in every way he could.

"On that note, I will leave you to it. If you fix the instability in the ley lines and deliver those responsible to me within the next two weeks, I will accept your apology," Lady Nerida said through the speaker.

Two weeks. Fuck. That was going to be tight. It also took them to the exact date he was supposed to be hosting the courts' rulers for his millennial celebrations. Celebrations he would now be organising without his damn seneschal.

"Fixing the damage here may not be enough to solve the damage to your stronghold," Mica warned the Water Lady.

"Then you will owe me. But I accept your proposed reparations for now," Lady Nerida said, disconnecting the call.

"I can have Zee here in under an hour," Bastion offered.

Turning to his people, Mica issued his orders. "Serena, can you take over stabilising the damaged tunnels and temporarily evacuating the residents? I won't risk our people again when we come up with a solution."

"Of course," she said, bowing at the waist. "Kaia can stay in my apartment in the Tree City until we're ready for everyone to return if that suits? I'll bring her back with me when I visit so the stronghold doesn't mope."

Mica glanced over at Ra and Bastion. "Is that acceptable? She will be safe."

"I trust Serena," Ra said.

"Good enough for me," Bastion said, a slight hint of challenge in his voice like Mica might still not trust Ra the way he should. Only time would prove him wrong so Mica ignored it.

"Elysia, I need you to take over planning the celebrations. I know it's the last thing on everyone's minds right now, but we need to send a strong statement to our people with this. I want you to review the guest list and festivities for opportunities to incorporate the other species of the global summit more fully. Keep a list of anyone pushing back. Once we've stabilised Earthshine, we'll need to check the loyalty of every member of my inner circle. I will *not* let this happen again," Mica said.

"It will be an honour, my lord," Elysia said, inclining their head.

"Excellent. Then you can all excuse me and leave us for the next hour while I feed my mate and make sure he is unharmed," Mica said.

"You can't just kick everyone out when they're helping you!" Ra said, but Mica could feel the fondness underneath the words through their connection.

"I will take you up on your offer of a guest room to nap and recover my strength," Kairon said, speeding across the room.

"I need to go and let Hel know everything's okay and fetch Zee," Bastion added, heading back toward the portal.

"And we're super busy now," Elysia said, pulling Serena toward the exit.

"So busy," Serena said, chuckling quietly.

At last, it was just the two of them left and Mica could do what he'd wanted all along and pull Ra into his lap so he could breathe in the man's scent until his brain accepted he was alive and safe. Ra cried out in surprise and then huffed against his neck as he straddled him, careful not to kneel on his wings.

Mica's hands stroked everywhere he could reach as he tried to reassure himself the healing had worked.

"How are you feeling?" he asked.

"Like I was punched in the soul. Also, super hungry," Ra said, groaning as Mica started kneading the knots in his shoulder muscles.

Letting his magic flow into the man on his lap, Mica bolstered Ra's energy reserves as best he could. Tilting his head, Ra drew him into a soft kiss and then another.

"I'll make you some food," Mica said, reluctantly getting to his feet but not letting Ra go.

"Put me down before you throw out your back, old man," Ra said, belying his words by wrapping his legs around his waist and clinging to him.

Mica snorted and dropped Ra on the nearest barstool before heading to the fridge to find something quick and nutritious for them.

"I'm sorry I didn't tell you about Kairon coming to visit," Ra said as he worked.

Mica glanced over at him. "I won't say it's fine because you know the tensions I'm trying to manage here, but I understand why you did it and I forgive you."

"I'll talk to you first next time. I swear," Ra said.

"And I will make sure my people welcome humans and everyone else into our lives."

Ra smiled tiredly at him and rested his gorgeous chin on his hand. "You can't promise that."

"No, but I can lead by example, and I can make damn sure they know what happens to anyone who threatens you or makes you feel unwelcome," he said.

"Are you really going to include more non-elementals in the celebration?"

"I'm going to include more non-elementals everywhere. I'll need your help with that. If you want to stay, that is," Mica said, focusing on plating their food so he didn't have to see the potential rejection coming.

"Are you asking me to move in with you for real?" Ra joked.

"Yes," Mica said.

"Get your sexy ass over here so I can answer you properly."

Stepping around the counter, Mica let himself be pulled between Ra's muscled thighs. Staring down into Ra's stormy eyes, he saw his future.

"I'll move in with you provided that means sleeping in your bed. With you. None of this not seeing you for weeks bullshit."

"Done," Mica said quickly. They'd still have to address the fact that Ra's first loyalty was to a rival court at some point, but this would be enough for now. He'd meant it when he said he trusted him.

Ra smirked and pulled over the plates Mica had prepared. "Let's hurry up and fix our Earthshine then so we can actually enjoy it."

Zahra's arrival put a stop to any immediate enjoyment they could've sought. He'd barely cleared the dishes before Bastion and the Soul Court magical engineer stepped into the room from the balcony where the portal had never closed. Kairon must have particularly acute hearing because he emerged only a minute later.

"Lord Mica. It is an honour to be back within the Earth Stronghold," Zahra said carefully, sweeping into an elegant bow.

Mica looked the engineer over for a moment, taking in their bright purple pixie cut and punk style that was so different from when they'd lived in his court hundreds of years earlier as he tried to decide how he wanted to play this. He knew Ra was close with them and he didn't want to create any tension between his mate and his friends. He must've waited too long because Ra elbowed him in the ribs. Hard.

"Be welcome, Zahra. I appreciate your willingness to answer our call for help. Please be reassured that you will not run into the one who caused your absence from our court while you are here. He was punished centuries ago and I made sure he has not set foot in the stronghold or surrounding cities since," Mica said.

Bastion nodded a silent thanks for his acceptance and he returned the gesture.

Zahra blinked in surprise, seemingly lost for words. "I ... thank you, my lord. I didn't know you'd done that. Please call me Zee. It's what anyone close to me does and if you're shacking up with Ra then we're definitely close by proxy."

Mica's lips twitched in a smile. He could see his sunshine's influence on the way Zee spoke. "Very well, Zee."

"Right. Now we've all made up, can we fix my Earth-shine all shiny and new so we can have a proper party?" Ra said, grabbing his laptop and setting it on the table.

The five of them lost themselves in deep discussion for long hours as Ra took everyone through the scans and what they'd tried so far. It was another eye-opening moment for Mica as he saw first-hand the growth of ideas and suggestions between them, each bringing their unique perspective. When they finally landed on a solution, it was painfully beautiful in its simplicity and yet he still was certain the elementals never would have come to it on their own.

Their fix was inspired by Soul Tower back in the City of Souls where Zee had grown living tendrils of metal over the soaring human building as a framework for Bastion's souls to reside in and protect them. Essentially, they would create a kind of tower that would stretch from the deepest parts of the earth where the stronghold resided, up through the caves and out into the open air above. Only this tower would be a giant spire constructed of earth magic and the precious metals and minerals surrounding them. The tower would be a beautiful space to occupy and a new bastion for the Earth Court but, more than that, with Kairon's healing expertise in its design, its magic would reprogram the broken ley line network, shifting key concentrations of power until balance was restored and the sentience's neural network could function healthily.

With his connection to the earth dragons that traversed the fault lines, Mica would form the roots of the spire by directing the wyrms to burrow a series of new tunnels to Kairon's precise specifications. The dragons themselves could affect the ley lines and, with the help of strategically placed sensors that the stronghold would use as a guide for where to focus its power as well, the new tunnels would form a strong foundation. Zee, along with the local engineers, would then grow the structure itself with the assistance of the stronghold as a new brain stem of sorts for their Earthshine.

The stronghold had been struggling against the missing parts of its whole ever since the contagion destroyed essential parts of its essence. They couldn't build a new sentience or replace what was lost, but they could give it a space that would shape it and keep it safe in the way it needed. Like a hermit crab finding a new home.

Speaking of homes, he added a few extra instructions to Earthshine as he explained what they wanted to do and tested how the stronghold felt about it. Its enthusiastic support had him grinning, as did the images it flashed through his mind of what it was planning.

"What's that smile for?" Ra asked, leaning over to kiss him.

"Earthshine's adding to your design," he said.

Everyone but Zee looked concerned at the potential

upset to their plans, but the engineer had already caught on to what was happening as the only other one around the table who could talk directly to the sentience.

"Oh, that's perfect!" Zee said.

"Would someone please share with the class?" Ra said.

"Mica asked if it could add a series of moving platforms and stairways, a bit like the elevators back home but operated by the sentience instead of electricity. It will mean you and any other folks without wings can traverse the Stronghold more easily without needing to rock climb or catch a ride," Zee explained.

"It's also made sure the acoustics and design of one of the levels will be perfect for you to start a permanent nightclub just like you have back home," Mica said, smiling as he felt his mate's surprised happiness. "Maybe you can start a global chain of inclusive dance venues. What are you going to call it?"

"Well, if we're going global, we need something in keeping with the original version—The Crypt. What does Earthshine think of keeping it simple and calling it The Spire?"

It's perfect, just like your mate, the Stronghold said into his mind, making him smile again.

"You have the Stronghold wrapped around your little finger, love. You could call it The Tornado and it would still be happy," Mica teased.

"Gross. Wash your mouth out! I'm not naming part of our Earthshine something that sounds like it's from the Air Court!" Ra said, slapping his chest playfully.

Grabbing his hand as he pulled away, Mica pressed a soft kiss to the inside of his wrist. "The Spire it is then," he said.

It took them the better part of a week to get everything in place. Elysia quietly arranged the transport of the traitors to Lady Nerida while he was busy, which was just as well. He couldn't look at them without wanting to murder them for what they'd almost taken from him and he'd promised they'd be delivered alive and intact.

The working to build the new structure would require all the powerful mages in the vicinity to contribute and Zee and Kairon continued to tweak and refine the design in consultation with the Stronghold right up until the final hour. With Ra's contribution mostly limited to modelling the changing scenarios, his mate had plenty of time to help Mica deal with the public relations fallout of handing over his own trusted advisors to the Water Court for punishment. He hadn't thought he could appreciate the human any more, but he was damn talented at this kind of thing, adeptly navigating a foreign court to help Mica regain the confidence of his people.

They slept in the same bed every night, but there was still the weight of their potential mating hanging over them. No matter how many times Mica asked, Ra was adamant he didn't want to put him at risk by tying their lives together. It was infuriating because it was Ra's life that was at risk while he didn't have access to the additional power and healing a mating bond would give him.

He would wear him down, though. They could both feel how much they wanted to finally succumb to this draw between them. Mica just had to keep showing him how perfect they were for each other. How perfect their future could be. Starting with the surprise he had planned for his mate once they'd completed the magical working to heal the Stronghold.

The day of the working dawned cloudy and warm, the surrounding jungle hidden by a thick layer of mist that made it seem like they were floating in a void. It was fitting really. It felt like they were awaiting a rebirth.

Mica had called the wyrms to the area the night before, and deep within the caves as the sun breached the horizon somewhere out of sight, he spoke to the earth dragons, weaving his will to become their own. Ra perched by his side, computer screen faced so they both could see as he relayed adjustments and instructions while he worked based on the feedback from the sensors, now heavily magically protected and reinforced. They weren't going to let them become a point of vulnerability again.

The final act of this phase of their working was to call on the oldest, largest wyrm to launch itself in a tight spiral up through the middle of the Stronghold. This part of the design had been inspired by his visit to Patuna Chasm with Bastion all those months earlier where he'd seen the huge limestone spiral left over after a battle of earth dragons in the distant past. It had looked like the central point of a shell and it was the perfect way to provide access up to their new Earth Spire.

Sometimes when he worked with the predatory wyrms, they fought him every step of the way. Not this time. He could feel their ancient calm embedding into the rock as they worked together. Could feel the pull on the tangled ley lines to shift where they needed to be. The wyrms instinctively knew their movements were contributing to the balance of magic that was essential to their wellbeing and they helped him every writhing tunnelling step of the way.

This kind of change didn't hurt the Stronghold. It wasn't like the contagion that had caused swathes of itself to simply cease to exist. The new tunnels and shifting rock were merely transformations. Growth and healing. They were a joint snapping back into place that had been dislocated so long you'd forgotten it could ever move. The final diving, screeching progress of the wyrm left a cylindrical hole from the sky to the deepest point of the cave system around which the new tunnel circled.

As the last rumbling rockfall drifted away, the engineers standing high above began their work, calling on the metals and minerals surrounding them to grow the Spire itself. Copper and tungsten tendrils spread like new shoots up the walls of the spiralling tunnel that he and Ra were slowly ascending as he let his own magic seep deep into the walls and floor around them while they walked.

"It's so beautiful," Ra whispered, his hands brushing against a vein of glittering mica.

Time seemed to blur as they climbed, the only sign of how deep they'd been the aching burn in his thighs. The spire that was being shaped from raw power and determination followed their path and it wasn't until they stepped out onto the highest point of the hillside over the caves that it breached out of the earth and the metallic structure started piercing into the air.

"Now *that's* an elemental home," Kaia said, slipping her hand into Ra's as she joined them. "Open to the sky, so Earthshine's people can fly in and out, but still accessible to everyone."

Serena must have brought the girl to observe as part of

her training. To his surprise, the electric blue of Kaia's wings flared bright as she lent some of her own power to the working. He hadn't realised she'd progressed so far and he could feel Ra's pride match his own as she lent her strength to her mentor, who was weaving metal like it was cloth overhead.

She is leaving a piece of herself with me for when she leaves one day, Earthshine said in his mind, both love and sadness in its voice.

The midday sun was beating down on them when the Spire was finally complete, a soaring, spiralling trunk of metal containing rooms and spaces they would fill with family and laughter. It might take a few more days to sort out some of the finer points like plumbing in time for the celebrations, but the structure was all there.

"Come with me, Sunshine?" Mica asked, holding a hand out to Ra.

Ra stepped into his arms and Mica launched them up into the sky to the highest point of the Spire where a large balcony extended off the new penthouse where they would make their home. Bastion had the right idea when he'd made his home in the highest building in his city, and now Mica could do the same.

"Mica, it's stunning," Ra said when they landed. "I thought this was going to be a gathering area."

Mica watched with a smile as his mate took in the incredible view of the surrounding countryside and the bright space inside that they could make their own. "No. There are plenty of other spaces for that. I wanted you to wake up to as much beauty every day as I will when I see you beside me. That is, if you'll have me."

Sinking to one knee as Ra turned back to him, he took a ring box from his pocket as his mate's eyes grew wide.

"What are you doing, love?" Ra asked, a rasp in his voice.

"You are the light in my darkness. You worry you will be my weakness, but you are my greatest strength. You once told me no elemental lord would be caught dead observing a human tradition. I need you to see that you are everything to me, not despite your humanity, but because of it. You are the partner I never knew I needed. The joy I never knew I was missing. Please do me the honour of marrying me by your customs? And one day I hope you will ask to mate with me by mine, but if you never do I will still be grateful every day that you chose to walk by my side and wear our ring on your finger."

They both knew what this moment meant. It was the moment Ra needed to choose whether to shift his home, his primary loyalty, to Mica and the Earth Court. Forever. But if he said no, Mica wouldn't give up. They would find a way. He couldn't live without his Sunshine.

"*Our* ring?" Ra asked, glancing down at the open box where two rings were nestled.

"I had Earthshine make it from tungsten metal from the heart of our home lined with a sliver of the oak you crafted your whiskey barrel from. A piece of you and a piece of me."

"Oh you beautiful, sneakily sentimental man," Ra said dropping down onto his knees in front of Mica and cupping his face in both hands. "Yes, I will marry you."

Unable to hold himself back any longer, Mica launched himself at Ra, sending them both falling to the terrace until Ra was pinned underneath him as they kissed each other breathless.

Ra's laughter as he gasped for breath had Mica drowning in love for the man.

"Aren't you supposed to be putting a ring on it?" Ra

asked, waggling his finger when Mica finally stopped kissing him long enough for him to speak.

He hadn't even noticed the box was still clutched tight in the hand he'd braced behind Ra's head.

"That would require me getting off you," Mica complained.

"As much as I would love to continue this right here, there are at least thirty of your people flying nearby and I'm pretty sure the engineers are blowing up your phone," Ra said.

Mica groaned, but the noise of his phone *was* starting to break the mood. "Fine. But I'm not letting you out of bed for the rest of the week once we're done," he said, leaning back until he could get to his feet and pull Ra upright.

Thankfully, the rings hadn't fallen from the box, despite his movements. Taking one of the bands from the box, he gently slid it onto Ra's finger, loving the way the dark multi-faceted metal contrasted with his fair skin.

"My turn," Ra murmured, taking the thicker band from the box and returning the favour.

"I love you," Mica said, as the warm oak wood lovingly carved by his mate nestled snug against his skin.

"Love you more," Ra said, sneaking another kiss.

CHAPTER 21
MICA

Sadly, Mica did have to let Ra out of his bed in the following week before the celebrations. They were both far too busy for more than stolen moments, but the bone-deep satisfaction of holding his fiancé in his arms all night and waking up to slow kisses and quick releases almost made up for it.

Ra had recruited his friend Esme to help with some of the tasks Wren would've otherwise been performing and it was just as well, because he wasn't sure Elysia would've survived the shock of discovering they needed to incorporate a wedding into their millennial party plans with only one week's warning. Neither of them had wanted to wait, nor could they be bothered trying to organise another international diplomatic event so soon after this one just so they could keep the other rulers happy when they tied the knot.

If he could choose, he would've kept the ceremony small and intimate, but that wasn't the life they lived. At least Ra understood after decades as the Soul Lord's righthand man. They had made sure to allow for a smaller gathering immediately after the ceremony for an hour before they re-joined the main celebrations. They'd kept the guest list for that one to actual friends and family. He'd just have to hope the other courts understood because he wasn't going to compromise on letting Ra enjoy a moment with his whānau.

The night before the celebrations, they finally managed to clear their schedule enough to eat a meal in peace. It was also the first night they would spend in their new penthouse at the top of the Earth Spire.

Rather than have a meal brought to them, they worked together in the kitchen to prepare the food. He lost track of the number of times Ra brushed against his wings or pressed against his back to drop a soft kiss on his nape. Delightfully torturous anticipation built between them as the night progressed.

As they brought the plates to the table, Mica sent a silent request to Earthshine that had the lights dropping until the only illumination was the sparkling glow of the minerals in the table and the veins running through the Spire's walls and ceiling. He wasn't the only one setting the mood, though. Ra must've spoken to the Stronghold when he was distracted because the room filled with soft music thrumming a strong beat beneath its melody. It was the same song he'd been playing when Ra had found him at the piano weeks earlier and he'd placed his mark on the man, now remixed with his mate's distinctive flare.

Reaching out, he linked his fingers with Ra's where they rested on the table, relishing the feel of the warm metal of their ring against his skin.

"Where did you get this recording?" he asked.

"Serena gave it to me. You didn't tell me you wrote that song," Ra said.

"Is it *our* song now?" he asked.

"I mean, I'm going to keep playing with it, but I intend it to be the soundtrack to every bond we form," Ra said, a slight hitch in his voice.

Mica froze in his seat as every part of him focused intently on the man beside him. "You mean it will be playing at the wedding tomorrow?" he clarified, trying not to get his hopes up if he was reading too much into this.

Ra nodded. "Yes, and this is the extended remix, so you have about..." He paused to dramatically check his non-existent watch. "...thirty minutes to complete our mating bond. Is that enough time? We can always put it on repeat."

"Sunshine—" Mica said, lost for words. "Are you sure?" He was barely restraining himself from scooping Ra into his arms but he needed to be absolutely certain.

Ra's reservations seemed to mainly be that he would put Mica's life at risk or that Mica might regret forming the bond. Mica had been keeping the connection between them wide open this last week so Ra could feel his every emotion and know exactly how much he cared for him. He'd also noticed the numerous conversations Ra had been having over the phone with Bastion about mate bonds. Even so, he hadn't dared to hope they would move this fast.

"I've never been more certain of anything in my life. When we welcome our guests tomorrow, I want everyone to know exactly how *mine* you are. It might not be long since you pulled your head out of your ass and trusted me, but it has been decades since I first started falling for you. I was wrong when I worried I would make you weaker. This past week has shown me this is how I can keep you safe and be the partner you need. You haven't had anyone to lean on for so long and I can be that for you once your people and the courts see our relationship in a way they understand," Ra said.

Every instinct was screaming at him to claim his mate already, but still he hung back. "I don't want you to do this just to satisfy my court," Mica said.

Ra snorted and pushed back the chair he was sitting on with his foot so he could straddle Mica's lap. "Shut up and listen. *I love you*. I'm done waiting and I'm not going to leave you vulnerable for a second longer. Bast pointed out to me that right now you would already die to save me, but I have none of the extra protections the mate bond will bring. We're going to fix that."

"This bossy side of you is kind of sexy," Mica murmured, kissing Ra's neck as he finally started to believe this was happening.

"There's nothing kind of about it. I'm sexy as fuck and you know it, so stop fighting this. I can feel how badly you want it," Ra teased.

Growling under his breath, Mica kept hold of Ra as he pushed to his feet and strode out toward the huge terrace just outside the living area, wrapping a glamour around them to keep them hidden as he went.

"Mmm ... I like where this is going. Which is where exactly?" Ra said as his hands slipped under his shirt to trace paths of raw desire across his skin.

Mica kept kissing every inch of exposed skin as they left a trail of discarded clothes behind them until they were both completely naked. Thank fuck he'd finally managed to convince Ra of the benefits of a fully elemental-tailored wardrobe so they didn't have to worry about inconveniences like zippers and seams.

"I'm going to claim you in the most traditional and ancient of ways. Under the stars with the sky above and the earth below as our witness," Mica growled, already lost to the intoxication of Ra's naked body pressed to his and the slide of their erections against each other.

"Wow. Your ancestors had a bit of an exhibition kink going on. I like it. But maybe we could grab the lube from my pocket before we get too far away from it?" Ra said.

"Okay, the artistic depictions of ancient matings might've skipped over that part," Mica said with a smile, looking down into Ra's storm-grey eyes twinkling with laughter as they reflected the moonlight.

"I'll hunt down the artists tomorrow and we can give them some feedback. It's important to depict sexual relationships in a healthy way," Ra said, sliding down Mica's body in a way that had him moaning before he went in search of the missing lubricant.

Mica paused and then threw his head back and let out a peal of laughter. This is what he'd been missing his whole life. This is what he needed. Joy. Fun. Love. That unique irreverence of his mate that made life worth living. That made life worth playing.

"I should ask you not to, but the artist Reagan is so pompous I'm actually looking forward to watching his face turn plum-coloured as he tries to figure out how to respond," Mica said, eyes trained on Ra's enticing backside as he leaned down to rifle through his abandoned pockets. Thank the earths elemental magic meant they didn't need to worry about transmittable diseases or who knew what else Ra would suggest Reagan add to those artworks.

"Success!" Ra cried, holding up a small bottle.

Using his supernatural speed, he crossed the small distance between them and wrapped himself around Ra's naked body, reaching down to take a firm grip on his erection as he started stroking him. His mate's head fell back against his shoulder and his arms dropped to his sides as he worked him, revelling in the growing arousal he could feel through their connection.

Reaching down to grab the errant lube bottle, he spun Ra in his arms so they could grind against each other as his now-slick fingers went exploring.

"Fuck, yes. I need you inside me now," Ra moaned as he teased against his hole.

"Patience, Sunshine. I'm not going to hurt you," Mica said, still stroking in tantalising circles instead of where Ra was increasingly desperate for him.

"Well, I'm going to hurt you if you don't hurry the fuck up," Ra groaned, the empty threat belied by the way his mate couldn't help but rut against him.

Huffing out a laugh he kept his touches light, worshipping his mate, until Ra's hand closed on the upper edge of his wing and dragged down in the perfect exquisite pressure on the sensitive surface.

The sensations made him lose all control. He had no memory of picking Ra up again, but as his fingers finally slipped into the tight heat of Ra's body, he knew he would remember the feel of him in that moment forever. With the help of his power, he hoisted Ra even higher, draping the man's legs over his shoulders so he could swallow his shaft in one deep moaning slide as he continued to work him over with his fingers, stretching him so they could finally come together in the way they always should've been.

Ra seemed equally lost to the passion between them, unable to do anything but tense and groan as Mica manhandled him into taking the pleasure he was offering.

"Sweetheart. Please. I need more," Ra finally managed to gasp out.

Snapping his wings out behind him, Mica slicked himself with more lube before tossing the bottle and lowering Ra down until his cock was pressed against his entrance.

"You sure you want this? There's no going back once I claim you," he growled against Ra's lips.

"Yes! Do it," Ra cried.

As he launched them into the skies above, he entered his mate's body with one powerful thrust that had them both screaming in pleasure. Every wingbeat as they soared higher seemed like it was driving him deeper inside Ra until he felt like they were one body, one soul. Raw power thrummed in the air around them as the stars became the backdrop to their desire. Earth magic pierced the sky like a copper beacon from the Spire as the Stronghold reinforced his magic with its own. Magic that was sinking into Ra's skin until it filled every part of him, tying them together.

Their flight might've caught Ra by surprise for a second, but he'd quickly adjusted. Ra's body was arching into him as he used his leg muscles for leverage to take Mica harder and further. Mica moaned as Ra leaned forward to suck hard on his neck. Yes. His mate wanted him just as badly as he did.

There was some debate on the nature of human magic, given there were no known human mages, but it wasn't something Mica had looked into. Whatever the truth of it was, he could feel a power unfurling inside Ra like a fern responding to the life-giving warmth and light as it reached back toward him. Ra had always been his sunshine, but, for the first time, Mica saw that he was Ra's as well.

His flight took them higher and higher until the world was far distant. The only link between them and it was the shaft of copper magic connecting from their Earthshine up to them. Hovering at the edge of the point where the air became too thin to breathe, they lost themselves in each other—heads swimming with the low oxygen, bodies burning with lust, and the essence of the magic they both contained weaving together until they could never be unravelled.

"I love you so much, my Sunshine," Mica gasped, his cock throbbing as he desperately tried to stave off his orgasm for another second, another breath. He didn't want this moment to ever end.

"Love you, too. Forever," Ra said, his muscles tightening around Mica's length like he might never let him go.

"Forever," Mica echoed.

With one final thrust, he felt Ra's orgasm rocket through him, dragging Mica along with him into pleasure he'd never felt before as it set off his own climax. As the mating bond finally clicked into place, their connection deepened until he could finally feel all Ra's essence, all his pleasure, as if it were his own. The aftershocks of their coupling held them in a state of shared euphoria long past the point he usually would've pulled gently free.

"Holy fuck," Ra gasped when the world finally started to come back into focus for them. "That was..."

"Everything," Mica finished his sentence for him.

"I've never had sex mid-air," Ra said.

"Good," Mica growled, nipping at his mate's neck as he tried to push back the jealousy that the man had had sex at all before they met.

"Aren't we supposed to have dive-bombed down to earth or something, though? I'm sure that's how it goes in all the romance novels," Ra said, distracting him from his possessive thoughts by making him laugh again. How did he do that with such ease?

"I enjoy aerial acrobatics as much as the next elemental, but I have no idea why you would want to focus on distance and wind speed and everything else required to divebomb proficiently while you were mid-orgasm, especially when you make me come so hard I almost black out," Mica said. "However, now that we're taking a brief pause, I'm happy to oblige."

That was all the warning he gave before tucking his wings in tight and plummeting them back down to earth head first. Ra's excited scream was quickly followed by breathless laughter as their feet touched back down to the Spire.

Welcome home, the voice of the Stronghold said into his mind.

Ra's eyes widened at the words and he realised his mate could finally hear the Stronghold, courtesy of their new mating bond. He knew Ra had wanted to be able to communicate properly with the sentience since he'd first stepped foot here, but a part of Mica was grateful his protective mate had never had to experience the broken, unstable darkness it had been. Ra cared too much and wouldn't have slept until they'd saved the Stronghold if he'd been able to feel it in his mind. This way, they had both been kept safe.

It would take time for the Stronghold to fully recover, but the difference in their Earthshine the second the Spire was completed was already like night and day. All that pressure now had a safe outlet and the murderous mood swings were a thing of the past. They would always mourn the part of the sentience that was lost to the contagion, but now it could finally heal and transform itself into something just as complex but new—the fractures in its essence repaired but still visible and somehow even more beautiful for it, like kintsugi pottery. Like him and Ra.

The energy he was no longer expending hiding and stabilising the fluctuating ley lines from its damage left him feeling almost giddy. Or maybe that was just a side effect of how fucking in love with his mate he was.

"This is so awesome! Thank you, Earthshine!" Ra said.

He'd have to teach the man how to speak to the Stronghold with his mind, but that was a task for another day. Right now, he needed to get them to their bed so they could pick up right where they left off.

His footsteps faltered as a thought struck him and Ra looked at him confused as he stopped and started laughing.

"What's so funny?"

"I just realised we're mated and engaged and I *still* don't know what name you were born with," Mica said.

Ra grinned. "I guess you've earned it, but you have to swear never to reveal it to anyone else."

"I promise, my love."

Leaning closer, Ra whispered in his ear and Mica's laughter only got louder as he finally learned his mate's full name. "That doesn't suit you *at all*," he said, tears forming in his eyes.

Ra shook his head ruefully. "Yeah, laugh it up. You better make it up to me when we get to the bedroom, though."

A shiver of desire travelled between them and Mica nestled his mate closer to his chest as he scooped up the abandoned lube while carrying Ra back into their penthouse suite.

Ra smirked at the move and ran his hands down his wings again making him groan. "Got some plans there, Mr Earth Lord?"

"Yes. They involve ravishing each other for the rest of our immortal lives."

CHAPTER 22
RA

Earthshine, could you please tell my mate that if he doesn't stop showing off that sexy ass of his, I'll take a bite out of it?

Was it mature to use the vast sentience of the magical Stronghold to tease his fiancé? Probably not. Was it satisfying as fuck to watch Mica stutter over his words to the Fire Lord before subtly adjusting himself? Absolutely.

Excusing himself from his conversation with the human leaders, he strolled over to Mica and nestled himself in under his arm, satisfaction thrumming through him as Mica extended his wing to wrap around his shoulders.

"Always such trouble," Mica murmured into his hair, kissing his temple.

"You *did* suggest I should practise speaking to the Stronghold silently," Ra pointed out.

The Fire Lord Tyson was giving them a strange look as they spoke, or rather, he was giving Mica a strange look.

"I can't say I believed the rumours until I saw it for myself," Tyson said.

"Which bit didn't you believe? The relationship or the mating?" Ra asked, wary given the Fire Lord's tumultuous history with his brother Bast.

"The bit where Lord Mica looks like he has actual emotions," Tyson said.

Ra smirked and sent a calming wave of reassurance to his mate who was bristling at the Fire Lord's tone. "Just imagine how far he'd be willing to go to defend his people with all those feelings," Ra said, keeping his voice carefully upbeat so he wouldn't cause any political issues with the warning. He wasn't going to let anyone think there was a weakness to exploit.

"Touché," Tyson said, inclining his head.

The official greetings passed in a whirlwind of more such empty flatteries and thinly veiled threats and, before he knew it, his mate had disappeared to get ready and Elysia was directing him and Bast toward the new ballroom for the wedding ceremony. The addition to the day's programme had caused more than a few murmurings and raised eyebrows, but there was no better way to show what their mating meant for the shift in the Earth Court than to hold a human ceremony in the midst of what had been an almost exclusively elemental event until a week ago.

Bast would be walking him down the aisle to 'give him away' as a symbolic display to the gathered elementals of Ra's loyalties shifting from the Soul Court to the Earth Court. He'd balked at that at first until both Bast and Mica had reassured him that neither expected him to choose one over the other. They were family. This was just about maintaining appearances for the delicate political balance between the courts.

"You ready for this? It's not too late to back out," Bast teased.

Anticipation and adoration rumbled down the connection between Ra and Mica that was now so deep he sometimes had to check whose emotions he was feeling at any given moment.

"I can't wait to be his husband," Ra said, his thumb stroking over the ring on his finger.

As the doors swung open and he finally saw the gathered crowd in the chamber ahead, tears gathered in Ra's eyes. At the far end of the aisle, Kaia's māmā Ana waited to perform the ceremony as celebrant, her back straight and her chin high as she stood before the gathered world elite. To Ana's right on Ra's side, Tir and Kairon stood where Bast would join them as his best people. They were all dear friends, but he had also wanted to send a message by having an elemental, a ceptae, and a vampyr standing by his side as he married the Earth Lord.

On Mica's side, Serena and Elysia were standing and, to Ra's surprise, so was Zee. Apparently, he wasn't the only one who'd decided to send a message to the gathered elementals. Some might say it was strange to be influenced by politics in this choice, but that was who they were and who they needed to be together in order to rule an elemental court. It also made his heart ache with pleasure that Mica had managed to include another of his friends in the ceremony.

The tears started falling for real when the Stronghold made the first notes of their song reverberate throughout the space and Ra realised that, rather than it being the recording he'd arranged, his mate was playing the hauntingly exquisite melody himself at a piano at the front of the room. Their eyes met across the length of the space and both Mica's mark on his arm and his collar at his neck warmed as earth magic stroked across his skin in greeting.

Kaia's slight form stepped out ahead of them as Bast tugged him gently to continue walking. Her electric blue and cream feathers flashed in the air as she preceded them. Sparkling flowers and birds streamed from her fingers to wend through the seats and flit above the heads of the guests as she wove her magic. Every single one was a shining replica of the native flora and fauna of Aotearoa. She was sharing the plants and birds of her home with the gathered world leaders and giving him this piece of his former life as he started his new one. They were illusion, not real, but they were even more beautiful for being so transitory—forming like miniature fireworks that drifted in the air before fading from view.

"Thank you, K-Bear. That was stunning," Ra whispered when they reached the end of the aisle.

"Thank you to you and Uncle Mica for everything you've done for me," Kaia said, flashing them a huge smile as she casually dropped in her adoption of Mica as part of her found family before taking her seat in the front row.

Everyone and everything faded from his awareness as his mate, his fiancé, the love of his life, stood from the piano to come join him, taking a moment to wipe away the tears on his cheeks gently with his thumbs before wrapping Ra's hands in his own.

As they stood vowing to love and honour each other into the millennia ahead surrounded by the people they loved most in the world, the last ache of any pain between them finally faded to nothing but memory. There was only room for love in their future.

The private gathering after the ceremony was the perfect

chance to hug his whānau tight and take a moment to get control of the tears of joy that kept threatening to slip free, and the long night of dancing that followed soon had him breathless and laughing.

"Mmm ... are you ready to head upstairs?" Mica asked when he finally took a break to lean against the wall and people-watch.

Tugging his mate close, he frowned a little as he watched Kairon and Nerida arguing on the other side of the room. What was that about?

"Is it rude to leave all our guests here so I can finally make love to my *husband?*" Ra asked back, but he was still watching his vampyr friend with concern.

"They'll be fine," Mica said, gesturing to Elysia to go and play peacekeeper before the flashes of blood-red and sea-blue magic surrounding the pair could become something more troublesome.

The plant mage quickly made their way to the Water Lady and had her pulled clear and dancing before any violence could ensue. Kaia did the same for Kairon. Finally satisfied their wedding night wasn't going to unexpectedly turn into a cage fight, Ra turned his face up to his husband and mate and pulled his head down into a long and filthy kiss.

His moan turned into a laugh of surprise as Mica scooped him up into his arms and headed toward the nearest balcony. Realising the couple was about to leave, their guests made way for them with cheers and catcalls.

"Carrying me over the threshold?" Ra asked with a grin. "I think it might be a bit late for that, given we broke in our new bedroom well and truly last night."

"I did not need to hear that," Bast joked from nearby as he and Hel came to bid them farewell.

Ra snorted. "As if I haven't caught you and Hel in the elevator more times than I can count."

"Mmm ... the elevator, huh?" Mica asked, a thrum of arousal coming down their connection.

"Maybe once the guests leave, love," Ra said with a smirk.

Bast smiled at them. "We just wanted to come and wish you all the happiness in the worlds in your marriage and your mating. We're going to miss you so much, but I knew when you left that you weren't likely to come home."

Mica put him down for a moment so he could pull Bast and Hel into a tight embrace. "I'll miss you too, bro. The Soul Court will always have a place in my heart, but Mica is my home now."

"As he should be," Hel said, sharing an understanding look with her mate.

"Welcome to the family, brother, and congrats," Bast said, turning to Mica and drawing him into a hug.

Ra smiled as he felt Mica's surprise through their bond. His mate wasn't used to the kind of family and open affection they had back in the Soul Court, but he was going to make sure the Earth Court became just as welcoming.

"The other courts are going to misconstrue this and think we're allying against them," Mica warned, but he didn't pull away.

"The other courts are going to have to find a way to accept the other peoples of these melded earths just the way we have," Bast replied.

"Well ... maybe not *quite* like we have," Ra added, his

eyes back on the way Lady Nerida was glaring across the room at the vampyr Kairon.

Hel shrugged, a wicked grin on her face. "You never know."

"As fun as it is to speculate on the sex lives of the other courts, I'd rather be enacting my own," Mica said, scooping him back into his arms.

With a final wave of farewell, Mica carried him out into the night to fly their way up to the tip of the Earth Spire where they could finally find the privacy to celebrate their marriage the way they'd been desperate to since the moment they'd said 'I do'.

As music and happiness thrummed through the structure and echoes of Earthshine's content seeped out into the earth to further heal the broken lines of power, they lost themselves in each other.

The potential for a mate bond between them was something fate had decided, but they had chosen this. Chosen each other.

And he would keep choosing Mica over and over again for the rest of eternity.

THANK YOU FOR READING! If you'd like to hear about my new releases and read the prequel short story of how Ra and Bastion first met, sign up to my newsletter through my website: www.melhardingshaw.com.

ABOUT THE AUTHOR

Mel Harding-Shaw is a paranormal romance and urban fantasy writer from Wellington, Aotearoa New Zealand. Her debut novel *City of Souls* won Agent's Choice in the RWNZ Great Beginnings Contest.

She's also a widely published award-winning writer of short speculative fiction as Melanie Harding-Shaw and has published five books under that name including a short story collection, *Alt-ernate*, and the witchy urban fantasy novella *Against the Grain*.

Mel won the award for Services to Science Fiction, Fantasy and Horror in the 2020 Sir Julius Vogel Awards. You can find her at www.melaniehardingshaw.com and on social media.